RADHIKA SANGHANI

V!RG!N

This edition published in Great Britain 2014
by Mills & Boon, an imprint of Harlequin (UK) Limited,
Eton House, 18-24 Paradise Road, Richmond, Surrey, TW9 1SR

ISBN: 978-0-263-24674-2

097-0814

Harlequin (UK) Limited's policy is to use papers that are natural, renewable and recyclable products and made from wood grown in sustainable forests. The logging and manufacturing processes conform to the legal environmental regulations of the country of origin.

Printed and bound by
CPI Group (UK) Ltd, Croydon, CR0 4YY

ACKNOWLEDGEMENTS

I could not have written *Virgin* without my girlfriends—you all know who you are. Your honest confessions about masturbating, finding semen in bath tubs and battling with your pubes have given me so much inspiration and endless laughter. Thank you.

To everyone who read *Virgin* when it was just the slightly weird book I was writing to cheer myself up—thank you so much for your invaluable feedback and for loving Ellie. That's you, Sarah Walker, Bex Lewis, Ella Schierenberg, Sarah Johnson, Rhiannon Williams, Olivia Goldhill, Andrea Levine and even Kim Leigh. Thank you, Rory Tyler, for being the only male I know who was brave enough to read *Virgin*. I know you're still not over the Mooncup.

I also really want to thank my parents. You had no idea I was writing *Virgin* until I told you it was being published. I know a lot of it has been quite a surprise to you and not what you expected I would write, but thank you for still being so proud of me and supporting me.

Thank you to my editor, Anna Baggaley, and everyone at Harlequin for carefully editing *Virgin* and loving it so much from the very start.

Lastly—none of this would have happened if it wasn't for Maddy Milburn, my agent. Thank you *so* much for believing in *Virgin* and making this all happen!

To anyone who has ever gone through the pain
of a Brazilian wax

CHAPTER ONE

Ellie Kolstakis
21 years old
Non-smoker
VIRGIN

I STARED IN HORROR at the words on Dr E Bowers' computer. The status of my hymen was plastered across her screen in capital letters.

V-I-R-G-I-N

The letters glowed luridly on the green computer screen, the kind used before Steve Jobs figured out Apple. They imprinted themselves into my mind in an eighties blur. A lump of anxiety lodged itself into my throat and my cheeks started burning. I felt sick.

My humiliating secret was all over my medical records and Dr E Bowers was going to see it. I didn't even know what the *E* in her name stood for but she was about to find out that in the two and a half years I had spent at uni, not a single boy had wanted to deflower me. Not one. I was twenty-one years old, and I still had my V-card.

'Ms Kolstakis,' she asked, pushing her rimless glasses up her nose, 'you're a final-year student at University College London, and you're here to register, is that correct?'

I forced my paralysed face into a smile and tried to laugh politely. 'Yep, I don't know why I didn't join earlier. I, uh, I think it's because I just didn't ever get fresher's flu, you know?'

She stared blankly at me.

'Um, also, you can call me Miss Kolstakis, or just Ellie, if you want,' I added.

She turned her head back down towards the forms, creasing her brow as she struggled to read my messy attempt at writing in block capitals.

I wiped the sweat from my palms onto my jeans and told myself to be calm. She was a doctor. She wasn't going to be shocked by meeting a twenty-one-year-old virgin. Besides, she was probably just going to ask me about the Kolstakis family history and the worst thing I would have to tell her would be about Great Granddad Stavros smoking a pack of cigarettes every day from the time he was nine. He didn't even die from lung cancer in the end; he choked on an almond at the age of eighty-nine.

She breathed in sharply. 'Mmm, oh dear—this isn't very good at all. You drink more than twenty units of alcohol a week?'

Oh, God. If she figured out I had deliberately rounded down by five units I would probably be on the first bus out of here to rehab.

Dr E Bowers cleared her raspy throat.

'Oh, sorry.' I giggled nervously in a way I hadn't since Girl Guides. 'I don't always drink twenty units a week. Obviously it's just during term time. We normally go out on Thursdays. Oh, and Mondays. Sometimes Wednesdays, but that club night is kind of full of freshers these days so we don't go as much.'

Dr E Bowers furrowed her forehead and pursed her lips together. She started tapping away at her keyboard and I held on to the edges of the chair with anxiety. I focused my gaze on her computer. The six letters were no longer there. She had scrolled down the page without commenting on them. I breathed out an audible sigh of relief.

A sentence appeared at the bottom of the screen. *Over twenty units a week, heavy drinker, binge drinks.*

'Wait, I'm not a binge drinker!' I cried. 'In fact, I'm not even a heavy drinker. I'm a normal drinker—I barely drink anything compared to my friends.'

'Ms Kolstakis, twenty units a week is still rather a lot. You should think about cutting down, or you'll be back here asking for a new liver in ten years,' she said severely.

She tucked her Princess Diana-circa-1995 hair behind her ears and continued, 'I see you've left this section about sexual health blank on your forms. Are you sexually active?'

I died.

Am I sexually active?

I couldn't even talk to my friends about just how *un*sexually active I was, let alone Dr E Bowers. Someone who wore glasses with no frames was never going to understand how traumatic it was to be a final-year student who had never had sex. I bet she lost hers through a hole in a bed sheet as they did in the Middle Ages. She stared into my eyes as though she could read my mind. I felt my body perspiring. I wished I'd worn a black top.

I fidgeted in my seat. 'Oh, right, well, I'm actually not really very sexually active so...I didn't bother filling in that section. I'm not pregnant, never have been and never will be at this rate!'

Her lips stayed in a thin line and she blinked her anaemic-looking eyes at me.

I made a mental note to stop trying to distract her with failed attempts at humour and quickly added, 'Honestly, I definitely don't have any STIs or anything. It's completely impossible.'

'Ah, so you've been tested recently for chlamydia and so on?' she asked.

'Well…no. I just *can't* have chlamydia. I'm…well, I'm a… I mean…' My voice broke and my words trailed into silence. I couldn't bring myself to say the word out loud. My best friends grew up just knowing this stuff and I'd spent the past three years hiding it from everyone I'd met at uni. I opened my mouth to try again but no words came out.

'Yes?' Dr E Bowers blinked and looked directly at me. 'You're a…?'

'I'm a v…a vi…' Great. On top of everything, I'd managed to develop a stutter.

I took a big breath and tried again. This time the words tumbled straight out of me. 'I've never had sex before so I can't have any STIs. Or STDs. Well, neither.'

She blinked again. 'But you are sexually active?'

Um. Does one failed attempt at a blow job and a few fingers jabbing into my vagina count as being sexually active?

'I don't know,' I replied miserably. 'I mean, I've never had sex but I've kind of been to third base.'

She sighed. 'Ms Kolstakis, are you sexually active or not? This is a confidential space. I just need to know whether or not to give you a chlamydia test.'

My stomach plummeted straight down into my five-quid plimsolls, taking my jaw with it. My own doctor didn't believe I was a virgin. 'No! I'm telling the truth, honestly. I've never had sex. I don't *need* a chlamydia test.'

She squinted at me as though she was looking for any traces of a post-coital glow on my face. 'Do you have a boyfriend at the moment?' she finally asked.

I lowered my eyes in shame. What kind of student was I, who had never had a boyfriend and was unable to answer a single question about sex when I was in my sexual prime?

'No,' I mumbled.

She turned to her screen and scrolled up without warning. I started in panic as the six letters emerged on the monitor. I threw my hands up to my face, shielding my eyes from the V-word.

She sat looking at the screen for twenty-seven seconds before she clicked it away and turned back towards me. Slowly, I lowered my hands from my flushed face.

She looked at me with something resembling pity. 'Right, then, Ms Kolstakis, I'm going to give you this chlamydia test to do at home. It is self-explanatory, but essentially you just use the cotton bud to swab your vagina and post it to the address in the pack. You should hear within a couple of weeks. Is that all right?'

I stared at her with my mouth gaping open. 'I… What?! I just told you that I've never had sex—why do I need a test?' I cried out.

'We offer free chlamydia tests for everyone over the age of twenty-one who is sexually active or has been in close contact with someone else's genitalia.'

'But you know I'm not actually sexually active.' I blushed furiously. 'I have never been, well…penetrated.' I stumbled over the last word.

Dr E Bowers raised her eyeballs to the ceiling. 'Ms Kolstakis,' she said, 'I am now well aware that you are a virgin. However, I advise that you take this free test I am offering you to ensure that you do not have chlamydia. It is still possible—though very rare—to catch it in other ways.'

'But what other ways? Surely fingers can't give you chlamydia?' I blurted out.

'No, they cannot. However, you can catch it from oral sex or if a penis has been around your vagina, even without penetration.'

How Dr E Bowers knew that James Martell's penis had touched my VJ but never actually gone in, I will never know. I stared at her mutely, impressed for the first time by her medical abilities.

She pressed the envelope into my hands with a knowing look. I stood up, clutching it. I could barely see past the bright green letters flashing in my head so I walked in an undiscerning daze back out through the waiting room. My throat felt parched and scratchy from mortification so I stopped off at the water cooler. As I poured myself a plastic cup of water, I felt something fall behind me.

I turned around in surprise and saw an upturned cardboard box lying in the middle of the room surrounded by small silver packets scattered all across the waiting room floor and under the waiting patients' seats. Oh, God. My satchel must have knocked it off the shelf behind me.

I closed my eyes briefly in shame before forcing myself to bend down and pick the box up. The waiting patients in the room were staring so I pulled my jeans up, hoping my faded M&S knickers weren't on show. Crouching on my knees and trying to pull my jumper down to hide my VPL, I started picking up the packets. I was half-finished shoving them carelessly back into the open box when it suddenly hit me. These weren't just shiny silver *packets* that I was picking up from under people's feet. They were condoms.

The irony was not lost on me as I fled the surgery, my eyes swimming in hot tears. I ran out into the street and chucked the brown envelope straight into the first bin I saw. My face burnt red-hot as I watched it sink in with the empty McDonald's paper bags, taking my dignity down with it.

I was nothing but a twenty-one-year-old VIRGIN.

CHAPTER TWO

LIFE AS AN adult virgin is more complicated than you might think. Obviously it is normal, there are thousands of us, and there is absolutely nothing wrong with it. Choosing when to have sex is a completely individual decision, and everyone is different. Some people choose to wait till marriage, and some just want to wait for the right person. Others are religious, and others are just too busy being successful in every other area of their lives to worry about something as minor as intercourse.

At least, that's what the internet said when I looked it up the second I got home from the doctors' surgery.

I knew Dr E Bowers hadn't even believed I was a virgin to begin with, because clearly no average-looking third-year university student who drank ten-plus units a week could still be a virgin. Except me.

I buried my head in the duck-feather pillow I'd spent a week's food budget on. I pulled my duvet over me to try to block out the six letters blinking over and over in my head: V I R G I N V I R G I N V I R G I N.

I hated the word. I hated it just as much as I hated the fact that I was one. It wasn't fair—why did I have to be the only non-deformed, non-religious girl who got stuck with an untouched inner lotus at the age of twenty-one?

I sighed loudly and let my mind go over the familiar responses to the 'Why am I still a v*****?' question that visited me as regularly as my period.

1. It was my parents' fault. They were education-obsessed immigrants who moved from Greece to Surrey and sent me to an all-girls school. Their plan was for me never to meet any boys so I wouldn't be distracted from their one and only goal for me: Oxford University. Result? I didn't get into Oxford and I didn't meet any boys, either.
2. I was a very unfortunate-looking teenager. By the time I figured out how to make myself look passable and wear a bra that gave me enough support to show off my 36D assets, it was too late. All the boys from the school next door already had girlfriends, and to them I would always be the slightly unattractive and quiet girl with big boobs hidden behind massive jumpers, and long dark curly hair that was more horizontal than vertical. It didn't help that all the other girls had figured out how to pluck their eyebrows and flirt while I was locked up in my bathroom with a bottle of bleach, battling my moustache. By the time I got to uni, I realised I had missed out on learning how to talk to boys. After a few minutes of my blunt humour and self-deprecation, they usually moved on to talk to real girls. Girls with minimal body hair, button noses and socially appropriate senses of humour.
3. My dysfunctional family. I was an only child, which meant most people assumed I had spent a spoilt, lav-

ish upbringing pleading with my parents never to have another child so I could have all their attention. The reality was that I spent my whole childhood avoiding my mum and dad whenever they were in the same room, which meant most of my formative years were spent on the swing in the back of the garden with my imaginary older brother, or reading books under my duvet. Consequently, I moved up to the top reading set at school, developed an over-active imagination and became obsessed with my friends' functional families. I couldn't figure out how all this linked to the 'why am I still a virgin' question, but it had to have had some kind of psychological impact on me. My latest theory was that it gave me a pathological fear of men.

4. I was a late bloomer. I spent every lunchtime listening to my friends talk about their first kisses and boyfriends but their lives always seemed so far removed from mine. Over the years, they moved on to second base, third base, and when they were all finally losing their virginity, I was still the only girl who had never kissed anyone. I sat on the socially acceptable side of the sixth-form common room. I hung out with the cool people and eventually managed to wear the right clothes, but somehow I didn't kiss a single boy until the ripe old age of seventeen. I didn't stop there, either—I begged him to have sex with me. He said no.

5. The Bite Job. It happened just before the First Kiss refused to deflower me and it is the reason why I have a fear of penises (penii?), second base, third base, rejection, teeth and pubic hair. It is my worst memory.

We were at Lara's eighteenth birthday and I was wearing a dress so low-cut you could see my bra. It was just like any other party, except this time, an actual boy came over to speak to me. James Martell. He was no Mark Tucker (Year Thirteen's own Brad Pitt from the boys' school) and his nose was, surprisingly, bigger than mine—but he was funny and had floppy blond hair. He took me upstairs to Lily's older brother's bedroom and drunkenly pushed me onto the bed.

We snogged. I mirrored what he was doing with his tongue and wondered why none of my girlfriends had ever mentioned how much saliva was involved. Then his hands started creeping into my pants. Any self-respecting girl who was having her first kiss would have yanked them back out, but not sexually starved Ellie. I let his fingers venture down into my VJ and let him poke away. I carried on shoving my tongue down his throat at full velocity and after a few minutes of discomfort in my sacred zone, he stopped. We went back downstairs holding hands and swapped email addresses.

We ended up chatting on the computer every night for two weeks until one Saturday evening when he invited me over. I was so nervous I ended up sitting on the loo excreting my nerves for an hour beforehand. After a second shower, I got the bus to his.

We sat in awkward silence for half an hour until he swooped in and started kissing me. We snogged on the sofa for a while before he put his hand down into my pants again. This time I was more prepared and didn't wince in pain when he started waggling his fingers around. The next thing I knew, he was pulling my dress over my head and I was naked bar my pink polka-dot underwear.

He pulled his clothes off, undid my bra and slid my knickers off. He stared in shock. After a few seconds of total silence when I wanted to curl up in a ball and die, he threw his head back and howled with laughter.

I froze. Why was he laughing at my vagina? I stood, paralysed with humiliation, and waited for him to speak.

His laughter died down. 'Wow, I knew you had some hair down there but I didn't realise you had a full-on *bush*. You're the first girl I've ever met with an unshaved vagina.'

I hadn't shaved. Why hadn't I shaved? Why hadn't I *known* I was supposed to shave?

He didn't seem to care very much because he carried on kissing me. Then he pulled his boxers off and I saw his naked penis staring at me. It was the first one I had ever seen and I kept trying to sneak a peek at it while we snogged. I felt it gently prodding my thighs and as we writhed on the sofa, I realised it was rubbing around my VJ.

I reached out and touched it. It felt alien and alive. I was about to move my hand away when he moaned in pleasure and I realised I was going to have to give him a hand job. I tried to remember what the girls at school had said, and with fear settling in my throat, I slowly began to move my hand up and down.

It looked like an extra limb and had the texture of an old cucumber. I had no idea how tightly to hold it, or at what speed I should be moving my hand up and down. What if he thought it was awful? What if he didn't come? What if he laughed at me again? I panicked. Without thinking I took my hand off his penis, broke away from the kiss and crawled down the sofa. I took it into my hands and slipped it into my mouth.

I felt my face getting hot as thoughts raced through my

head. I tried to make my mouth fit around him and began moving my head backwards and forwards. The minute I started I knew it was a mistake. I had thought it would be easier than the hand job but I could not have been more wrong. I had absolutely no clue what I should be doing. I opened my mouth wider and pushed forward, when suddenly I heard a loud yelp.

I stopped what I was doing and dropped his penis in shock. I looked up and saw him try to pull his face into a smile.

'What's wrong?' I asked, though I didn't want to know.

'It's just, um, you bit me.'

I felt bile rise in my throat and wanted to throw up and cry in the corner. Feeling my skin prickling with humiliation, I laughed shrilly and said, 'Oh, sorry.'

I wanted to leave but there was no escape. If I ran away, everyone at school would know. I took a deep breath and went back down to his penis. I tried to carry on like before but this time I wrapped my lips around my teeth. It was so uncomfortable it had to be wrong. I tried to go down deeper and then gagged. I swallowed the urge to throw up and carried on. How was I going to finish?

I pulled away from his penis. 'James, let's have sex.'

He laughed awkwardly. 'Um, are you serious? I thought you were a virgin.'

I flushed fuchsia. 'So? I'm seventeen. I'm ready.'

He looked at the floor. 'Ellie, we've only kissed a few times. I can't take your virginity.'

'But…I want you to. Please?'

He squirmed. 'I can't. Not like this. Your first time shouldn't be like this.'

Standing, I pulled on my pink dotted knickers and did

my bra clasp with numb fingers. I ignored his protestations and left.

I never saw James Martell again. I avoided the parties that I knew he would attend, and I blocked him on instant messenger. He didn't try to call me and I never did anything more than kiss someone ever again.

Once I got home from the GP surgery, I lay down on my bed and felt a familiar wave of disgust flood over me. Only this time it wasn't just because of The Bite Job. It was mixed up with Dr E Bowers.

I always knew it was weird that I was a twenty-one-year-old virgin, but it hadn't *really* hit me until I saw those green capital letters screaming at me from my medical records. I wasn't even eligible for a chlamydia test. Dr E Bowers had given it to me either to make up a quota or because she thought I was a religious nut-job who didn't want to go the whole way but secretly gave head to every guy around. If only.

I sat up straight in my bed. This was it. I was in my final year of university and I would never be surrounded by so many horny men again. This was my last opportunity to lose my virginity and I had to grab it now. I had to ditch my V-plates by the time I graduated in summer—which meant I had four months to finally understand what an orgasm was and to learn how to give blow jobs.

I took a sharp intake of breath and visualised my future.

In June, I would go back to Dr E Bowers, get a chlamydia test and make her swap VIRGIN on my records for SEXUALLY ACTIVE. The next time I came into contact with a condom, it would not be falling off a shelf in the doctor's surgery; it would be on an actual penis. And this time, it wouldn't just rub around my vagina *à la* James Martell; it would be going straight in there.

CHAPTER THREE

'OK, OK, SO HAS everyone got some kind of alcohol? There's some more vodka over here if you need any.'

Kara, a pretty brunette who used to wear Topshop in her hometown but had swapped it for vintage clothes and brogues when she came to London, poured generous amounts of vodka into all our glasses.

Somehow I had been invited to an end-of-term party at Luke's house, just before we broke up for Easter—Luke being the leader of the 'cool' group in my English Literature course. I didn't own any vintage clothes whatsoever so I never really felt like part of the group and didn't fully understand why they invited me to their parties. Maybe some of them thought my general uniform of jeans and woolly jumpers was a deliberate anti-fashion statement. Obviously they were unaware that dresses and fur coats made me look like a sad transvestite trying too hard, and high-waisted things just accentuated the birthing hips I may never have a chance to use.

'Can we just start already?' shrieked Hannah, who was wearing the vintage white nightdress she wore day in and day out, a strand of fake flowers around her head. 'I'll go first. Does everyone remember the rules?'

Without giving anyone a chance to respond, she lurched on. 'So obviously it is called Never Have I Ever, so when the person says something like, "Never have I ever shagged someone who was married," then if you have done that, you drink. If you haven't done that, you don't. Even if you are the person who said it, you still have to drink if you have done it.'

'Hannah, we get it. Just start,' moaned Charlie. 'And can you please start with something better than shagging someone married? That's so boring.'

Hannah put on a deliberate pout. 'Well, why don't you start, Charlie?'

He grinned, rubbing his hands together. Charlie was the joker of the group, and he liked nothing more than being given the spotlight so he could make everyone groan and laugh over his filthy sense of humour. This was his prime opportunity. I gulped as I tried to mentally prepare myself for what was coming. If I managed to make my face look calm and unbothered, no one would know that I would be lying through my teeth.

'All right, so, never have I ever fucked someone in a public place.' Without waiting for anyone else to start drinking, Charlie raised his glass and downed it. Everyone rolled their eyes until he shot them the cheeky grin that had probably made so many girls want to shag him in public in the first place.

I hesitated over whether to drink. I needed to choose wisely. I couldn't just develop a new personality for this game; I needed to think which sexual things I would have done if I had lost my virginity years ago like everyone else. A brief layer of sweat formed on my top lip. It was too late to drink now so I put my glass down and looked around to see who had drunk.

Eight people raised their glasses, and six of us hadn't. I breathed out in relief. I was one of six, which made me normal, kind of, and there was always safety in numbers. With the edge of my sleeve, I wiped the beads of sweat off my top lip.

Hannah—who had drunk—started waving her arms around and said, 'OK, my turn! So, never have I ever cheated on anyone.'

Some of the boys sighed in boredom, but even Charlie refrained from criticising this, probably because he was just as curious as everyone else to see who drank. I started to wonder if I could drink for this one. Obviously I hadn't actually ever had a boyfriend to cheat on, but back when I was messaging James Martell during those two weeks pre–Bite Job, I once got drunk and accidentally snogged someone else at a party. I think it lasted two-point-five seconds, and I have no idea who it was, but it was definitely cheating.

Feeling confident and sexually active, I drank some of my vodka and Coke. Three other people drank with me, and ten did not. Oh God, I was in the minority. This was dangerous, because someone could ask me about my story, and what exactly would I—

'Ellie! I can't believe you've cheated on someone! That seems so unlike you! So tell us, who were you dating, and who did you shag?' On cue, Hannah interrupted my thoughts and brought me crashing back to the reality of Luke's living room with its vinyl records stuck to the walls.

Shag? Surely cheating could include snogging, right? Why did EVERYTHING have to be about sex?

'Oh God, um, it was ages ago. I was seventeen, and I

was dating this guy called James Mar—' I paused, suddenly remembering that Joe, one of the guys in the room, had gone to the same school as James. Hopefully he would have no idea who I was talking about, especially because I was trying to pass off this casual fling (could I even call it a fling?) as a *bona fide* relationship.

'So, yeah, I was dating James, and I hooked up with someone else. When I was drunk, at a party. Not very exciting.' I laughed awkwardly.

Hannah looked at me with raised eyebrows and did a feminine snort as she turned away, literally flouncing her hair. I'd thought only shampoo models did that.

Marie, a Belgian ex-model with a block fringe, asked, 'So, it is my turn now?' All the boys looked up at the sound of her accent and grinned their assent. 'OK, so I have had anal sex.'

I choked on the pretzel I was eating and coughed. No one noticed because all the boys were grinning and admiring Marie's looks while Hannah shrieked about her getting the rules wrong and ruining the game. I grabbed my glass and drank quickly, feeling better as the bits of pretzel were flushed down my throat.

I looked up to see who had actually drunk for this, wondering if Charlie would. I saw Hannah staring at me with her beady eyes as she shrieked, 'Oh, my God—Ellie just drank, as well! So that's five of the boys, Marie, Emma and Ellie. Wow, Ellie, you're such a dark horse.'

All of them were staring at me. I saw Charlie's appreciative expression, and something like lust spreading across his face. I felt the blood drain out of my cheeks and tried to force my face into something resembling a smile. I shrugged as I fake-smiled too brightly and reached back into the bowl of pretzels.

'So, who did you do it with?' asked Hannah persistently. I could have killed her.

Luckily, Emma—the only girl there whose clothes looked way more Topshop than charity shop—came to my rescue. 'Uh, I thought we were playing Never Have I Ever, not Twenty Questions,' she said.

Hannah shrugged and Emma carried on. 'But if we are allowed to ask questions, then why don't you tell us your cheating story? You already made Ellie tell hers.'

Hannah looked confused. 'Um, I didn't drink for the cheating one.'

Emma's hand flew to her mouth. 'Oh, my bad. I got confused with the question. For a second, I thought it was about being the person who slept with someone who was already in a relationship…like you did with Tom. Oh shit, I've said too much,' she finished as Hannah's face went purple.

Kara turned around in shock. 'TOM, AS IN, MY EX-BOYFRIEND TOM?' she screeched.

Emma shot me a wink and I let out a yelp of laughter, which no one noticed because they were too engrossed watching Kara scream at Hannah. I grabbed my coat and bag and slipped towards the door, using this as the perfect escape opportunity. I was about to leave when Emma snuck out from behind me.

'So, how much fun was that?' She grinned.

'You saved me,' I replied gratefully.

'From that skank? I know, I can't stand her.'

I stared at her with my mouth wide open. 'No way, are you serious? I thought everyone loved her. She's so pretty and confident and has the Shoreditch style down to a T.'

Emma rolled her bright blue eyes. 'OK, so she's pretty, but it seems like she only owns one dress and her personality is so grating it hurts to be around her for more than an hour.'

I started laughing, surprised. Who would have thought anyone else could see past Hannah's fake-flower headband into her unhippy heart? 'Oh my God, I couldn't be happier you just said that,' I cried. 'I thought I was the only one who hated her.'

Emma grinned through her thickly coated red lips. 'Trust me, you're not alone in this, babe. Anyway, we should go for cocktails and share our anal sex stories.'

I made a strangled, yelping sound and Emma looked at me questioningly. Oh God, to lie or not to lie?

I compromised with a half lie. 'Um. That part wasn't actually true. I've never had anal sex. I just drank because I was choking on a pretzel and then it was too late to say no.'

She threw her head back and let out a throaty cackle. 'OK, wait, so why didn't you just tell Hannah you accidentally drank and didn't mean to admit you took it up the bum?'

I flushed at her very visual words. 'I guess I wished I was the kind of girl who, uh, took it up…there,' I admitted. For a second, it had been kind of exciting to have Charlie look at me as though I was shaggable.

'Babe, anyone can be that girl. I'm sure the guys are queuing up to do you up…there.' She grinned.

I looked at her doubtfully. 'They're not.'

She dismissed me with a wave of her hand. 'You must be going to the wrong places. Next weekend, you're coming out with me. Text me,' she said, blowing me a kiss as she turned back to the party, sashaying on her five-inch-heeled boots.

She left a trail of Miss Dior Chérie in her wake and I

couldn't help imagining what it would be like to be Emma. Maybe if I started wearing perfume instead of the strawberry body spray I bulk-bought two years ago, *I* could have casual sex stories and stand up to Hannah Fielding.

I looked down at the soggy pretzel I was still holding and realised I had a long way to go.

CHAPTER FOUR

I WOKE UP with a loud groan as I remembered what had happened at the party. My eyes were still glued together with sleep so I groped around blindly for my mobile and called Lara, my best friend.

She was my first port of call whenever something humiliating happened to me. I turned my horrible luck with men into funny stories for her so we could laugh about them and help me forget how much it hurt deep down. The Bite Job had given us enough ammunition for years.

Lara had given up her V-plates a year earlier than the legal limit, at the age of fifteen. He was called Marc, went to a school near ours in Guildford, and it only happened once. She was never exactly sure if it counted as sex, because even though he had penetrated her, it only lasted a couple of seconds and he didn't go fully in. Marc never called again.

Now she had moved on and was living my parents' dream by studying law at Oxford. Although her Facebook relationship status was still single, she had been having an on-off thing with a guy called Jez for three years. They'd met at the start of her gap year and had been having casual sex ever since. I wished I'd taken a gap year.

She picked up the phone on the fifteenth ring. 'Ellie, thank God you called. I'm having a crisis.'

I pulled the duvet over my head. 'Me, too. I played Never Have I Ever with the hipster crew and I told them I had anal sex.'

'Why would you say that—you haven't even had *real* sex.'

'AND YOU THINK I DON'T KNOW THAT?' I yelled down the phone at her. She responded with silence and I sighed despondently. 'Anyway, I give up on my life—it's too depressing. What's your crisis? I hope it's worse than mine. I need major distraction.'

'Trust me, it is. I'm home for Easter and want to see Jez but, as usual, he is being a dick and won't reply to my messages. So now I'm in central London just waiting for him to reply so I can see him tonight.'

'Wait—so you're in London with no plans? Why don't you come over to mine?'

'Well, I'm kind of already on my way.'

'I can't believe you assumed I'd be home alone with nothing to do.'

'But that's exactly what you are doing.'

'OK, point taken. Anyway, I hope you're willing to ditch Jez, because I have a proposition for you and it involves going out tonight.'

'But what if he calls and wants to see me? I don't know if I can go *out* out tonight.'

'Lara, come on. He is ignoring you, which he does every few weeks, so you can't just be at his beck and call. Embrace your inner feminist, stop being his booty call and come out with me tonight to help me lose my virginity.'

She started laughing. 'Are you kidding? You want to lose your virginity *tonight*? To a stranger?'

'Yup.'

'I'm not helping you get deflowered by a one-night stand. You've held on long enough so you may as well last a bit longer for The One.'

'I am so bored of that phrase,' I retorted. 'Do you know how many websites have advised me to keep on waiting? WikiHow's entire virginity page is full of Hare Krishna crap like that.'

'Did you actually search for virginity advice on Wikipedia?'

'See how desperate I am?' I pleaded in my best whiny voice.

'Promise you'll never do that voice again and I'll consider it.'

'Oh, fine. Have you brought any chocolate with you? I'm going to need calorie support for when I tell you about last night.'

'I'm on a diet again.'

'Are you kidding me?! You're a size eight—you don't need to diet.'

'I know, but I feel kind of gross and I was planning to see Jez tonight and I didn't want to be bloated.'

'Lara, you're speaking to someone who had to buy size twelve jeans the other day—and they still left imprints on my legs when I took them off. Do not even think about saying you feel fat. Besides, do you want to end up looking like those anorexic A-listers in magazines? They're completely airbrushed and no normal humans look like that and—'

She groaned through the rest of the rant I recited to her every time she tried to diet. We had both decided long ago never to become girls who only ate celery and used their diaries for cumulative calorie counting, but occasionally one of us lapsed and found the willpower to start dieting. It was normally Lara.

'OK, OK, I'm sorry,' she said. 'I'll see you in five with chocolate.'

We sat looking doubtfully at the pile of clothes on the bed. I had no idea what to wear. *Cosmo*'s *'What to Wear for Any Occasion'* guides were open on twenty website tabs but none of them had a *'What to Wear for Finding a One-Night Stand to Lose Your Virginity to'* page.

'Once we've chosen where we're going, it will be easier to choose an outfit,' said Lara.

I sighed and fell back onto the pile of discarded dresses on my bed. 'The thing is, I don't want to lose it to a skanky student, especially because I might see him again, so we can't go to a student place….'

'OK, why don't we go somewhere a bit nicer?' she suggested. 'In Mayfair or something? Lots of people from my uni go out round there.'

Normally the thought of going to those clubs made me come out in a cold sweat. Hordes of Oxbridge graduates in designer clothes would make me stick out like a sore thumb. However, I had already tried the typical student clubs and had no luck whatsoever.

I shrugged. 'You know what? Fuck it. I'm desperate. Let's go to a posh club.'

She whooped and I carried on. 'Besides, I may as well get deflowered by someone who can actually afford to buy me a drink. Hell, if I shag someone wealthy with connections, I might even get a writing internship out of it.'

Lara stopped cheering. She crinkled up her perfect-sized nose and stared at me. 'Are you sure you're not being a bit, um, *blasé* about this whole breaking-your-hymen thing?'

I exhaled loudly. 'Look, I know I sound a bit crazy. But honestly, it just feels like a burden now. Even if I did meet the right guy, he would run a mile if he found out I'm still a virgin. It just makes me look weird—kind of like I saved it for him. If I can get rid of it with an ONS, then I'll feel so much freer after, you know?'

'Did you just abbreviate one-night stand?'

I ignored her. 'I promise I won't regret it. I've thought about it a lot and I know it's the right choice for me. I just want to get this humiliating experience over with as soon as possible. Please help?'

'Oh, fine. Let's go to Mahiki. Prince Harry and his friends go there so at least you'll lose it to someone who can pay for an abortion if you need one. Besides, it's cheaper on Mondays for students.'

Hours later, Jez still hadn't texted Lara back so she decided she would look for an ONS of her own to take her mind off him. We decided to wear black to respect the impending death of my virginity and picked out two short dresses from my wardrobe.

'OK, so if I'm planning on getting down and dirty tonight, I need to shave my legs.' I paused and then carried on. 'And more important, what am I meant to do with the hair down *there*?' I whispered. 'You know what happened last time.'

Following the Bite Job, I had decided it was time to get rid of my pubes. A quick poll had revealed that all my classmates had been shaving their vaginas since they turned fifteen but no one had thought to tell me. I realised where I had gone wrong in leaving my pubes *au naturel.* I was too embarrassed to ask my friends for more info so I researched the topic online. It didn't take long to learn the difference between a Hollywood and a Brazilian. Every website and magazine said that the *au naturel* vagina had only been acceptable in the seventies.

I realised I had to sort out my bush immediately because if I ever met another guy—or, more likely, got run over and had to wear an operating gown in hospital—I would be a laughing stock the minute they took my pants down.

I began my task right away. I ran a bath, and with grim determination climbed into it, brandishing my pink Venus razor. Shaving cream was too expensive to bother with, so I took a deep breath and reached for the shower gel. It was empty. Typical.

There was a bottle of shampoo and conditioner on the side. Conditioner was basically the same as shower gel, right? I figured it would be fine and slathered it all over my pubes. Then, without really knowing what I was doing, I started to shave the triangle area. My never-cut pubic hairs immediately got tangled in the razor and it started yanking them painfully. I persevered for twenty minutes before I realised I should have trimmed them to start with. I grabbed some nail scissors and started.

I finished snipping away with the scissors and went back to the razor. This time it was much easier, and the hairs disappeared. It got trickier around the more delicate areas, where I tried to pull the skin taut for a cleaner shave. When I got to the lips, I was navigating in total confusion. I was so terrified of cutting something important that I just left all the hairs on the side of the clitoris. I rubbed around with my hand to check if there were any other obvious patches I'd missed, but I couldn't find any.

Until I headed down south and realised with horror there was a line of hair going up to my anus. I had no idea if you were meant to get rid of this bit, too, but figured I may as well finish what I'd started. I held my bum cheeks wide open and leant forward in the water, wishing I hadn't put so much bubble bath in. I held my breath, carefully shaving upwards. It was hard to keep the razor close to the skin but I managed to get most of it off. I swapped sides and then breathed out in relief. I felt as though I'd just had a gruelling Pilates class.

I was about to climb out of the bath into the comfort of my dressing gown when I remembered Lily saying the lips were the one area where boys didn't want hairs in case they went down on you. There weren't exactly any boys queuing up to go down on me—but then, I reasoned, they wouldn't if it got around that I had a hairy vagina. With a resigned sigh, I pulled the lips apart as far as I could and found the hairs growing only a few millimetres away from the clitoris.

Picking up my razor again, I slowly started steering it around the delicate parts, wishing I had invested in a special bikini razor.

Then I screamed. I had cut it. I had actually cut my clitoris.

I grabbed the shower head and turned the cold water on max. It numbed my vagina, and gradually my cries turned into self-pitying whimpers. I had another peek at it and it looked OK. It was only a tiny nick. I thanked God that I hadn't accidentally lopped the whole thing off. I got out of the bath and dried myself gently before limping off to bed.

By the next day, I'd forgotten about the cutting incident. It seemed to have miraculously healed and I spent the entire morning feeling deliciously smooth. I even spent a full twenty minutes admiring my naked body in front of the mirror. The mass of hair that had used to terrify me and make me feel anything but sexy was gone. Post-shave I felt like a New Woman.

A few hours later, everything changed. I sat on the loo to pee and screamed in agony. The urine was trickling against my cut and it was more painful than anything I had ever experienced. I couldn't pee without crying. I was fucked.

The only option was to dehydrate myself and not pee. I wandered around school for the next couple of days in a state of hell. Dante's seventh circle of hell had nothing on my life post-shave. I was thirsty, faint, and had to stop wearing mascara because I cried so much every time I peed.

On top of that, the hairs had already started to grow back as stubble. It was itchy as hell and I couldn't stop scratching. I had to hide in corners in public to scratch my vagina, and I winced whenever the outer lips rubbed together. In the mirror, it looked as hideous as it felt. The stubble made my poor lady bits look like a middle-aged man's beard.

It took four days for the cut to heal and I spent every evening writing *I hate my life* all over my diary in five different felt tips. Eventually I worked up the courage to tell Lara exactly what had happened and she laughed so much she cried.

When I mentioned it again four years later, she was still laughing.

'Oh my God, I totally forgot that,' she sniggered.

'It wasn't funny,' I snapped. 'It was agony and I'm never letting a razor go anywhere near my vag again.' I paused. 'So what do I do instead?'

'Why don't you use a cream?'

I raised my eyebrows at her. 'I can't really see a cream having much effect down there. The hairs are kind of thick.'

'No, it's fine. The creams are designed to work on all types of hair. Why don't you go ahead and trim, and I'll go to the supermarket and buy the cream?'

'OK, but if it goes wrong, I'm blaming you,' I warned as I chucked her my wallet and walked into the bathroom to start the preparation. I hated trimming my pubes. I didn't know what length to trim them to, and Lara was useless in this area because she was so fair her entire body was hairless. I doubted she had ever had to decide which hair removal method was best because she definitely didn't have any. I'd noticed in Year Seven when we changed for swimming.

I started trying to pull the hairs together in clumps so I could trim them in mini sections. I channelled my inner hairdresser, sectioning the hair in between my fingers and cutting the ends of it. I snipped away as best I could, struggling as I did the lips. The hair fell away into the loo bowl and eventually I was left with a relatively evenly trimmed vagina. I leaned over so my head was in between my legs. Then the door swung open.

'Jesus, Ellie, what are you doing?'

I snapped my head up and pulled my dress back down. 'What happened to knocking? I was checking for stray hairs but I'm tempted to give up on them now.'

'Yeah, you can just get them with this,' she said, as she triumphantly waved a tube of hair removal cream and a bag of M&M's. As I reached for the chocolate she threw the cream at me.

'I figured we'd need extra chocolate for this. We can eat them while we're waiting for the cream to de-hair you.'

I rolled my eyes but dutifully pulled my dress up. Lara groaned, 'Ellie, I seriously wish you wouldn't just whip all your clothes off without some kind of warning.'

'What? I went to an all-girls school.'

'We went to the same school.'

'Exactly, so you should be fine with it. How much of this stuff do I put on?'

She examined the packet. 'Right, you need to make sure all the hairs are covered, so I'd just put loads on if I were you. And then we leave it for ten minutes but you'll probably need fifteen because it says leave it on for two minutes longer for tough hairs.'

'Twelve minutes, then.'

'You're standing in front of me with your vagina out. Trust me, you need fifteen.'

I slathered the white cream, which stank worryingly of chemicals, over my pubes. Then I sat on the loo with my legs spread wide open so the cream wouldn't wear off against my thighs. Lara was lying in the empty bath, passing me M&M's.

'I don't understand how a cream can be as effective as a wax wrenching the hairs out. How can this stuff do the same thing?' I asked.

'Judging by the strong smell coming from between your legs, there are enough chemicals in there to burn them off.'

'Ohmigod, do you think that if I leave it on for too long it will burn me?'

'Nah, probably not. Shall I check the instructions, though?'

I tried to reach for them to chuck over to her but I couldn't without getting off the loo. Instead I held my hand out for more M&M's.

'What does the timer say?'

Lara glanced at her iPhone and announced, 'You officially have forty-five seconds and then you're free to wash it off.'

I jumped up in excitement and gestured for her to get out of the bath.

Gingerly, I switched the shower on and did a silent prayer. I moved the shower head down and waited for the hairs to wash away.

Two minutes later, I was still waiting. Panicking, I started to rub them, and a few came off in my hand. The rest stayed, so I rubbed harder. A few more came away, but after five minutes of frantic rubbing, I was left with a vagina scattered with small patches of pubes. It looked like a sad, bald potato sprouting hairs.

CHAPTER FIVE

WE SPENT TWO HOURS and a bottle of wine consoling me. But by the time we tottered out of my room, we were both snorting with laughter.

'It looks like one of those Mr Potato Head toys,' sniggered Lara. 'With a receding hairline.'

'Here's hoping some lucky man in Mahiki is into the sparse-pubes look.'

'Yeah, you never know, it could be some kind of fetish.' She giggled.

'Poor vagina,' I said, as we hobbled to the bus stop on our high heels. It was cold so we wore coats but left our legs bare for sex appeal. I wished I hadn't relied on alcohol to keep me warm.

'If we were rich, we could get a cab,' said Lara as we finally sat on the 390 towards Green Park.

'But you can't down vodka-lems in a cab,' I reminded her.

'You aren't allowed to drink alcohol on public transport either, Ellie.'

'Seriously?'

'Yes, you idiot.' She rolled her eyes at me as I handed her the plastic water bottle we had filled up with vodka and a tiny bit of lemonade. She glugged then gagged and

I obediently repeated the procedure. We carried on like this until we got to the club and wobbled inside, where we showed them our university cards and were only charged a fiver each.

'Oh my God, have you ever seen so many designer clothes? I feel like I've just walked into an Abercrombie catalogue.' Lara looked around in disgust at the mass of blond people surrounding us.

'I know. If I cared enough this would definitely give me an eating disorder. How am I going to find my devirginiser when I'm surrounded by this inbred gene pool?'

'Alcohol?'

The club was packed with Oxbridge graduates tanned from weekend trips to St Tropez. We headed over to the bar and within seconds, a couple of men were buying us drinks. They were old, slightly balding, and were tucking a bit more than their shirts into their trousers, but as they were happy to splurge their cash on us, we ignored the natural layers bulging out of their waistbands. They bought us whatever we wanted, but drew the line at twenty-quid piña coladas that came in real pineapples. Lara and I spent the next few hours rolling our eyes and getting drunker, while the men carried on chatting and skirting around the topic of their families.

'So, Ellie,' asked the fatter of the two, pulling me out of my daydreams, 'do you want to dance?'

I widened my eyes at Lara and before I had time to mouth 'help' at her, she grabbed my arm and dragged me away. 'Just off to the loo.' She smiled sweetly at the disappointed men.

'Oh my fucking God, I can't handle them any more,' I groaned as I collapsed onto an armchair in the bathroom.

'Tell me about it,' she cried. 'I swear I can see the hair on their bellies *through* their shirts. And have you seen Mike's sweat patches? I actually thought his shirt was grey until I saw the collars.'

I stared at her blankly. 'Which one's Mike?'

'Are you kidding me? The one who just asked you to dance, Ellie.'

'Oh, the fat one,' I said. 'What's the receding hairline one called?'

'Andy,' she said, as she layered more mascara onto her lashes. 'Have you been listening at all?'

'Um, I know they work in real estate, or finance, and probably have two depressed wives at home,' I replied.

'Ugh, this is so miserable,' she moaned. 'Let's just get one more drink out of them, and then go dance. If I have to hear one more thing about Andy's BMW Z4 Roadster I'm going to drown myself in my vodka-lem.'

'Yeah, I don't care about video games at all,' I agreed.

There was a moment's silence as Lara turned to face me. 'You know he was talking about his car, right?'

'Oh fuck. I thought it was some kind of PS4,' I admitted.

She snorted with laughter and pulled my arm, shaking her head. 'This night is ridiculous. Fuck it, one more drink and then we're off to find some actual fitties. Deal?'

I nodded reluctantly and let her lead me back to the balding forty-year-olds.

'Girls, you're back,' cried the fatter one. 'We bought another round, and some tequila shots.'

Lara and I glanced at each other and shrugged. 'To us,' she announced before we downed our glasses. I grabbed the lemon and started sucking it dry when I felt someone staring at me. He was wearing chinos, a blue denim shirt, and had the most symmetrical face I had ever seen. I choked on the lemon skin. I had found the perfect person to deflower me.

I fluffed up my hair, wiped away any smudged mascara from beneath my eyes and gave him my best smile. He smiled back, and I clutched the edge of the table to support myself. I turned to Lara to share my excitement with her, and then slowly, my smile dropped off my face as I realised she was smiling at him, too, and—oh, look, he was smiling back at *her*, not me.

My stomach sank in disappointment and rejection, and I turned back to the balding men and my vodka-lem. By the time I had downed the entire thing, Lara and the amazing guy were sipping out of piña colada pineapples and leaning against each other. I caught her eye and she mouthed *sorry* at me, even though she still had a huge grin on her face.

Andy or Mike nudged me and made a seedy joke about our foursome becoming a threesome. I realised I had to get out of there. I turned away from them, mumbling something about needing to go to the loo, and slipped outside.

I leant against a cold brick wall, too miserable and drunk to feel the cold. This whole idea had been stupid. Deep down, I'd known that from the start. But I had secretly hoped I would find a cute guy who would take me home, buy me breakfast in the morning and fall in love with me. Obviously, though, it was pretty, blonde, clever Lara who had found the ideal guy—and she didn't even need one.

Everyone around me was laughing and chatting happily as they smoked their way to lung cancer. I felt so alone. That was the worst thing about my unwanted virginity—it made me feel so lonely. Lara hadn't been a virgin for years and I was the only one out of our school friends who still hadn't had sex. When we met up for people's twenty-first birthdays, everyone shared stories about their boyfriends or regrettable one-night stands. It was standard uni experience stuff but I could never join in. They all gave me pitying looks—*Aw, still a virgin, Ellie?*—and I used self-deprecating jokes to hide how much I cared. Secretly I wanted to be just like them.

'You all right there?'

I turned around in surprise. There was a boy standing there, grinning at me. As my alcoholic daze cleared up a bit and my eyes adjusted to the light, I saw him properly. He was wearing a grey hoody and he had a flippy, emo fringe with a lip piercing. He was the only person at the club who didn't look as though he'd walked off a yacht, and even the barmen were better dressed than him. He was also the only person who had come over to talk to me willingly.

'Just a bit cold,' I said, trying to force my face into an attractive pout.

'Do you want a cigarette?' he asked.

'Sure,' I said and took the one he offered me.

I lit the third cigarette I had ever smoked in my twenty-one years, breathed in sharply and coughed. A lot. He looked over at me with raised eyebrows, so I rasped, 'Sore throat.'

'Yeah, must be the cold.' He grinned. 'Happens to me all the time.'

I took another drag, swallowed the cough rising up my throat and nonchalantly flicked the ash from the tip of the cigarette onto the ground.

He looked amused.

'So, have you…been here before?' I asked.

'Are you asking me if I come here often? Original chat-up line,' he said with a smirk.

'You're the one who came up to me,' I reminded him.

'Fair point. No, I have never been here before, if you can't tell by my general appearance. What about you?'

'Me neither,' I said, wondering what it would be like to kiss someone with a lip piercing. Would it get in the way?

'So, do you want to go back inside?' he asked.

I shrugged and threw the cigarette onto the ground, following him back down the stairs. We got to the bar and I waited for him to ask me if I wanted a drink. He said nothing so I bought myself a ten-quid vodka and lemonade, trying not to wince as I handed over my debit card. He bought himself a beer, and we leant against a fish tank in the middle of the club.

'So, are you here alone?' he asked.

'I'm with a friend. You?'

'Yeah, same, but he's pulled so I'm alone.'

'Cool, that's, uh...good for him.' I nodded, wondering how much of this static conversation I was going to have to put up with. He paused and looked into my eyes.

After a couple of seconds of intense staring, he leant in and kissed me gently on the lips. It wasn't bad, until he stirred his tongue into action and started sliding it in. I felt the familiar rise of panic at not knowing what to do and tried to keep calm.

Even since my first kisses with James Martell, I'd never really figured out how to do it. When I was young and practised kissing on my hands, I knew deep down that when it happened for real, I would magically know what to do, just like a Hollywood heroine.

But the magic had never happened. Lip Piercing started rubbing his tongue against mine. I felt the metal of his piercing rub against my gums. I was tempted to run my tongue over it but instead I resorted to my fail-safe move of copying what he was doing. As always, it didn't really work and my slightly oversized nose bumped against his. We switched sides and I braced myself for the tongue again.

I tried to remember the advice from a YouTube video I once watched. I started to massage his tongue with mine. Was I meant to go over and around it in a circular way, or go to the side of it? Was I meant to withdraw my tongue back into my mouth afterwards?

Closing my eyes, I hoped for the best. After a few minutes, he seemed to figure out that kissing with tongues was not my speciality and went back to lip kissing. I breathed a sigh of relief that we were done with tongues.

'Ellie!' Lara crept up behind me. She was grinning wildly and her long, silky hair was all mussed up. Her voice was girly and unnatural as she squealed, 'This is Angus. He's at Oxford as well, and get this—we have so many mutual friends!'

Obviously Angus went to Oxford. I gave him my best fake smile and turned to Lara, asking, '*Why have you suddenly become a posh dick?*' with my eyes.

She ignored my look. 'So, who's this? Aren't you going to introduce us?'

I pulled Lip Piercing towards me. 'This is, erm…' I looked at him and he looked blankly back at me. After a few seconds of social embarrassment, I glared at him. 'Well, aren't you going to say what your name is?'

He looked taken aback and stuttered, 'Uh, yeah, it's Chris.'

Lara air-kissed him before turning back to Angus. They went over to the bar and I was left with Chris. I looked down and saw he was wearing Converse. Angus had been wearing beautiful suede loafers. I sighed, but Chris grinned and pulled me towards him. We started kissing again and I wrapped my arms around him, trying to let myself enjoy it. He may have been the only misfit in the club, but at least he was a misfit who fancied me.

We were interrupted by bright, glaring lights. Chris broke away from me. 'Oh shit, the club's closing. I'd better find my friend and head off,' he said.

'Oh God, yeah. Me, too. I need to find Lara.'

'OK then, see you,' he said and walked off.

My mouth dropped open in shock. I wasn't expecting him to suggest a spring wedding, but he hadn't even bothered to ask for my number or to kiss me goodbye. His brief positive impact on my self-esteem slid away and I felt ten times uglier than I had at the beginning of the night. It had been more fun getting ready at home with Lara than it was to take part in this meat market.

Suddenly, I couldn't believe I'd been considering giving my virginity to a guy I met in a club, who had a *lip piercing*, no less. And he didn't even want me. I felt a tear stinging my left eye and stubbornly brushed it away. I wasn't going to cry over some unattractive emo.

Then another tear came. I sat on a leather sofa in a dark corner of the club. I knew I would be able to laugh about this tomorrow with Lara, but right now it wasn't funny. It just validated all the insecurities I'd tried to banish along with my moustache in Year Ten. Why had I expected more?

This was what happened on every night out I had pulled, since starting uni. The guy just left, or took my number, promising to arrange drinks, which he never did. I shouldn't be surprised—I was used to it. I closed my eyes and stayed there alone until the urge to cry lessened and I got up to find Lara.

She was outside snogging Angus. I stood there, waiting for her to kiss him goodnight. The bouncer looked me up and down and winked. 'You going home alone, darling? You don't have to, you know.'

Of course, the only person who wanted to take me home was the old, overweight bouncer. He started leering down my dress, so I pulled my coat over my shoulders and turned away. My drunkenness faded into acute sobriety as I walked towards the bus stop. Lara and Angus followed, hand in manicured hand.

CHAPTER SIX

THE MORNING AFTER, I woke up to find myself splayed out across my double bed. I yawned widely and stretched my arms across the mass of pillows under me. Then I sat up straight. I was in the middle of my bed, which I was meant to be sharing with Lara. Where the hell was she?

I grabbed my silver metal glasses from my bedside table, which I wore strictly only in the privacy of my bedroom, and I hobbled towards the window to pull open the thick curtains.

'OWWWWWW, GET OFF ME!'

I screamed in alarm at the unfamiliar male voice coming from my floor, and jumped over him to the window. I yanked open the curtains and blinked as light flooded the room. My eyes gradually adjusted and the fuzzy male lump on my floor turned into Lara curled up on the floor with Angus-from-last-night. His face was bright red where I had stood on it and he was rubbing his eyes angrily. Lara was lying next to him on her front, naked apart from a black bra. They had my throw draped over them, but it was only half covering Angus' Male Zone.

I stared in silence at them as my brain took in the scene. Slowly, I asked, 'Why are you both on my bedroom floor?'

Lara groaned and rolled over onto her back. She pulled the throw over her body, leaving Angus totally exposed, and I tried not to stare at his trimmed blond pubes creeping up his six-pack in a snail trail. She yawned loudly and said, 'I can't believe how uncomfortable your floor is. You could have given us your bed.'

It all came back to me. Last night at the bus stop, Lara had begged me to let Angus come back to mine, because he was in London visiting a friend so they couldn't go back to his. I had been so depressed and drunk that I had agreed, on the condition that they couldn't have my bed. Clearly they had accepted my offer.

I stared at them wordlessly, then looked down at myself to check that I wasn't also half-naked. I was wearing an oversized T-shirt and last night's black knickers. Wordlessly, I climbed over them, went into the bathroom and closed the door.

My head was throbbing and I had just found my best friend lying naked on my tiny bedroom floor with a guy I had fancied. I was hung over, jealous and irrationally angry.

I needed to shower away my feelings and last night's sweat before I went back out as a normal, happy-for-my-best-friend human being. I pulled my T-shirt over my head, slid my knickers off and climbed into the bathtub.

As my second foot touched the bottom of the tub, I slipped backwards, falling onto my back with a thud. I screamed in pain and swore as loudly as I could.

Rubbing my sore back, I sat up and inspected my hand. It had some white stuff on it and I realised it was probably the hair removal cream from yesterday that I had spent hours washing off.

Then a horrendous thought came to my mind. There were

other things that looked white and gloopy. Sexual things that had nothing to do with my hair removal cream. OH MY MOTHERFUCKING GOD. Had Lara and Angus come in here to have sex in my bathtub while I slept alone next door?

I looked closer at the white stuff but I'd never seen real semen before, not even in all its dried up glory, so I was clueless. I scanned the rest of the bathroom for other evidence. Lara's lacy Calvin Kleins were scrunched up on the bath mat. My worst fears were confirmed.

I screamed as loudly as I could until my screams turned into hysterical sobs. I wiped my hands on the sides of the bath. I could hear Lara banging on the bathroom door and calling out to me, but I ignored her and turned the shower on.

I stood there for what seemed like forever, letting the hot water wash away my hangover and humiliation. Lara hadn't really done anything wrong, bar the whole sex in my bath thing, but this entire experience just made me feel so… rejected. She and I had gone out together to have fun and meet cute guys, but I was the one who genuinely wanted to take a guy back home. Except, obviously, it was Lara with her perfect nose, long blond hair and Oxford education who was taking the men home—even though she was still technically seeing Jez. I knew I was being the bitchy girl who couldn't handle having a prettier, more successful best friend, but that thought just made me cry more.

Forty-five minutes later, I walked out of the bathroom, now cocooned in my dressing gown. Lara was sitting, fully clothed, on my bed. She was alone. As I walked in, she looked guiltily up at me. She sat in silence, waiting for me to say something.

I gave in. 'So, has Angus gone?'

'Yeah. Ellie, I'm really sorry. I shouldn't have brought him back here—that was really weird of me.'

'Don't be silly. It's fine.'

'No, it's not fine. We— Oh God, I have to admit something to you.'

'Go on, then.'

She shuffled on the bed, fidgeting with her hair, which still looked shiny and glossy, and then took a deep breath. 'We had sex together. In your bathroom.'

I waited a few minutes to let her suffer, and then calmly said, 'I know. I found the evidence.'

Her face wrinkled in confusion and then crumpled in shock. Her hand flew in front of her mouth and she groaned. 'Fuck, is that why you screamed? Shit, Ellie, I'm so sorry! This is so embarrassing. I feel so bad. It's just, I was so drunk and we really wanted to have sex but we didn't have anywhere to go….'

I sighed. 'It's fine, honestly. If I were you, I probably would have done the same—except I would have washed the bathtub afterwards.'

She lowered her face in shame again. 'I know. I'm a bad person. I'm sorry. I owe you.'

I sat down on the bed next to her and knew I had already forgiven her. 'Anyway, let's just forget it. How was it with Angus?'

She brightened up and smiled happily. 'He was really nice. We swapped numbers and made plans to go for coffee next week. He's doing his Master's so he's a couple of years older than us, but he seems like a really decent guy.'

'Better than Jez?'

She snorted, 'Babe, even your emo from last night is better than Jez. What was with that, anyway?'

'Uh, well...after you heartlessly abandoned me, I had to fend for myself, and I guess drunk Ellie couldn't find anyone better to hang out with. So, that happened.'

'I guess the mission failed, then?'

I nodded, scrunching up my face. 'I think it was for the best. I can't really lose my virginity like that. I don't think I'd mind losing it to a total stranger, but last night was kind of seedy....'

'You're right. And you know what? I'm proud of you for not giving in. I'm sure you could have easily gone home with the emo guy, but you didn't, so well done for resisting,' she said.

'I guess,' I replied uncomfortably, deciding I didn't need to admit to her that Chris hadn't actually offered me his services. Or a drink.

'No, seriously, Ellie. I'm glad you didn't lose your virginity to some stranger. I know you feel like it makes you different because everyone we know has had sex, but being different really isn't a bad thing, you know.' She paused, and then added, 'Besides, it's better to be a virgin than to have sex in your best friend's bathtub, like I just did.'

I felt my skin prickle and I crossed my arms. It was all right for Lara to say being different was a good thing, but she had never had to make up lies during Never Have I Ever or sit in silence while our school friends giggled over awkward sex stories. She got to *have* awkward sex with Jez—and Angus, too, apparently.

'How is being different a good thing?' I asked.

'I don't know.' She sighed. 'I guess...I wish I hadn't thrown my virginity away on a total dick, and you haven't, so that makes you different. You have morals. It's a good thing.'

'I didn't have a choice, remember? The dick I tried to give my virginity to said no.'

She rolled her eyes, 'Ellie, that was, like, four years ago. You need to get over the James Martell thing.'

I winced.

The James Martell 'thing'?

'Um, Lara, you know how horrible that was for me. The Bite Job was awful—you can't deny that. And then he totally rejected me. I couldn't just "get over it".'

'He was a decent guy, Ellie,' she said, her tone irritable. 'If you hadn't been so terrified of seeing him again, you probably would have ended up going out, and eventually losing your virginity to him in a really nice way. Instead, you just totally flipped out about it all.'

'What do you mean?' I asked in a slightly strangled voice, knowing I wouldn't like the response.

She sighed. 'Don't hate me for saying this, but I think you're scared.'

'Scared?! How can you say that?' Hurt welled up inside me. 'Lara, it's so easy for you. You never had to worry about any of this, and OK, so Jez is a bit of a dick to you, but you both clearly really like each other and you've been seeing him on and off for years. It's different for me. You have no idea how hard it is to be alone when everyone around you is in a relationship or living single life to the max and sleeping with the whole university.'

'But you're not alone, are you?' she snapped. 'You have your friends, you're doing well at uni—but you're just obsessed with finding a guy and losing your virginity. If you forgot about that for one second, you might actually enjoy your final year instead of freaking out the whole time.'

I felt tears start to sting the back of my eyes. 'Do you ever think for a second that I *do* try?' I asked her. 'That losing my virginity is important to me because it would help me finally fit in? You fit in without even trying. I don't even understand *why* I'm a virgin. No one we know has ever had an issue losing their virginity—more often, they regret losing it to the wrong guy. You had an opportunity with Marc but the only one I've ever had was with James Martell. Maybe I fucked it up because, yes, post–Bite Job I was scared of seeing him, but I was seventeen. Since then, no other guy has been interested in me so I've never had an opportunity to try again. Lara, I try *so* hard to meet men and none of them ever do anything more than kiss me—exactly like last night. *You* just go out to a club and a hot guy comes over and flirts with you. I get stuck with the old men and emos, and then my best friend has sex in my bathroom with a stranger. Do you not understand why I feel alone?'

'Oh my God, why do you keep going on about the bathroom thing?' she asked, her voice becoming shrill and high. 'I'm sorry that Angus preferred me to you. Maybe it's because I'm not so desperate.'

I felt as though she had whacked me across the face. 'Desperate? You actually, genuinely think I'm desperate? How can you say that?'

She looked guilty but the apology I expected didn't come. 'Well, I just think you're a bit…I don't know, obsessed with this whole thing. You wanted to lose your virginity to a guy in a club.'

'So?! It's *my* choice,' I replied, trying not to cry. 'Lara, you can't judge me when you've never been in my position.' I closed my eyes tightly and blurted out something I regretted immediately. 'Why have you suddenly decided to care about it, anyway? You never have before.'

Her mouth dropped open. 'I'm sorry, Ellie, but are you suggesting I don't *care*? I'm here for you whenever you need me. I drop everything every time you have a crisis, which is pretty much every other day.'

My hurt morphed into anger. 'So? We're best friends—that's what we do. OK, fine, I have a lot of crises, but they're not serious. I don't…I don't mope about them or anything.'

She cried out in disbelief, 'Please, Ellie. You are so self-pitying. And you know what? You can be really selfish, too.'

'*I* can be selfish? Look who's talking! We spend hours talking about Jez every couple of days, analysing his text messages, and going on and on about the latest news at Oxford when I don't even go there, and I don't care about the people there.'

'Exactly,' she spat. 'You don't care about the people in my life but you expect me to care about whatever guy recently smiled at you on the tube, or the people you hate in your English course. It's almost like you're jealous of me.'

We stared at each other, and our words seemed to echo around the room. This was our first fight. I didn't know how much of it we meant. Was it true? Was I selfish? The silence was unbearable. I finally understood the phrase about cutting the tension in a room with a knife.

She stood up abruptly. 'Whatever. I'm leaving.' She grabbed her bag and coat, and walked out of my room, slamming the door behind her.

The minute she left, I burst into tears and all the anger dissolved into hurt and regret. She was right—I did self-pity and mope and I *was* selfish. But wasn't everyone? And how could she say those things to me? Didn't she care that she had just hurt me more than any boy ever had?

I curled into a ball on my bed and began to cry very quietly. My wet hair soaked through my dressing gown, but I barely noticed. Lara thought I was desperate.

CHAPTER SEVEN

SHE STILL HADN'T CALLED. It was Wednesday and I didn't know whether to stay in my Camden room or go back home to Guildford. Lara would be there, too—or maybe she had gone back to Oxford to be as far away from me as possible. We'd never had a falling-out before.

In the cold light of day, a bit of the anger had come back. The things she had said were so hurtful, and so…true. She had blurted them out without caring how I felt, and I'd been just as bad. I couldn't face her and I couldn't even begin to start processing the thought of an apology. I had spent all of Tuesday crying, eating my feelings and distracting myself with movies. Now I had an ice cream hangover and couldn't spend another second in my own company.

The only option was to pack up my stuff and head home in defeat for the Easter holidays, but I couldn't bear the thought of sitting around in Guildford with nothing to do. The only reason I normally went home was to spend evenings with Lara, watching films and lounging in the park. I couldn't face going back yet. At least if I stayed in London, I would be surrounded by people. I needed a distraction, to spend time with someone different so I wouldn't have to think about Lara.

Suddenly I remembered Emma. If she was still around, maybe we could have our promised drinks. Before I could change my mind, I reached for my phone and sent her a text asking if she was free. I hadn't even had a chance to put my phone down when it buzzed with a reply.

Yes! So glad you texted. I say we get a late pub lunch and start drinking immediately afterwards. Girly cocktails?

Perfect. Where shall we meet?

See you at The Rocket at 3pm?

Done!! x

Feeling proud of myself for taking the initiative and doing something with my day, I showered quickly and decided to walk the thirty minutes to the pub to work off some of yesterday's calories. I'd forced myself into my favourite black skinny jeans and even though it had taken me half an episode of *Friends* to do them up, they were finally covering my cellulite and inspiring me to walk briskly. I flicked around on my iPod until I found my *Fuck You, World* playlist. It was a relic of my teen angst days but I needed to re-embrace life. And dancing to The Killers was the easiest way to do it.

Forty-five minutes later I arrived at the pub and collapsed, exhausted, into a booth. I had just ordered tap water when Emma walked in. She gave me a hug, enveloping me in flowery perfume, long feathery earrings and her jaggedly-cut blond hair. Thank God I had worn my favourite jeans and black suede boots with gold studs, because otherwise I would have been seriously underdressed. Emma was wearing a chiffon cream shirt over a black bra, paired with jeans, heeled boots and a furry leopard-print coat.

'So, have you ordered yet?' she asked. 'I'm craving a full fish, chips and mushy peas with a proper sticky toffee pudding.'

'That sounds so good. Except I ate a whole tub of Ben & Jerry's last night.'

She looked at me sympathetically. 'Ouch. Who is the bastard?'

'I wish it was a guy.' I sighed. 'Long story short, she is—or maybe was—my best friend from school, who just decided to tell me everything she's secretly disliked about me for years, out of the blue, *after* having sex with a guy I fancied in my bathtub while I slept obliviously next door.'

'Whoa, sounds like you've had a rough few days.... Who was the guy? Was he fit, because if he was, then surely the bathtub sex is excusable?'

'I guess so, yes. I mean, neither of us knew him. We just saw him in a club, fancied him, and he chose her.'

'And then went back to yours and your friend got it on with him in your bathtub? Classy girl,' she said, shaking her head with an admiring smile. 'Babe, you could blame her for this, but I think what's happened here is you've made the classic mistake of having a best friend who gets all the guys. You need to go out there and get a new best friend—preferably an uglier one.'

I snorted with laughter but she grinned at me and carried on.

'OK, maybe that is a bit drastic. But you know what? There are so many girls like this out there. Pretty girls who get all the guys without lifting a finger and then rub it in their friends' faces. Bitches.'

I laughed. 'OK, I feel like we're not talking about my friend any more. Do you have direct experience of this, Emma Matthews?'

Emma rolled her eyes. 'Do I? At school I was second to Alex, because she was blonder than me and had bigger boobs. That's all the Portsmouth guys cared about, by the way—some cultural context for you. You'd do really well there,' she added, making me blush as she looked down at the cleavage I'd tried to hide with a high-cut top. 'But anyway, then I realised that all those years of rejection and being second choice had taught me loads. Ten years later, I am now oblivious to rejection and I can proposition a man without really caring what he says back.'

I looked at her with unadulterated awe. 'So, you ask men out?'

'I've been known to do so. And for the few who say no, the dozens who have said yes and given me some of the best nights of my life have made it worthwhile.'

'I'm officially impressed,' I said. 'The closest I've ever come to asking someone out was when I asked a guy called James to take my virginity when I was seventeen and he said no.'

She burst out laughing. 'Oh, wow, that kind of rejection is enough to put anyone off. Seventeen, huh? That's kind of late to lose your virginity. We all lost ours before fifteen, but then half of the girls in my year at school got pregnant before A-Levels. So I guess we aren't really a fair reflection of the greater world.'

They all lost their virginity at fifteen? Oh God, I was a circus freak. A cable TV channel was probably going to end up doing a documentary on me. The twenty-one-year-old virgin.

I forced a smile. 'Ah, well, I don't think anyone at my school has ever got pregnant before being respectably married to a doctor or lawyer, aside from Molly Hanson in 1984, who ran off with a teacher after he got her pregnant in sixth form. Since then, the school hasn't allowed male teachers under the age of forty unless they're gay. They're scared the girls will run off with them.'

'They have a point. I definitely would have run off with Mr Branson if he'd asked. It's only because he was so good-looking that I was motivated enough to get an A in Physics. So anyway, when did you lose your virginity after the big rejection?' she asked, drawing out the last three words with dramatic pausing.

I flushed red. I didn't want to lie to Emma because she was so open with me. But I couldn't tell her I was a virgin… especially since she clearly didn't know anyone who was still a virgin post-GCSEs. But how would we ever have a proper friendship if she didn't know the one defining detail about me?

I quickly blurted out the truth before I lost my courage. 'Well, it never actually happened for me,' I admitted. Her face screwed up in confusion as her mind started to process what I said. She was judging me, and oh my God, I was freaking out. I rushed on, 'Well, until a few months later when I got drunk and that was that.'

She grinned. 'Ah, the classic drunken first time. Happens to us all.'

I plastered a bright smile on my face and hated myself for being too weak to stick to the truth. 'Yup! Though I can't say I've had many repeats of it, so I'll have to live vicariously through you.'

'Ugh, I know. There is a major male drought going on these days. But is there anyone in the English course you fancy? Charlie, maybe?' she asked with a knowing smile.

I wrinkled my face up in disgust. 'God, no! I could never keep up with his filthy sense of humour.'

'Yeah, I know, right! It's like…what is he trying to cover up with it? I reckon all those stories are just there to hide the fact that he has got a little secret of his own—a very, very little one.'

'Are you trying to tell me he has a tiny dick? How would you know that?' I asked her in shock.

She laughed and tapped the side of her nose. 'I have my sources. Let's just say I overheard Marie saying something to Fiona.'

'Marie and Charlie? You have got to be kidding me,' I gasped.

'Marie and everyone, more like. The girl is a serious player—and that means something, coming from me.'

We ordered our fish and chips and carried on gossiping well into the sticky toffee puddings and our second mojitos. I felt a bit guilty for lying to the most open person I'd ever met, but I figured the second I slept with someone, the lies would be true, and she would never need to know about the half lie.

'Anyway,' Emma said as she spooned the last bit of caramel sauce off her plate and threw her spoon down in triumph, 'we got so distracted that I forgot to be more supportive about your fight with your friend. What actually happened?'

I groaned. 'It's too depressing to relive.'

'Do it.'

I took a deep breath. 'OK, but remember…you asked for this.'

'Disclaimer accepted. Spill.'

'So, we went out on Monday night to Mahiki. I was craving a man and she's already seeing someone, so we went out to try to find me a guy. A couple of disgusting old men bought us drinks and we took full advantage. Then we both saw the perfect guy, but of course blond attractive Angus preferred blonde attractive Lara, so they hooked up. Meanwhile, I got distracted by an ugly little emo boy and snogged him, even though he was the only person not wearing a designer outfit.'

'Whoa—first, what are you trying to say about blonds, Miss Kolstakis? Second, I can't believe you were in Mahiki and you managed to find an emo.' She laughed. 'I admire your skills.'

I raised my eyebrows at her. 'A skill? I feel like it's more like a curse.'

'I don't know…I'd much rather be with someone a bit different than another typical Oxfordite.'

I paused and briefly wondered if I would have enjoyed being with Angus. He had been pretty rude when I stood on his face. 'I don't know,' I said. 'I give up on men. Especially because I then got very drunk and agreed to let Angus stay with Lara in my tiny en-suite bedroom. And when I woke up I stood on his face, realised that they were both NAKED and then…and then I decided to shower it all away and slipped on what I thought was hair removal cream. But as I was lying flat on my back in the bath, crying out in pain, I realised that I had slipped on Angus' come.'

Emma spat out her drink and burst out laughing. I grumbled at her to stop enjoying my humiliation so much, but after my attempts failed, I grudgingly joined her and we laughed until we were both close to tears.

'That…is just…*so* funny,' she said, gasping for breath. 'How do these things happen to you? Even the situation where you accidentally told the whole of UCL English Literature class that you loved being bummed even though you never have been.'

'I didn't exactly tell them I *loved* it….'

'Yeah, sorry, the rumours going round are a bit different.'

I froze. 'Please tell me you're joking.'

'Oh, come on, it's not that bad. I think even Charlie has a newfound respect for you. The boys all fancy you now.'

'Am I meant to be flattered that they now only fancy me because they think I'm a dirty sex maniac?'

'Excuse me,' said Emma as she plonked her glass back onto the table. 'Don't knock anal sex until you've tried it.' She paused, and then lowered her tone. 'Except, it can have slightly disastrous consequences.'

I stared at her, picturing her and an unknown man covered in poo. 'What?' I asked in alarm.

'That girl Alex I was telling you about? The first time she did it, they were at the guy's house and his dad walked in. The guy was so terrified he pulled out immediately, just as she clenched in panic, and…her rectum dislodged and came out with it. The dad had to drive them to hospital.'

I gulped, mentally vowing never to have anal sex.

'That's…that's awful,' I whispered, trying to erase the very vivid image from my mind.

She nodded slowly. 'If it hadn't happened to her, I never would have believed it. It sounds like one of those urban myths, but, unfortunately for Alex, it was true. Some might call it karma,' she added with a grin.

I let out a shocked laugh.

'Anyway,' she said, 'I'm so glad we're hanging out. You're definitely the most normal person I've met in our course so far.'

'Same here,' I said, smiling at her warmly and realising how true it was. 'Although, that's really not saying much,' I joked and she rolled her eyes at me. 'Honestly, though, sometimes I feel kind of distant from the rest of them. They're fun and everything, but I'm never sure how much I have in common with them,' I admitted.

'I know,' she cried out. 'Like, why do we always have to drink red wine and pretend we hate pop music? Sometimes I just want to embrace my inner mainstream self. In fact,' she said as she raised her glass in the air, 'here's to not being cool and not giving a fuck.'

We clinked our glasses together laughing and she called the waiter to bring us more cocktails. He was young and cute, and I shot him my most flirtatious smile but he didn't seem to notice. Emma, meanwhile, was beyond subtle smiles and eye contact. She flirted openly with him, and wrote her number on the bill when we paid two hours later. When we left, she winked at him and he grinned back at her.

'I can't believe you did that, Emma. You're so brave,' I lisped as we left the pub.

She laughed. 'He was so cute I had no choice. My inner lust for him was so overpowering that I just fell prey to my desires. Here's hoping he calls....'

'Will you care if he doesn't?'

'God, no! He's a waiter in a bar. There are hundreds of those all over London. Who cares if one of them doesn't fancy me back? He might have a girlfriend already, or be gay—except I do have a pretty good gaydar—or he might just not like blondes.'

'You're my new idol, Emma,' I said as I tripped over a jagged paving stone.

'Oh-kaaay, little lady, that's good to know. But I reckon we should get you home before you throw up all over your new idol.'

'I'm not that drunk,' I said, as she bundled me into a cab and told the cab driver an address that wasn't mine. I laid my head on her furry leopard-print coat and closed my eyes.

CHAPTER EIGHT

I WOKE UP with a headache and saw flashing lights in front of me. I blinked a few times and realised they were fairy lights. Different-coloured ones encased in paper stars, carefully positioned to illuminate a life-sized poster of Rihanna. I looked down and saw that I was stripped down to my underwear and my half-naked body was barely covered by a zebra-print duvet cover.

'Emma?' I called out, my voice creaking as though it hadn't been used in days.

The door creaked open and she rolled in, wearing a hot-pink dressing gown, carrying two floral mugs. 'Hiya! I brought tea.'

Gratefully I took a mug from her and eased myself up onto my elbows, wincing as a sharp pain shot across my head. 'Thanks so much for letting me stay here yesterday.'

'No worries. There was no way I was letting you go home alone in that state. Anyway, I don't know if you can stomach it but there's kind of a party happening tonight that you should totally come to.'

'You've got to be kidding. I feel like I'm dying.'

'It's the Easter holidays! We have no lectures, and as you told me about a million times last night, you officially have nothing to do back in Guildford. So I can't think of a single reason why you shouldn't come.'

I groaned. 'Emma, I'm an emotional wreck. My best friend doesn't want to know me any more, I spend my free time eating ice cream alone, and when I do persuade someone to hang out with me, I don't shut up about all of the above. Why do you want me to come to this party with you?'

'Stop self-pitying, Ellie Kolstakis,' she said in a mock-mum voice, before putting her cup down and looking me in the eyes. 'When you're not moaning about how crappy your life is, you're hilarious and loads of fun. So I think you should have a shower, then come sit on the sofa with me and watch that new series everyone is obsessed with, and then we can get glammed up and hit the party. How does that sound?'

'It definitely sounds more appealing than going back to mine and packing up all my stuff to take home.'

'Exactly. And then I promise you can go home to your family tomorrow and I'll leave you alone. For now, though, take these.' She threw me a towel and some tracksuit bottoms. 'Get showered up. I can't wait to put you in one of my outfits tonight. You're going to look *so* hot.'

I raised my eyebrows at her and walked out of her room, trying to cover my underwear-clad body with her towel. She called out after me, 'It's the door on the right. My housemates have all gone back home for Easter, so don't worry about anyone walking in on you showering. Feel free to enjoy that shower head however you want, babe!'

I ignored her tip and had a very uneventful shower. We spent the entire day watching a new series about terrorists and the CIA whilst eating carrot sticks and hummus. After seeing Emma's fridge, which looked like an aisle from

Whole Foods, I now understood why she was still a size six and I wasn't. The other day's fish and chips had clearly been her day off weight-watching.

When the evening came round, Emma led me up to her room and forced me into trying on dresses that wouldn't go up past my bum.

'Emma, this is getting embarrassing now. I'm a 36D with a sometimes-size-twelve bum, and I'm not going to fit into your clothes. Please can we give up?'

'You're only a couple of sizes bigger than me. We can definitely find you something. Ugh, I'm so jealous of your bum. I wish I had one. Mine is just flat.'

'Stop trying to make me feel better, Emma.'

'No, I'm serious! Beyoncé is my hero and I dream of having curves like her. In fact, let me prove it to you,' she said, suddenly starting to rummage through her drawers. After a few minutes she triumphantly pulled out a pair of large knickers. 'There!'

'Are those Spanx? Those suck *in* your fat, Em.'

'Nooo! Look, they're padded pants! They have all this padding at the back to give you a structured bum,' she said, waggling her tiny posterior at me.

I burst out laughing as she pulled the pants on over her black thong and began dancing like her bum idol in the new music video everyone was talking about.

'OK, point proven. I will squeeze myself into one of your insanely glam dresses if you go out wearing those pants.'

'Ellie, I already wear these as many times as I can before I have to do a whites wash. Oh my God, I've had a brain-wave. I think I have a very, very cool chiffony dress lying around somewhere. It wouldn't only fit you—it would look amazing!'

After a fifteen-minute search, which uncovered numerous sparkly ones instead, Emma found the dress she meant and I put it on.

I looked critically at myself in her full-length mirror. I was expecting it to hang shapelessly from my boobs, which were hooked up in my most industrial, thick-strapped bra. Instead, it gave me a feminine shape. It was black chiffon, sleeveless and even made my legs look shapely. It was covered in a dark blue peacock print and Emma had persuaded me to wear it with her black, five-inch-heeled ankle boots. She had even cajoled me into putting on a pair of long silver earrings, to which I had agreed only as a compromise after refusing to wear two huge peacock feathers dangling from my ears. My long brown hair still looked a bit out of control and there was nothing that could be done about my prominent, straight nose, but the dress did detract attention from the centre of my face.

'You look amazing, Ellie,' remarked Emma as she surveyed my body.

'I guess I look as good as I'm ever going to,' I admitted and she rolled her eyes.

'You need more self-confidence, babe. Embrace your hot bod and work those curves,' she said, as she rummaged distractedly in her drawer.

I raised my eyebrows. She thought *I* had a hot bod? She was wearing black velvet platform heels with tiny coloured gems all over the heels and a skintight cotton dress that she wore braless and tightsless with the peacock earrings I had rejected. Standing next to her, I felt like a nun, but when we walked into the party—at her friend Amelia's house—I was relieved I'd gone for a more toned-down look. Most people there were the typical hipster types: the guys in checked shirts and skinny jeans, while the girls wore oversized jumpers and boots with tiny floral dresses underneath. I was grateful I had listened to my inner Greek mum and worn thick black tights.

Emma was the only one who looked as though she had walked out of a Soho nightclub, but she seemed oblivious to this and ran towards Amelia, shrieking, 'OH MY GOD, HI!' as we walked in.

Amelia had short dark hair that suited her elf-like face, piercings all up her ears, and she was wearing a man's denim shirt with ripped tights. She and Emma looked as though they were from different worlds—or opposite social scenes at the very least—but they hugged as though they had been friends for years and started sharing stories with each other so loudly the whole room turned to stare.

I smiled politely when Emma remembered to introduce me, and then decided to disappear for a while so they could catch up without the awkward friend hovering behind them. I mouthed something about coats and a loo to Emma, before slipping off in search of company—or, if that was too optimistic, in search of somewhere to hide.

I walked around with my coat slung over my arm, scanning each cluster of people to see if I recognised anyone. Even though everyone there was a third year student at UCL, I realised I didn't know a single person and was forced to give vague *I'm actually looking for a friend and totally belong here* eyes to anyone who gave me a questioning look. Once I had given out the look-over ten times, I decided to give up. I chucked my coat onto a pile of khaki anoraks in a bedroom and took refuge in the bathroom.

I hated forcing myself to speak to strangers at parties. All my teenage insecurities came flooding back the second

I became the new girl or walked into a room full of people I didn't know. I put the toilet seat down and sat on top of it. Emma's flippant remark about me needing more self-confidence drifted into my head. I thought I had ditched the low self-esteem levels that had haunted me through school when I was surrounded by impossibly attractive girls and their boyfriends who hadn't ever fancied me, but I clearly hadn't. I couldn't even admit I looked good after spending two hours getting ready.

I needed to sort myself out or my entire life was going to pass me by. While I was moping around and wishing someone would shag me, everyone else was moving on and *carpe diem*–ing. Maybe Lara was right and I should stop blaming my virginity for every problem I had. I sat up straight. I needed to take a leaf out of Emma's book and get over my teenage bullshit.

I stood up and walked over to the mirror, scrutinising my face. My thick dark hair was not as out of control as I always assumed it was, and fell over my shoulders in acceptable waves. I'd refused Emma's fake eyelashes but after seeing her with a full set, I had compensated for my short ones by piling on layers of mascara. The result was that I now had long eyelashes, satisfactory hair and an impressive outfit. I gave myself a small smile and started a version of the same self-help speech I'd been giving myself since I was thirteen and saw it in a copy of *Just Seventeen* magazine.

'I, Ellie Kolstakis, look amazing. I am a beautiful, confident individual and I can have anything I want. I will go downstairs, I will be amazing and I will be brave. I am incredible.'

I couldn't help grinning widely after the speech. It worked every time. I didn't care how lame, clichéd or romcom it was—the self–pep talk was a tried-and-tested method. It had a good success rate for a reason and I was damned if I was going to miss out on it. I winked and pouted at myself in the mirror until I realised how ridiculous I was and quickly left the bathroom. I shut the door and found myself face-to-face with my all-time favourite person.

'Oh my God, Ellie,' said Hannah Fielding, who had swapped the flowers round her head for a piece of fabric tied into a bow. 'I can't believe you're here. I've never seen you at one of Meely's parties before.'

'Yeah, well, I don't really know, erm, Amelia very well, but I'm here with Emma. In fact, I should probably find her—I've been ages.'

'Yeah, I've been waiting ages. I could have sworn I heard you speaking to someone in there.'

I shrugged my shoulders and held out my phone weakly. 'I took a phone call while I was in there. Anyway, so good to see you. I'll see you later, I'm sure.'

I turned and bolted down the stairs before she could say anything else. I put my head into my hands, wanting to curl up in a corner, but then I saw Emma. I was still on the staircase, so she couldn't see me from my vantage point but I saw her walk over to a very attractive guy and start talking to him. At first he just looked pleasantly surprised, but within seconds his body language suggested he was interested. OK, I understated—he looked as though he was ready to throw her over a banister and shag her immediately.

How did Emma find it so easy? She didn't even let people like Hannah bother her. I trudged down the rest of the stairs, suddenly feeling the effects of my motivational speech slowly ebbing away. I poured myself a glass of vodka with a few drips of orange juice.

I was gagging after my first sip when I saw a guy standing in the corner of the room on his own, his arms crossed. He wasn't very attractive—his face was kind of squashed-looking and he was very pale and freckly. On top of that, he looked pissed off. He was wearing a dark red zip-up hoody and had a book poking out of his pocket.

He looked like a pretentious idiot. The perfect guy on whom I could practise my confident new persona.

Without letting myself think, I decided I'd walk over and say hi. I could feel my little enzymes and cells inside urging me on. *Come on, Ellie, you can do this,* they yelled. *You don't even particularly fancy him—you have nothing to lose.* They had a point.

I closed my eyes and quickly walked over before I had a chance to convince myself not to. The blood pounded in my veins as I approached him.

I smiled. 'Hey, I'm Ellie.'

He looked up at me suspiciously. 'Hey. I'm Jack.'

'Hi! So, how do you know Amelia?'

'Who's Amelia?'

'Oh, um, she lives here and it's her party. I thought maybe you're a friend of hers.'

'No, I'm just here with a friend, Eric.'

'Oh, right, I don't know him.'

'Yeah, he's dating a girl who told him to come. Hannah Fielding?'

Of course he was dating Hannah. Fucking typical. 'Yeah, I know her. We both study English together. How do you know Eric?'

'We work together.' He shrugged.

I smiled. 'Oh, cool. What do you do?'

'I work in graphic design.'

I winced. He was giving off strong *leave me alone* vibes and the monosyllabic responses suggested he definitely didn't want me here and was about to reject me. *Come on, Ellie! You're beautiful and brave,* I yelled at myself inwardly. I gave it one last shot.

'Graphic design, cool. What kind of stuff do you do?' I asked optimistically.

'Well, I really hate the idea of working for the commercial side of things, so I'm working for a small start-up in Shoreditch.'

Typical. This guy was a total cliché and I was ready to bail. Then my new mantra popped into my head—*What would Emma do?*

I opened my mouth and a stream of words fell out. 'Right, and you like underground music, you hate girls who wear fake eyelashes or nails and you secretly want to be a millionaire—but in the meantime, it makes you feel better to say you hate capitalism or whatever.'

He stared at me in silence with his mouth slightly open and he looked like a confused goldfish. Fuck, why had I just done that? I was an idiot. Emma never would have said all that.

I tried to undo the damage. 'No, wait, I didn't mean it like that. Sorry, I got carried away. I'm sure you're nothing like that. It's just that a couple of people here are, and I kind of assumed you would be, too, but that's just me being stupid. Ignore me, really.'

Why did I have so much verbal diarrhoea? I cringed at what I had just said, and hoped he wouldn't think I was deranged. I thought about trying to explain what I meant, but at the last minute, his face broke into a half grin. I breathed a sigh of relief.

'Yeah, you're right. I guess I am a bit of a pretentious twat. I bet capitalism and commercialism would look pretty fucking great if I was a millionaire,' he admitted. 'Especially because I'm definitely not a millionaire, and just had my wallet stolen today—which is why I'm in a shit mood. Sorry. I don't normally go to parties and stand alone in a corner being unfriendly.'

OK, so he knew he was being unfriendly before and he didn't normally respond with less-than-five-word sentences. This was positive news. I figured he wasn't rejecting me, so I asked him what happened, and let him tell me his ten-minute sob story about getting pickpocketed on the 176 bus to Penge. We sat down on the sofa together and carried on chatting.

It turned out Jack was twenty-six, originally from Nottingham but lived in South London, loved philosophy and art, hated all the music I loved and kind of *was* the Shoreditch stereotype I had guessed he was. But we still ended up talking for hours, and he laughed at all my jokes, even the ones I didn't realise I was making.

'Do you want a drink?' he asked suddenly.

'Sure, I'd love another…erm, vodka and orange?' I said, looking doubtfully at the remnants of the pale, sickly looking drink left in my glass.

'Is that what that is?' he asked, nodding his head wisely. 'Wow, I'd forgotten the crap that students drink. Luckily, I bought a bottle of Beaujolais before my wallet got stolen, so shall I pour you some of that instead?'

'Uh, yes, please,' I said, impressed by the fancy bottle of red that he pulled out of a canvas bag.

He started pouring the wine into two cups when Emma

swooped up, a cup in her hand. 'And one for me please, thank you very much.'

Jack looked a bit taken aback but went along with it when he saw Emma envelop me in a bear hug. 'Sooo, are we having fun, Ellie? Oh my God, I met the nicest guy. He is so much fitter than yesterday's barman, who still hasn't texted—what a wanker. Anyway, so Mike, the new guy, is a total cutie.'

'I saw,' I said, raising my eyebrows at her. 'There was some major flirting going on there.'

'Not just over there,' she added, grinning, and looked pointedly at Jack.

I flushed red and quickly said, 'Yeah, OK. So, Jack, this is Emma. Emma, Jack.'

She turned to face Jack and gave him a full hundred-watt smile. 'Glad to see Ellie's getting to know the only guy at this party who brought decent drinks with him.'

'Well, hey, someone had to.' He grinned back at her.

I felt the familiar Lara-jealousy creeping into my stomach as I realised they were flirting with each other, and even though I didn't fancy Jack, I really didn't want to be the rejected third wheel again. Except I had forgotten that Emma wasn't Lara. When Jack had finished pouring her drink, she winked at me, blew him a kiss and disappeared with the drink in hand.

'So, that was Emma!' I said brightly, recovering from my temporary lapse of self-esteem and inwardly telling myself off for ever having doubted her.

'She seems fun.'

'She is. Hey, what's the mysterious Eric like?'

'Not so mysterious at all, really,' he said, gesturing towards a tall dark-haired guy standing at the back of the room with his arm around Hannah. Eric was very good-looking, at least six feet tall, with stubble. He wore a T-shirt with an image of headphones printed around its neckline, and he looked bored. Hannah was welcome to him.

'So, do you know Hannah well?' he asked.

'Um…' I paused. 'Well, we've had a lot of classes together these past few years, and we have a lot of mutual friends so I guess I know her well enough. We don't really hang out one-on-one, though. Ever.'

He laughed. 'OK, I get it. You're acquaintances more than friends. To be honest, I don't really get on too well with her.'

My face shone with delight but I quickly forced it into a concerned expression. 'Oh, no way, how come?'

He grinned. 'Don't play innocent. I can see that you don't like her. It's written all over your face.'

Ah. 'Well, I mean we just don't have much in common. Like…I'm a nice person and she's not.'

'Ouch! Where did that come from?'

'I honestly didn't mean to say that.' I gestured towards the now-empty glass I was holding. 'I think maybe it was the wine that said it.'

'Then I think we should fill that up again. This is getting entertaining.'

'Getting? Excuse me?' I asked, raising my eyebrows. Oh my God, I was flirting. Emma's dress was clearly giving me all of her vibes. I was on a roll.

'You're right,' he said, smiling at me. 'This has all been fun. In fact, hey, do you want to maybe do it again?'

Oh my God, he was asking me out. An actual, real guy was asking me out. A twenty-six-year-old MAN was asking me out, and he had a job. I bit my lip to hide the elation bursting out of me, and as casually as I could, replied, 'Sure.'

He grinned back at me. 'Cool, do you want to give me your number, then?'

I read my number out to him and saw him pause when he was about to type in my name. Oh God, I knew there had to be a catch. He had managed to forget my two-syllable name.

He looked up. 'Erm, how do you spell your name again?'

I sighed. 'It's Ellie. Which is E-L-L-I-E because there really isn't any other way to spell it. I can't believe you forgot my name.'

He flushed red. 'Sorry. Can I blame this on the Beaujolais, too?'

I made a mental note to research this wine, and a couple of others while I was at it, so I could look a bit more sophisticated on our date. Oh my God, DATE. I beamed and took his number happily.

'So, I'd better go find Emma,' I said finally.

'Yeah, it's like— Wow, it's 1:00 a.m.,' he said as he looked at his watch. 'We've been chatting for about three hours now.'

'Shit, Emma's probably furious,' I said, whilst my insides danced for joy at the fact that a guy had asked for my number after spending three hours chatting to me exclusively.

'I wouldn't be too sure. Isn't that her on top of that guy?'

I glanced over to where he was pointing and burst out laughing. 'That girl is amazing. I hope that guy realises how lucky he is.'

Jack smiled uncertainly so I quickly carried on. 'Anyway,' I said, jumping to my feet, 'I'm going to go and intrude on that because I'm exhausted and need to go home.'

He got up and smiled at me. 'Good luck. It was good to meet you.'

He put out his right arm and as I was about to walk up to him for a hug, he clenched his hand into a fist. I stared at it. Why was he screwing his hand into a fist? Jesus, was he going to punch me?

Alarmed, I started to step back as he raised his fist. He reached out towards me and bumped his fist against my right hand, which was hanging limp by my side. Had he just fist-bumped me goodbye? All thoughts of a goodbye kiss slowly evaporated.

'Um, OK,' I said slowly. 'I'm going to go now, so bye, then.' I looked at him expectantly, giving him one last chance to kiss me or, at the very least, hug me.

He lifted his eyebrows and smiled, before turning away and walking towards Eric and Hannah, who were now snogging on another sofa. I looked down at my right hand and sighed. So much for my romantic goodbye.

CHAPTER NINE

FOUR DAYS LATER, I was at home with my mum, living in a state of limbo. Jack still hadn't texted me. I was trying not to think too much about it but every time my phone beeped I jumped and had to restrain the wild feelings of hope every time I read the message and it wasn't from Jack.

I was starting to wonder if I was untextable. On Day One, I had fully expected a message but there was nothing. Then I thought, *OK, maybe he doesn't want to come across as too keen*, so on Day Two I figured he would get in touch to hang out that Saturday night. On Day Three, I remembered all the dating books said to wait three days, so I expected a message, assuming he was just following the three-day rule.

But…nothing. And now it was Day Four and I had never heard of a four-day rule. Getting a message from him was starting to look highly unlikely.

Despondently, I put on *Dirty Dancing* and curled up in my dressing gown. I was nearing the end when my mum walked in with a worried expression on her face.

'Elena, what is wrong with you? You look like you are having a fit.'

I froze with my arms stretched out and one leg pointed as I wobbled in the middle of the living room trying to imitate Baby's dancing. I turned to look at my mum standing with her arms crossed.

'What? Why are you staring at me, Mum? I'm just watching *Dirty Dancing*.'

'Elena, you are standing in the middle of the room dancing to a film and I can tell you have been crying. You have spent all weekend alone. It is the Easter holidays—why aren't you out with your friends?'

'Uh, because when I go out you tell me I'm out too much, and now that I'm home, apparently I'm home too much?'

'You need a balance. All you have done these holidays is watch movies and cry. Can't you go out with Nikki Pitsillides? She's such a nice girl.'

'She has a boyfriend, she's busy, and FYI, she's not such a nice girl. Her boyfriend's a total druggie.'

My mum looked at me with pity in her eyes. 'Elena, my darling, you need a boyfriend.' She turned around, sighing and shaking her head as she walked out of the living room, muttering in Greek.

I froze, totally gobsmacked. Then I ran into the hallway and yelled out to her, 'Mum, I just told you that Nikki's boyfriend is a total drug addict, and all you can say is I should get a boyfriend, too? Can't you just be glad I'm not taking MDMA in my room with my twenty-five-year-old unemployed boyfriend? What kind of mum are you, telling me I need a boyfriend? I'm at university and I don't inject heroin. YOU SHOULD BE PROUD OF ME. I'M A DREAM DAUGHTER AND ANY NORMAL PARENT WOULD BE GLAD TO HAVE ME.'

There was silence from upstairs. I kicked away in frustration at the inflatable Pilates ball I'd ordered off the internet and never used.

When your mum told you that you needed a boyfriend, and wouldn't even mind if he was a drug addict, you had to accept things had got pretty bad. I trudged down to the kitchen and opened up the freezer. I took out a spoon and a tub of peanut butter ice cream. I sat in the living room with the ice cream, gorging.

Why had Jack bothered to ask for my number if he wasn't going to text me? Would anyone ever want me like Patrick Swayze wanted Jennifer Gray?

I wanted to call Lara but we still weren't speaking. The fight had been over a week ago. This was the longest we had ever gone without speaking, and every time I thought about it, I felt a black hole inside me that ached. I couldn't deal with the fact that she hadn't bothered to text, call or even tweet me. OK, theoretically I could get in contact with her just as easily as she could message me, but I was scared that she was still furious. Besides, she was probably all loved up with Angus and didn't have time to chat.

I was halfway through the tub of ice cream when my phone beeped. I rushed to grab it and my stomach sank when I saw it was an email. It was from UCL's student magazine. I scanned it disinterestedly but sat up straight when I read the next line.

We are looking for a new columnist for *Pi Magazine* and would love for you to try out. Our last columnist, Will, has had to unexpectedly drop out so we want to find someone new ASAP.

If you enjoy writing, have something to say on a variety of topics and can convey your thoughts in an interesting and humorous way, then this is for you.

Please send us a 400-word column on the topic of 'anarchy' by the end of the week, and if you're successful we'll get back to you and let you know if you're *Pi Magazine's* new columnist.
Thanks,
The *Pi* team.

Oh, my God. A student columnist…that would be amazing. I had always wanted to write professionally but had never had the opportunity—or the courage—to do so. I'd entertained the idea of joining the student magazine back in Freshers' Week but I'd been too scared to apply. You had to give a one-minute speech in front of the entire editorial team and the thought had been enough to completely put me off. Sending in a single column entry was definitely a preferable option.

I felt my heart rate increase as I thought seriously about doing it. I loved writing. Going into journalism and having a *Sex and the City*–style column (once I'd actually had sex, of course) was my dream. It had always seemed pretty unreachable but this seemed like a good place to start.

Without giving myself time to talk myself out of it, I grabbed my laptop. I could do this. I had opinions. I could definitely think of something to write about anarchy. Um, the Sex Pistols? Punks? Mohawks?

Anarchy column entry—Ellie Kolstakis

The Sex Pistols brought anarchy to the UK. I know it already existed in other forms—take stoned hippies clutching daisies, or the late 18th-century French who took anarchy to a whole new level, guillotining poor Marie Antoinette, who only wanted cake…

I sat back and smiled with pride. I had an introduction. Now I just had to write another…oh, 356 words, if I counted the title. That would only take half an hour or so, and then I could watch *Downton Abbey* repeats all night. Perfect.

Three hours and four green teas later, I scanned over the 402-word entry to check for errors. It was finished, edited and as good as it was ever going to get. My pulse quickened with nerves as I clicked 'send' but the adrenaline felt good. I had no idea if it was the sort of thing they were looking for, but at least I had finally tried. Maybe being untextable would prove to be a good thing—this lack of dates just meant I had more time to write.

I woke up the next morning feeling rejuvenated. After sending in my column entry it had suddenly hit me that my only current graduation plan was to lose my virginity. But being deflowered was not a career. The realisation inspired me to get the laptop back out again and put on my *Motivation* playlist. I ended up applying for twenty internships at media publications before I eventually passed out with exhaustion.

Now I was still feeling the positive after-effects of my hard work. OK, so it was Day Five and Jack still hadn't texted. There were plenty of reasons why that could be and I didn't have to sit around waiting to find out if he ever would. I was a modern, independent woman, just like Beyoncé, and I could ask a man out. Easy.

Sitting on the tube into East London, I felt like a deranged idiot. Instead of just asking Jack if he wanted to go for drinks like a normal person would, I had invented a reason to be near his office in Old Street station and was on my way there. I was one move away from being a verified stalker and getting a criminal record.

My mind wandered back to the text I had composed just before getting on the underground.

Hey Jack, it's Ellie. Do you fancy going for a coffee today? I'm in Old Street, so maybe round there?

Oh God, I felt sick again. The tube pulled into the station. Doom built in my stomach as I ascended via the escalators, and the signal bars on my phone crept upwards. It beeped. It was a message from him.

Sure, how about 3pm at the Shoreditch Grind?

For a split second I felt pure euphoria, until it hit me—I was going to go for coffee with him. Alone. The nerves washed over me, and I felt the urge to be sick. It was 2:30 p.m. so I had half an hour. I saw the edgy-looking coffee shop opposite the station and decided to sit in there and wait for him.

I ordered a large cappuccino and for once, I didn't have to fight the urge to order a brownie. Then I sat down and waited the longest thirty-five minutes of my life.

Eventually he pushed the door open and walked in, scanning the room. 'Hey!' I called out in a weirdly high-pitched voice.

'Hey, Ellie, how are you?' he asked as he came over and gave me a hug. Thank God—I'd been terrified he would do another fist bump. Or maybe that was waiting for me at the end of our date?

'Good, thanks. You?'

'Yeah, not bad. I'm going to grab a drink. Do you want something?'

'Oh, I'm fine, thanks, I just ordered a cappuccino.' I indicated my cup. It was empty, apart from a bit of cold coffee at the bottom. He looked at it and then looked at me with his eyebrows raised.

'Are you sure?'

'OK, erm, maybe a tea, please. Earl Grey.'

He walked over to the barista and I suddenly panicked—should I offer to pay him for the tea? If it was a date, he should probably pay, right? I forced myself to think calmly and take out my wallet. If Lara had gone up to get my drink, I would give her the money for it, so why should this be any different, I reasoned.

By the time he came back with the drinks, I was waiting for him with my wallet in my hand. 'Thanks, Jack, how much was it?' I asked.

'One-ninety,' he said, without missing a beat.

'Right, cool, OK, here's two pounds,' I said, as I handed him a two-pound coin and thanked God I had offered to pay as he had clearly expected it. He took the coin and reached into his pocket for a ten-pence piece. I took it wordlessly and wondered if this was normal. He sat down and I smiled at him, taking in the fact that he was wearing the exact same outfit from five days ago.

'So, how have you been?' he asked, and I hurriedly moved my eyes away from his clothes and focused on his face.

'Not bad, thanks. I've just moved back home for the holidays, so I've spent the past five days acting like a moody teenager while my mum yells at me.'

'Oh, really? What is she yelling at you about?'

'Um, everything? Just typical Greek parent stuff,' I said,

trying to avoid telling him how my mum thought I was doomed to a life of singledom and weight gain. 'Anyway, how have you been?'

'Yeah, pretty good, thanks,' he said. 'Work is pretty average, but I'm doing a lot of writing in my spare time and hoping to get some of it published. I actually already write for an online magazine, so that's going pretty well.'

'Oh, really? I just applied to write a column for my student magazine!'

'No way, that's pretty impressive. What kind of stuff would you write?'

'Well, the theme was anarchy so I wrote something about what anarchy means nowadays and how it's pretty much gone. I compared it to stealing *pains au chocolat.*'

He laughed. 'OK, that's not what I was expecting, but I'd love to read it. You should email it to me.'

I raised my eyebrows. 'You'd really want to read it?'

'Yes, definitely. It sounds really interesting. I think it's very cool you write.'

I blushed. 'Thanks. I'll send it to you. Anyway, what kind of stuff are you writing?'

'Mine is more of a political satire. It's about the futility of our existence and the fragility of our manmade political systems.'

'So, pretty much the same sort of thing as me, then?' I quipped.

He laughed again. 'Yeah, not quite. I'm trying to illustrate how all the political parties are essentially as distorted as each other, and it doesn't matter if you vote Labour or Conservative—they all want the same things.'

I blinked slowly at him, trying to absorb what he had just

said. 'So, you're basically saying all politicians are idiots and nothing is going to change.'

'Uh, yeah, I guess,' he said. 'But obviously there are a lot of layers and I'm trying to show how one politician is the same as any other.'

'Yeah, that sounds pretty, um, sensible,' I said, feeling totally out of my depth and praying he would stop discussing politics any second.

'To be honest, I'm a socialist. A working-class socialist,' he continued, staring straight into my eyes, as I returned his gaze wordlessly. What the hell was I meant to say to that?

'You're…working class? But you do graphic design. And didn't you say you have an art degree?' I asked him.

'Yeah, but my parents were northern miners. It's my background and my roots,' he explained, moving his arms around passionately.

I was confused. 'OK, but surely that doesn't make you working class, too? Like, you've had a decent education and now you have a profession that isn't really working class.' He looked at me as though I was an idiot. I needed to prove I had a brain or he would get bored of me. I sat up in my seat and tried to force myself to be clever. 'I feel like these class distinctions are just really outdated, you know?' I said.

'No, I really don't agree,' he said vehemently. 'I think the class system prevails as a sub-layer in society. In the United Kingdom, and pretty much all western countries, it's the underlying foundation of civilisation.'

Oh God, the conversation was getting heavy and I was out of my depth. In a last-ditch attempt to save it, I joked, 'Wow. OK, I'm going to need a dictionary to start translating what you're saying now.'

It was clearly the right thing to say because he laughed.

'God, yeah, I've got a habit of doing that. Sorry. So, yeah, I really think class systems are still an integral part of our society but I wish they weren't, which is why I'm a socialist.'

Oh no, he was still going. And it didn't even make sense any more. With my face scrunched up in confusion, I asked, 'But…you just said you think political beliefs are all the same. So why do you have one?'

There was a twenty-second silence, and then he grinned at me again, staring straight at me with his sparkling green eyes. 'I talk a lot of crap, don't I?'

Thank God he knew. I giggled in relief and shrugged my shoulders. 'I think we all do, but you really have a gift for it,' I teased.

'And you have a gift for getting to the core of things without batting an eyelid,' he said. 'I've dated so many girls, but most of them are such intellectuals that we go round in circles for ages, but you…well, you're kind of different.'

Oh my God, had he just implied that we were dating? Wait, did he just say he didn't think I was intellectual? 'Um, thanks?' I said uncertainly.

He laughed. 'No, it's a good thing. I'd love to chat politics with you more often. You obviously have quite good insights and aren't the type of girl who is going to spend an entire coffee date discussing *X Factor* for three hours.'

Shit, he really didn't know me. 'Of course not. Who actually watches that trash?' I giggled nervously.

'God, I know. My ex-girlfriend used to live with a bunch of girls who were obsessed with it. She and I ended up spending all our money at The Ritzy, watching decent films to try to undo the damage it caused.'

'What's The Ritzy?' I asked, my voice suddenly small and quiet from the mention of his ex-girlfriend.

'Oh, it's a cinema in Brixton, near where I live. It's cool—we should go sometime,' he said, smiling.

I smiled back. 'Yeah, that sounds good.'

He cleared his throat. 'Anyway, what were you doing in the area today?'

'Oh, right,' I said with a little laugh. 'I just had some errands to do, like buying things I need. Pretty much doing anything I can to escape the boredom of Surrey and avoid revising for my finals.'

'I see. Well, I'm glad you were around. Sorry I didn't text you—I've had a crazy week and was going to wait for the weekend to see if you wanted to do something when I had more time.'

I felt a warm glow rise inside me and chastised myself for going crazy about the five-day thing. I couldn't think of a suitable response so I just smiled at him and hoped he would carry on. Luckily, he did. 'So, do you want to do something this Friday?'

I was just about to agree when I remembered that Emma was coming home from her trip then and we had arranged to meet up. Typical that the only social plan I had for the entire Easter holidays was on the one day when a boy had asked me out.

'I'm sorry,' I said, my eyes looking down at the floor, 'I can't. But any other day is fine with me.' Damn, that sounded desperate. 'I mean, most days. When is good for you?'

'Oh, no worries. What about Saturday night?' he asked.

'Yeah, OK, Saturday works. I mean, you're tearing me away from the new episode of *Gossip Girl* but I can probably cope.'

His eyes narrowed in curiosity. 'You watch that trash?'

Bugger. 'Um, yes,' I admitted. 'It's important to be a well-rounded person, right? Especially if I want to be a journalist. I can't just watch *Newsnight*. I have to keep in touch with popular culture, as well. As much as it pains me to watch beautiful people wearing stunning clothes and having fun, with addictive drama going on in their enviable lives.'

He laughed. 'It seems like I'm not the only one who talks a lot of crap. I'm getting the feeling that you love this show and it's not the only American drama you're addicted to.'

Shit, how did he know? I hoped he didn't realise I had never watched an episode of *Newsnight*, either. 'OK, I love crap TV,' I confessed.

'I watch *The Simpsons* and *South Park*. Does that count as crap TV, too?' he asked.

'Totally,' I said, smiling. Maybe we had more in common than I thought.

He looked at his watch and sighed. 'Shit, as much as I'd like to sit here and discuss satirical cartoons with you, I've got to get back to work. It's been fun, though,' he said.

'Oh, yeah, I'd better go do my, um, errands,' I replied. We got our coats and walked out together, my heart beating with anticipation and nerves as I prepared my right hand for a fist bump, praying he would do something normal like hug me.

We stood outside in the cold, looking at each other in awkward silence. 'It's been really nice, Ellie,' he eventually said.

Then, next thing I knew, his pale face leaned in towards me. I could see every freckle and every pore and suddenly his pink lips were on mine. I stood, frozen in shock, as his lips planted themselves onto mine. As he kissed me, I started to come back to life, and slowly kissed him back, trying not to think about the fact that we both tasted of stale coffee. I made my lips move against his, and when he tried to put his tongue in, I ignored it so blatantly that it eventually withdrew.

After a few minutes, we stopped kissing and pulled away. I looked at his green eyes, smiling directly at me from their crinkly corners, and I felt something in me melt. He was really attractive up-close and he actually liked me.

'I'll text you,' he said, and I jumped as his words pulled me back to reality. 'And I'll see you on Saturday.'

'Yeah, sounds good,' I said, and smiled at him as he hugged me and walked away, putting his hand in the air as a kind of wave.

I turned around and walked back to the tube, a huge smile glued onto my face. He had kissed me! And I had my first proper date lined up. A grin broke out on my face and I couldn't wipe it off for the entire one-and-a-half-hour train journey home. I couldn't believe we both loved writing—and, OK, so I didn't really understand his, but it sounded incredibly intellectual. And he loved cartoons. At this rate, he might actually become my boyfriend one day.

I did a tiny jump when I ran up my driveway. My mum almost fainted with shock when I hugged her as I walked into our house. *Fuck you, Nikki Pitsillides, with your druggie unemployed boyfriend. I have a date with a graphic designer who thinks I'm clever and funny.*

I'd found my devirginiser.

CHAPTER TEN

I RAN INTO Emma's arms, hugging her happily. 'Oh my God, I have so much to tell you!' I squealed at her.

'Me, too, babe!' she said, hugging me back just as hard. 'Spanish guys are beautiful, and oh my God, are they talented.'

I laughed and we sat down on a velvet banquette in a new French café that had just opened in Soho. 'Tell me everything,' she said. 'You saw that guy, didn't you?'

'Maybe.' I grinned. 'We went for an impromptu coffee, and at the end, he kissed me! And he asked me out—you currently have the privilege of liaising with a woman who has a real date tomorrow night.'

'AAAAAAH!' she screeched, making everyone in the quiet café turn to stare at us. 'I'm so happy for you. This is so exciting. What's he like, where are you going and how was the snog?'

'It was amazing,' I gushed. Then I paused. 'Except…he has a bit of a tendency to be a bit pretentious at times. I don't really get all the political stuff he talks about.'

Emma nodded wisely and clasped her hands together like a sage. 'Let me impart some of my wisdom. What you have here is a classic case of unrealistic-expectations-that-Disney-gave-me.'

'What are you on about, Em?'

'Look,' she said, spreading her hands out, 'you watched Disney films growing up, right?'

'Obviously. I used to wish I was Jasmine from *Aladdin*.'

'Exactly, like most girls. We all wished we were Disney princesses and we believed our Prince Charming was going to swoop in on his magic carpet or whatever. But, unfortunately, Walt Disney has made an entire generation of independent women turn to jelly the second they meet a decent guy because they pray to God he is going to be their Aladdin. And he never is, because no men are going to live up to their cartoon representations.'

I leant back against a satin cushion and pondered this. 'OK, I see your point,' I said cautiously. 'Men aren't going to be as amazing as we want them to be, because we're probably nothing like the princesses, either. But, surely we will still meet incredible guys one day?'

'Yes, I fucking hope so,' she said. 'But *how* incredible? We just don't know. And I, for one, am not going to spend my twenties, AKA my hottest years, waiting for a guy who may or may not exist. Instead I'm going to have as much fun as possible, and date the most decent guys I can find. You've just got to remember that guys will have their faults, but so long as they seem nice-ish and you're attracted to them, the rest doesn't matter. You're only twenty-one, babe. That's so young. I'm basically a granny compared to you. But those two gap years were worth every second,' she added wistfully. 'Anyway, at the end of the day, just enjoy it while you can and if this guy is nice, go for it. Nice is rare these days.'

At the end of her pep talk, she collapsed onto the sofa.

'Oof, that tired me out,' she said. 'What do you think of Auntie Emma's wisdom?'

I sighed and leant my head against the cushioned wall. 'I don't know. I guess you're right. He is definitely very clever, and he's really funny. I love when he smiles. It's just that I don't know how much we really have in common when he talks about the intellectual stuff.'

'Men love talking bollocks. They all do it. Just carry on with him, and each time he goes down that road, cut him off or change the topic and he'll eventually figure out you don't want to hear it.'

I felt better. Emma was right. My expectations were too high and Jack was lovely and that was all that mattered. 'OK. Advice accepted. I'm going to enjoy the fact that I finally have a proper date. Anyway, tell me all about Marbella!'

She grinned, and turned to face me. 'Which one do you want to know about first?'

I let Emma's stories transport me from my ordinary life to a glamorous one in the sunshine, where hot thirty-something-year-olds asked twenty-four-year-old girls out and took them for drinks. On a one-week holiday—with her parents and older brother—Emma had managed to go on two dates with two different men and sleep with both of them. I had no idea how she had managed this, and absorbed everything she said to me with admiration and wonder. All she had done was smile at these guys on the beach and they had come up to her, flirted and asked her out.

The girl had a gift. She regaled me with tales of Antonio, the Spaniard, and Carl, from Yorkshire, and I let myself live through her. She was only a couple of years older than me but her life sounded so fun and exciting, like something straight off TV or out of a Carrie Bradshaw column.

'Anyway,' she said, when I had finally heard every detail about Antonio's talented tongue, 'I'm done boring you to death with my Spain goss. Tell me about your date plans with Jack.'

'Well, it's tomorrow and we're going for dinner but he hasn't told me where we're going yet.'

'Oooh, dinner. He must be planning to get lucky if he's bothering to take you out for dinner,' she said. 'Are you going to go back to his if he asks? Are you gonna shave in case?'

'No, and I don't think I can. I've, um, had some bad experiences,' I said, averting my eyes from hers. 'Let's just say I'm not very skilled with a razor blade when it comes to my vagina.'

She started giggling and when I looked up at her questioningly, she replied, 'Babe, I meant your legs.'

'Ah,' I said sheepishly. 'I think I can probably handle shaving those. But honestly, Emma, removing hair down there is a fucking nightmare for me. Shaving isn't my forte, those hair removal creams don't work and I'm out of options here.'

'Well, I go to a salon and get waxed every month. It's kind of expensive, so that might put you off, but other than that it's the perfect option because you just lie on a bed, raise your legs, and they take care of all the dirty work.'

'How expensive?'

'My salon does a Brazilian for thirty quid, which is expensive, I know, but they use this really good sugar wax and it lasts for weeks,' she assured me.

'Thirty quid?! I could buy about four dresses with that,'

I said, my mouth wide open. Then her words sank in and I raised my eyes to meet hers in confusion. 'Hang on, you get a Brazilian? Why do you do that over a Hollywood?'

She shrugged. 'Personal preference, I guess. I just think having it all off makes it look too bald and I feel so pre-pubescent. It's kind of creepy, isn't it? Like, suddenly we're young girls having sex with older men. It makes me feel illegal and not in a good way.'

The colour drained out of my face and as I sat there thinking about what she said, I wanted to give up once and for all with pubes. Why were they so sodding complicated? Emma picked up on my confusion and touched my arm. 'Don't worry, babe, loads of girls have Hollywoods. It's normal.'

'But do they?' I blurted out. 'I have no fucking clue what other girls do. This is my problem. I can't handle pubes any more. Magazines go on about Brazilians and Hollywoods, but no one actually tells you what everyone else is doing down there. You can see boob jobs, and haircuts and whatever, but you can't see vaginas and it means that I have no idea what lies beneath for half the population. WHY DOES NO ONE EVER TALK ABOUT THEIR PUBIC HAIR-STYLES?'

My voice had reached an anguished crescendo and the entire café turned to stare at us but I hardly noticed.

Emma sat back and a thoughtful expression came to her face. 'God, you're so right. I hadn't really thought about it too much—I just get Brazilians because you can't leave it natural, and a Hollywood seems a bit weird to me, so I figured this was in the middle. Besides, loads of porn stars have it, guys like it and it's easy for wearing bikinis and stuff. But, fuck, why don't magazines talk about it? I would *love* to know what the rest of the world is doing down there.'

I nodded fervently. 'Exactly. Magazines are just hypocritical. They're meant to tackle female issues but none of them write about how awkward it is to shave your vagina. They don't even rate hair-removal products for how well they work on the bikini zone. They just focus on the safe zones like legs and underarms. It drives me crazy.'

Emma's eyes lit up in excitement. 'Oh, my God. We need to publicise this to the world. We need to be the new teenage agony aunts to help all those thirteen-year-olds figure out how to de-hair their vaginas.'

Her enthusiasm was infectious and I started to think our idea could definitely work. 'Yeah, you're right. Some kind of blog about vaginas and sex and awkward things that answers all the questions the NHS government sites won't even consider asking.'

'Oh…I forgot about all those other sites,' she said. 'Don't they basically do the same things? That would be so annoying if our idea already exists.'

'Trust me, Emma. This is totally my area of expertise. I have looked up everything there is to look up and there are *no* websites that answer even half of the questions I have. Well, had. Mainly had, obviously. Besides, it would be so good to have it all in one authoritative source to keep coming back to, instead of just trying out a different website each time.'

She nodded thoughtfully. 'OK, well, let's do it,' she said. 'So, we're thinking a blog. Um…a vagina agony blog that's totally based on our own experiences. A vlog? Or, um…'

'Oh, my God,' I blurted out. 'Like…a vlog for virgins. Everyone writes sex blogs, but no one ever writes about being a virgin.'

'Virgin?' she asked in confusion.

My face went blank and pale. 'Um, like, we could pretend we're virgins?'

She looked at me.

How the fuck was that the best lie I could come up with?

I could feel my face heating up with humiliation. Neither of us spoke and I bit my bottom lip. Oh, God. I was going to have to admit I'd lied to her—that not only was I a virgin, but I was a virgin who had *lied* about it. I'd fucked up our friendship. She opened her mouth to speak and I interrupted. I had to tell her. She deserved to know the truth.

'I lied to you, Em,' I said, looking down at my cappuccino and feeling very sick. I closed my eyes. 'I'm a virgin.'

Emma was mute. I tentatively opened one of my eyes into a kind of squint. She was sitting there, staring at me. I couldn't read her expression. Oh, God. My body was tense when she finally spoke.

'But why didn't you tell me?' she asked, her voice softer than I had ever heard it. 'Did you think I'd…judge you?'

'No!' I replied, horrified. 'Of course not. It was totally just a thing in my head and no reflection on you at all. I'm just a weird, embarrassing freak and didn't want to tell you because I was scared you'd feel uncomfortable around me…and I didn't want you to think you couldn't talk about sex around me,' I admitted. I then added in a small voice, hoping I didn't sound like a pervert, 'And I liked hearing your stories.'

I felt my cheeks burning and I knew my face was about to start clashing with the purple velvet sofas but I couldn't stop talking. 'I was just so embarrassed, Emma,' I said, trying to swallow the sick feeling inside of me.

She looked straight into my eyes and I shifted uncomfortably. She hated me, I could tell. I'd officially ruined our friendship.

'You bloody idiot,' she cried and crushed me in a huge hug. I couldn't physically breathe or move but I felt light with relief. I shut my eyes and breathed in the smell of Miss Dior Chérie. I felt so much better.

Emma broke away, gazing fondly at me. Her eyes looked cloudy. 'Ellie, you're so weird sometimes. Of course I don't care that you're a virgin. Why would I?'

I looked down at my hands and picked at my chipped nail polish. 'I don't know.' I shrugged. 'Just, you don't know anyone over the age of fifteen who is still a virgin.'

'Yeah, because I went to the sluttiest school ever,' she said. 'There are loads of older virgins out there. If a person wants to wait, that's their decision and I respect it. Of course I would.'

'No, but…' I sighed. 'I don't *want* to be a virgin. I'm not like those moral people who want to wait for The One. Obviously I would love for it to be a boyfriend, but realistically, it hasn't happened yet so why would it happen now? At this point, I would take any offers. Well, most,' I added.

She stared at me in confusion. 'Wait,' she said. 'I don't get it. Are you waiting for a particular reason? Did it never almost happen with someone drunk or something?'

I sighed. It hadn't and I didn't really know why. This was it—the big question that I never really knew the answer to. Lara thought it was because I was scared. I thought it was because I was scarred post–Bite Job, but really, it seemed as though it was just bad luck and a severe shortage of opportunities.

'I guess…I guess because I went to an all-girls school?

I was kind of a late bloomer, and then there weren't many opportunities,' I explained.

'But what about uni? Freshers' Week?' she asked.

'I snogged random guys but none of them ever asked me to go back with them,' I confessed.

'Maybe they could sense you weren't slutty?' she suggested.

I looked up. This was a new theory. 'Wait, that's a thing?' I asked curiously.

'Yeah, definitely! I mean, a guy can tell if you're the kind of girl who's going to go home with him or not. They could probably sense…well, not your virginity, *per se*, but that you weren't really easy. It's a good thing, Ellie,' she said encouragingly.

'Huh,' I replied. 'I don't know. Lara thinks I give off desperate vibes. That's what our argument was really about,' I admitted. 'And that night out? I made her come with me to find someone to lose my virginity to. I've kind of sworn to myself that I'll lose my virginity by graduation so I can take a chlamydia test like a normal person.'

Emma snorted with laughter. 'Wait? You want chlamydia?'

It was my turn to look at her as though she was crazy. 'Obviously not. I just want to be eligible to do the test.'

She looked at me in bewilderment. 'You're going to have to explain.'

I fidgeted uncomfortably in my seat. I had never really explained to anyone why I was so desperate to lose my virginity. My girlfriends from school kind of understood it because at one point they'd been in the same position. Even if it was a while ago.

'Well, I guess…it feels like ever since we hit sixteen—or

actually, thirteen for my friend Lily—that everyone started this whole thing about losing their virginity,' I said. 'It was like, I don't know, a competition. Then all the conversations were about sex, and I couldn't join in. I felt so…out of it. Now everyone's having one-night stands and getting with their friends with benefits. And again, I'm the only one who can't join in. It's lonely…and honestly? I want to fit in.'

'Ellie,' she said, touching my arm with concern. 'I'm really sorry if I ever made you feel like that by going on and on about sex.'

'No,' I cried out, hitting her arm. 'You're my friend and I love hearing your sex stories. You show me what I'm missing and what my life will be like one day.' I grinned.

She looked worried. 'It's…not always as glamorous as it sounds, though. I know girls like me who have had abortions, and then girls who actually *got* chlamydia but realised too late and now they're infertile. Seriously, El, how come you want to do this chlamydia test so desperately?'

'It's a symbol,' I explained. 'You can only do the chlamydia test once you've had sex, right? And the majority of university students have had sex, which I'm missing out on with every day that goes by, so for me to be like everyone else and be able to relate to my friends' stories, I need to have sex and do the test. It represents the dream.'

'Chlamydia?'

'No, *sex*. I've heard it's meant to be pretty good.' I smiled with a faux-nonchalant shrug.

She laughed. 'OK, well, I love a challenge so you've come to the right place. I'll help you lose your virginity and we can vlog about it.'

My eyes widened in alarm. 'Um, I'm not blogging about my virginity to the world.'

'Why not?' she suggested reasonably. 'You're the one who wanted to help other people like you. I bet there are loads of twenty-one-year-old virgins who don't want to feel alone. We can discuss pubes, too….'

'Oh God, pubes,' I groaned. 'I forgot about them. I need to figure out what to do with mine before we start vlogging about my virginity and vagina to the world.'

'Well, why don't you just try a Brazilian wax for now?' she suggested. 'I reckon that would be the easiest option, and they still leave a largish chunk of hair down the middle, so it doesn't feel pre-teenage.'

'But it just seems so painful,' I moaned, wincing at the thought of a beautician ripping the hairs out of my bush.

'No pain, no gain, Ellie. Now, about this vlog of ours…'

CHAPTER ELEVEN

WE SAT ON Emma's zebra-print bed, surrounded by copies of *Cosmo* and educational pamphlets about sex she'd bulk-grabbed from the doctors' surgery. I'd refused to go back in and had waited outside next to the bin where I'd chucked the brown envelope.

'So, shall we just call it a vlog?' asked Emma as she looked up from her notepad. 'Like, vlog.com?'

I shrugged my shoulders. 'Yeah, why not. It's a vaginal/virginal blog. A vlog. It doesn't have many SEO words in the website, though—like, no one is ever going to search for the word "vlog". Unless it means something weird in Czech.'

'SEO?' she asked blankly.

'Search engine optimisation. It's like, you want to have really searchable words all over your site so people can find it when they search for it,' I explained.

'How do you know that?'

I flushed slightly. 'What? Everyone knows that. I'm not some kind of tech geek.'

'Well, if you are, I'm fucking impressed. And definitely glad one of us knows something about setting up websites. So, what's the vlog going to focus on?'

I lay back onto her mass of cushions and sighed. 'I don't

know. It needs to be, like, a grown-up, modern, accessible and very graphic version of the problem pages from teenage magazines.'

'Oh my God, do you mean the ones that closed down?' she asked excitedly. 'I loved those, like *Mizz*, *Sugar*, *Just Seventeen* and stuff.'

'Tell me about it. We used to read them out at lunchtime at school. They had the best agony-aunt things, and "confession" series. We used to read aloud the problems people wrote in and laugh at how cringeworthy they were—while secretly feeling glad whenever the agony aunt assured them they were normal. Or maybe I was the only one who secretly thought that,' I added as an afterthought. 'Did you?'

She laughed. 'Yes, obviously. I was always convinced I had a wizard's sleeve.'

'A what?'

'It's like, a bucket vagina?' She looked at my blank face and sighed. 'It's basically where you have a "loose" vagina and it's not that tight. I thought my flap bits were too long, as well.'

'Oh, my God,' I said. 'I never thought of that.'

'Neither did I,' she admitted. 'Until all the local boys started using the words as insults and it got round that Lucy Palmer had a wizard's sleeve. Then I freaked out that I had one, too. And honestly, I think maybe my flaps *are* bigger than most people's.'

'Em, this is perfect,' I cried out.

'It really isn't. Smaller ones look nicer,' she said.

'Noooo. I mean, this is great material for a blog post—or vlog post, sorry. We don't want to make it just a blog for sexually confused virgins. We want to just make it a vaginal blog, for anyone who's ever panicked about the state of their vagina, or anything related to it. Stuff like this about the shape of it, and other things to reassure people they're normal and not alone.'

Her eyes lit up. 'Yeah, definitely. And that line you just said about being panicked over your vag has got to be our tag line.'

'Ooh, it can go in our "About Us".'

'Yeah! But, just to clarify, we can still do some posts about you being a virgin, right? I feel like all the other twenty-one-year-old virgins out there need to know they're not alone.' Her face momentarily clouded with worry. 'You don't think the virgins in their late twenties will feel neglected, do you?'

'Nah, all the advice we're going to give out is pretty universal, right? Like, when it comes to the shape of your vagina, age doesn't really matter.'

'OK, so does this mean you'll do it? You'll vlog about your virginity?'

I let out a dry laugh. 'Who knew my virginity would become so in demand? But OK. I'll do some virginity posts. Can we also do some on pubes, though? And awkward body hair?'

'What a surprise that you want to do a post on pubes.' She grinned. 'But yes, obviously. It's funny, I always got a Brazilian and didn't really think too much about it until I met you. But, you're right, like why am I getting a Brazilian? Did I naturally think, oh, why don't I just wax off my entire vagina and leave a thin strip in the middle? It's not exactly natural, is it? It's...well, it's a bit porn star.'

I nodded vigorously. 'I know. I blame porn for giving us this crisis. Why can't it just be like the seventies when it was normal to have a bush? It's going to be so expensive to get waxes all the time.'

'Yes, and men will never know the pain we go through,' she said darkly. 'It definitely has a lot to do with porn and I guess the whole Hollywood industry thing, too. Like, all the glam people in films have pubeless vaginas.'

'Exactly,' I cried out. 'And, even worse, lingerie ads. They always have pictures of women in lacy underwear with nothing but skin showing underneath the pants. I mean, when I was, like, thirteen, I assumed that's how all women naturally were and that I was a complete freak for having this growing mass of hair.'

She laughed. 'No way! I had that exact thought when I watched my first porno. Although, to be fair, as much as I blame porn for doing this to us, it definitely came in useful in Year Eight.'

'For what?' I asked curiously.

'Well, to know what a penis looked like,' she said matter-of-factly. 'Did you not do that? I thought everyone did. I mean, how are you going to know how to give a blow job if you don't research it?'

I had a flashback of my Bite Job and nodded. 'I totally feel your pain. I wish I'd thought to look at porn—I really fucked up when I first tried.'

'Trust me, you weren't the only one,' she consoled.

'You bit him, too?' I blurted out.

She burst out laughing. 'That's amazing. It's definitely going in the vlog. I didn't bite my guy but I'd heard you were meant to cup the balls with your hands while you did it, and I definitely cupped way harder than you're meant to. In fact, I squeezed them so hard he almost fainted and lost his boner immediately.'

I laughed but made a mental note to be careful about cupping balls.

'I know…thirteen-year-old me was very embarrassing,' she said. 'In fact, I remember when I was even younger and people used to talk about blow jobs. I had no idea what they were. I actually thought that a blow job meant you had to blow into a guy's penis to make it bigger….'

Emma was thirteen when she gave her first blow job? A full four years younger than I was, and she'd clearly managed to do it more than once. I really had been a late bloomer.

'Well, as always, I can beat you on the embarrassing scales,' I replied. 'When I first heard about a blow job I thought it meant blow-drying a guy's pubes.'

Emma howled with laughter and rolled back onto the cushions next to me. 'Ellie, that's…that's so… Just, why would you even think that?!'

'No one ever told me what it was,' I said. 'I just used my very literal initiative. In the same way I did with most sexual stuff. It's just not the sort of knowledge you can get from romcoms or wherever.'

'Fuck romcoms,' she said with such forceful assurance that I gulped on the green tea I was sipping. 'They're all lies, and I'm so bored of the whole scenario where the pretty girl gets burnt by a guy, then gets a personality, makeover and some confidence, and then he comes crawling back. That's not realistic.'

I nodded enthusiastically. 'Yes! Where's the rejection and the humiliation? That's the stuff I can relate to, not amazing book deals that come out of nowhere and random trips to Hollywood. Chick lit these days is just as bad.'

'I know, right?' she replied passionately. 'OK, I like to

read *Bridget Jones* as much as the next person, and I used to love the *Shopaholic* books, but what is with the sickening happy endings? And these perfect men—where the fuck did they come from?'

'Yeah, and did you ever read those teenage novels? The ones about snogging and first boyfriends.... I mean, *seriously*. These girls just know exactly what to do with a guy—their only dilemma is whether to lose their virginity or not—and they seem to never have a shortage of whom to pick. I mean, my friends and I were discussing in major detail how to give hand jobs while these fictional girls magically knew exactly what to do.'

Emma laughed. 'You're so right. This is all going to be such great material for the vlog. It doesn't even feel like work—although it will look so productive on our CVs. Except maybe we should do it anonymously. What do you think?'

'There is no way I can put that on my CV,' I said firmly. 'Anon is definitely the way forward.'

'What if we just use our initials? So you can be EK and I'll be EM.'

'OK,' I said, nodding. 'That's doable.'

'Cool, so shall we get back to CEO words?'

I shook my head at her. 'SEO words. Let's just keep it simple. I'm thinking we set it up and pick a standard template for the layout. Then we can just do a post whenever and add more stuff as we go along. Sound good?'

'Sounds perfect.' She grinned.

The Virgin Entry

Welcome to our vlog.

If you've clicked on our About Us, you will know that a vlog is a blog for people with vaginas, or anyone who wants to read about them. But before we start delving into the depths of our vaginas, we should introduce ourselves. We are—anonymously because we're discussing our sex lives (or lack thereof)—EK and EM.

EK is a 21-year-old virgin who isn't sure why she hasn't lost her V-plates yet, and desperately wants to. She is not religious; she's not waiting till she is married; she's not waiting for The One; she's not expecting her deflowerer to propose immediately; and she's not frigid. She is just unlucky.

EM is 24 years old and the opposite of a virgin. She proudly calls herself a slut and is on a campaign to rid the S-word of its negative connotations and make it unisex: i.e. 'Oh my God, they're such sluts. Cool.'

There you have it. One of us is a virgin and one of us is a slut. The two are not mutually exclusive and regardless of our experiences, we both have very similar views on the world of sex, virginity and vaginas. Ultimately, we're both just 21st-century girls who grew up with *Cosmo*, *Vogue*, TV, Facebook and romcoms. We are part of the generation who have been seriously fucked up by media, but also the generation of women who have more opportunities than our mums and g'mas ever did.

So. This vlog is here for anyone who has ever felt temporarily panicked about anything related to a vagina. It is a website, a forum, a social network where you can see what we have to say about taboo topics that no magazine would dare to publish. We are not afraid to say what needs to be said. In the most graphic way we can think of.

So if ever you have felt confused/alone/upset/stressed/angry/worried because of something remotely sexual, we're your girls. Whatever you've felt? We've felt worse.

CHAPTER TWELVE

LYING ON MY BED and staring up at the Peter Andre poster I had stuck on my ceiling aged eleven, I thought about my date with Jack. He had texted me with a firm plan for tomorrow. We were going to have dinner at a cheap sushi restaurant and go for drinks after. According to Emma, this meant that he was hoping to get lucky, so I should avoid the wasabi sauce because it was the Japanese equivalent of garlic. If having S-E-X was a possibility for tomorrow night, then I needed to be ready and sort out my VJ.

I groaned in misery at the thought of waxing, which seemed too painful to contemplate, braving the cream again—although this time I would have to leave it on for double the time—or accepting my doomed fate and going back to shaving.

Then I remembered the interlinked traumas of my cut vagina, itchy stubble and James Martell crying with laughter at my unshaven haven. I had to get a wax. I couldn't blow it with Jack just because I didn't like the thought of spending my student loan on an hour of excruciating pain.

Emma had recommended her thirty-pound-a-go salon but I was sure I could find one that did waxes a bit cheaper. I grabbed my laptop and started searching. Eventually I found a place in Bloomsbury that did a Brazilian for eighteen quid. That was pretty much half the price of Emma's and it was near the British Museum so it wasn't going to be a dodgy backstreet alley.

Feeling very proud of my thrifty self, I called up before I could lose my nerve and booked myself in for an afternoon appointment. That way I could go just before our date and have a perfectly smooth vag for Jack. Now all I needed to do was trim the damn thing.

The next day, I walked into the salon cautiously, pushing open the pink door and trying to ignore the tacky leaflets stuck all over it. It was a hairdresser's salon on the ground floor and there was nobody at the reception desk, just a woman with a peroxide-blond head cutting a man's hair on the other side of the room.

'Hiya, love. Give us a second,' she called out to me. 'What is it you're in for?'

'Um, a wax,' I replied, hoping I'd come to the right place.

'A Hollywood, is it?' she bellowed.

I blushed furiously, and shook my head silently, praying she would stop speaking about waxes at the top of her voice. She seemed to take my hint because she put down her scissors and crossed the room to me. The man in the chair had turned around—showing himself to be Eastern-European-looking and middle-aged—and was now watching the whole scene with an amused smile on his face. Fantastic.

'No, it's actually for a Brazilian,' I said in a hushed voice as she reached me and started flicking through an A4 notepad.

'Oh, a Brazilian! Why didn't you just say so?' she asked,

her voice still as loud as before. 'Oh, wait, is that going to be just a normal Brazilian you want, or a Playboy Brazilian?'

'A Playboy Brazilian?' I answered, confused and wondering if she wanted me to have a Playboy Bunny etched onto my vagina.

'Yeah, you know, a Playboy wax. It's a type of Brazilian wax but instead of leaving a thick runway strip, we just leave a smaller area of hair. Honestly, babe, I totally recommend a Playboy—they're all the rage these days and I'm sure your boyfriend would love it.' She winked at me and threw her head back to screech in laughter. 'Don't you agree, Stan?' she called out to the man in the chair. He looked me up and down and smiled, showing his crooked yellow teeth, before nodding slowly.

I flushed under his lewd gaze and quickly said, 'Fine, that's fine. So, where do I go?'

'Oh, just down those stairs. Yasmin will take care of you when you get down there. Second door on the right,' she said, flicking her hot-pink nails in the direction of a wooden staircase.

I ran down the stairs without thanking her and prayed that a Playboy was what Emma would have recommended. The name sounded like something she might go for, and a smaller area of hair sounded good. Besides, I had been so uncomfortable up there that I would have agreed to anything—even having a hair bunny marked out onto my lady bits.

'Hello?' I asked, creaking open the second door on the right.

'Oh, hiya,' said a young, dark girl with curly black hair. 'I'm Yasmin. Come in.'

I breathed a sigh of relief as I saw that she was dark-skinned and probably had thick pubes, as well. That meant she wouldn't judge me. She smiled supportively. 'OK, so do you just want to undress and lie down on the bed for me? I'll be back in a couple of minutes,' she said.

I nodded mutely but as the door closed behind her, I began thinking about what she had said. I had to undress and lie on the bed, which sounded pretty simple, but just what did 'undress' mean? Obviously I had to take my shoes and socks off, which I did, and then my jeans. But then, standing there in my black knickers and polka-dot jumper, I wondered how much more to take off. I should probably leave my top half on, because it wasn't as though she would need to access those parts, but what about my knickers? Would she want to navigate around them, and just sort of pull them to the side, or should I just take them off and lie half-naked on the bed?

I heard a knock on the door, and she called out, 'Can I come in?'

Fuck fuck fuck. 'One sec,' I replied as I made a split-second decision and pulled my knickers off. I jumped onto the bed and lay down. 'Ready!' I called out, trying to hide the shrill panic in my voice.

She pushed opened the door and walked into the room, smiling at me. 'OK, great. So Roxy tells me you want a Playboy?'

'Um, I think so,' I said. 'It's a type of Brazilian, right? Would you recommend it?'

'Oh, I don't know,' she said, with a slight laugh. 'I reckon a Playboy should be just fine. OK, so just spread your legs out as wide as you can and I'll start.'

Feeling very awkward, I pulled my legs apart as much as I could and displayed the inner workings of my vagina. She brought a pot of wax towards me and slathered a hot blue strip onto my skin with a wooden spatula. She leaned between my legs as she did so and I prayed to God it didn't smell. I had washed it as much as I could, but as my mum had told me I shouldn't use soap down there, I was stressed that a pure water wash hadn't left it clean enough. I mean, if I didn't use shower gel all over my body, that would just be uncomfortable for everyone, so surely not using it down there would be the same?

Suddenly a bolt of white-hot pain soared up my body, pulling me straight out of my thoughts, and I screamed.

'Sorry, did that hurt?' she asked. 'It should get less painful. Just hold your skin taut and do it as tight as you can. That should help.'

I looked down and saw a patch of hairless skin in between my legs. It was pale and already covered in tiny red dots. Whimpering slightly, I pulled the skin tight around the next waxed area and breathed in and out deeply, preparing myself for the next bolt of pain. Sure enough, a second jolt of agony spread through my body as she whipped the strip off my sore skin. The nerve endings down there felt frayed and I couldn't help yelping out in pain again. I closed my eyes and tried to think calming thoughts while my hands mechanically moved around my vagina, pulling the skin taut for the next minutes of agony.

After a while, she said, 'OK, I'm going to need you to pull the lips open so I can get right in there and take the hair off the sides. Pull one knee up like that, and then… Yep, that's it. Push your knees far apart.'

My knees were bent and spread out, my hands were pulling my labia open and my body was so contorted I felt as if I was doing intermediate yoga over her paper-clad bed.

'Is this, um, right?' I grunted, focusing all my energy on maintaining the pose.

'Perfect,' she trilled as she slathered the wax onto my most delicate bits. My eyes opened wide in horror as I saw the white strip descend onto the fragile-looking skin and she ripped it off abruptly. I howled in pain and felt tears in the corners of my eyes.

'Sorry,' she said, not looking sorry at all. 'The hairs are pretty thick down here, so it's going to hurt a bit, but I'll try and get them all off for you.'

Try?! She was a trained beautician—at least I hoped she was—so surely she was accustomed to getting the toughest hairs out. There was no way I was going to leave with patches of pubes over my VJ.

'I've got most of them out now,' she said, after five more strips yanked my poor pubes out. 'Turn on your front now, and rest on your hands and knees.'

Resisting the temptation to lie there stroking my raw skin, I obeyed her and turned onto my front. Then I pulled myself up onto my hands and knees, doing the Pilates table pose on her bed.

'Can you just use one hand to pull your bum cheek to the side?' she asked casually.

I gingerly removed my left hand and pulled my left bum cheek to the side as requested, wobbling slightly on my right hand. She put more wax down my bum crack and I breathed slowly, preparing myself for the pain.

'You didn't trim down here,' she tutted in annoyance. 'The hairs are going to pull. Next time you need to trim all the way in the G-string area.'

She ripped the strips off and the pain wasn't as bad as I had expected. The skin must be tougher here because it felt kind of cleansing. She did the other side, and I wobbled less as I leaned on my left arm and held the other cheek open. I tried not to think about the fact that she could see parts of my body in more detail than I would ever be able to.

'There we go,' she said. 'Now lie on your front and let me pluck out any stray hairs.'

She got out some tweezers and began pulling little hairs out. I craned my neck downwards in curiosity, as the thought of tweezing down there had never crossed my mind.

'Lie back,' she snapped and I quickly rested my head back down on the bed, where the tissue paper had scrunched up and I could feel the cold leather of the bed against my skin.

'OK,' she said eventually. 'Let me just rub some aloe vera onto the skin and then you're done.'

She squirted freezing-cold liquid onto my skin and started rubbing all over it. I tensed up as she started to rub on the lips and wondered if this counted as sexual harassment. *Was I being molested by my waxing lady?*

'Lovely,' she said. 'I'll see you upstairs to pay when you're changed.'

She walked out of the room and I immediately sat up straight to look down and see the finished result. The entire vagina was bare, with tiny red dots all over the pale white skin. It looked like a plucked chicken, apart from a tiny patch of black hair in the middle. Was this what it was meant to look like? Emma had insinuated there should be a thick strip of hair down the whole thing but mine just looked like a tiny rectangle.

In fact, I thought as I tilted my head, my VJ looked as if it had a little moustache on it. A Hitler moustache.

'So, that will be…twenty-four pounds for the Playboy, plus ten for the G-string area,' the peroxide bitch said as her pink acrylics tapped away on the calculator.

I stared at her in shock. 'What? No, I thought it was eighteen quid.'

'Oh, no, that's just for a normal Brazilian. As you can see, the Playboy Brazilian takes more hair off so it's twenty-four. A full Hollywood is twenty-six, you see. Then, because you've had all the hair off at the back, too, that's another tenner,' she explained.

Silently I handed her my debit card and paid thirty-four pounds for my Hitler moustache. I didn't say another word to her, and barely mumbled 'bye' to Yasmin as I escaped from the shop and let the flyer-clad door swing shut behind me. I pulled my phone out from my bag and rang Emma immediately.

'Heya,' she answered. 'All ready for the big date?'

'I have an emergency,' I blurted out. 'I just went to a salon and got a Playboy Brazilian wax and now my vagina has a tiny Hitler moustache in the middle. The rest of it looks like it has acute chicken pox. Please tell me this is normal.'

'Oh-kaaay. The chicken pox thing is definitely legit—mine always looks gross afterwards but the red dots will disappear soon. But the Hitler thing? I don't understand, babe. Didn't you get a normal Brazilian like we discussed?'

'It went wrong,' I wailed. 'She told me a Playboy was the best type of Brazilian. And it hurt so badly, and it looks so weird.'

'OK, calm down. I'm sure it isn't as bad as you think. Why didn't you just get them to take the little bit of hair off, and have a Hollywood?'

I stopped mid-step. 'Fuck. I don't know. I should have. I can't go back in, though. I just can't. It was so embarrassing and so gross.'

'Where did you go?' she asked.

'A depressing place in Bloomsbury that was freezing cold and cost thirty-four quid.'

'You should have gone to my salon! It's cheaper and really nice and— Oh my God, please tell me your beautician used sugar wax?'

'What's sugar wax?'

'It's the one where they layer it all over you, and then peel it off at the end. They don't use strips so it hurts waaaay less.'

'My beautician used strips,' I moaned.

'Oh, Ellie,' she said. 'Don't worry, you'll be fine. Are you on your way to meet him now?'

I looked down at my Casio watch. 'Yep, and obviously I'm early. He's going to think I'm so keen.'

'Just go hang out in the loos and make yourself look even more beautiful than you already do,' she suggested.

'OK. Thank you.'

'You'll be amazing. Good luck!'

My Hair Lady

Everyone knows women have pubes, leg hair and even underarm hair. But we want to focus on the neglected body hair that everyone ignores. The hair that sprouts up in places we never knew the names of until we looked them up frantically on the internet to check that we were normal. So, these are places that we have found noticeable body hair growing on our own bodies.

NB: EM is blond so she will never really understand the pain of this as much as EK, who is dark-haired and of Mediterranean origins. However, EM insists that even though her hairs are blond, they are plentiful and long.

Arm hair. Everyone has arm hair and it shouldn't be a thing, but for some reason, salons have decided it is normal to offer arm waxes and every model is airbrushed to hide her arm hair. EM's mum even tried to make her wax off her downy forearms so she would look more 'feminine' at a family wedding. She refused.

Nipple hair. This is a thing. We both have fine—or even not-so-fine—hairs growing on our areola (that's the name of the outer ring bit). We haven't checked the biological reason for this but are positive there is a good one.

The snail trail. It's normal, it's natural and we all have it. If you can work yours along with all this other hair, we are majorly jealous and admire you.

Toes and finger hair. There was a scene in *Miss Congeniality* that showed Sandra Bullock getting all her digits waxed so she could be transformed into a beauty pageant winner. It was shit. We're going for the *Little Miss Sunshine* vibe instead.

The 'stache. Both of us have hair on our upper lips. EK used to bleach hers but realized this left a blond downy patch on her face that was still very visible. She now waxes it, as does EM.

Cleavage hair. So, this is a thing we've only just discovered on ourselves. Maybe it's a sign of late puberty (yes, we are in our early 20s), but both of us now have very faint hair down our cleavage. Who knew?

CHAPTER THIRTEEN

I WAS IN SOHO and still had half an hour before meeting Jack. There was a pub nearby so I decided to go inside and use their loos. I ran upstairs, crinkling my nose at the smell of beer-stained carpets, and locked myself in the single loo. I pulled my trousers and pants down, then froze as I realised my best black lace knickers were stuck to my vagina. I yanked at them, and they tore away from my skin. The lace was still intact and they hadn't ripped but there were three bluish blobs covered with black fluff on my vagina.

Oh my fucking God. The wax hadn't all come off on the strips, and it was stuck on my skin along with knicker fluff. I rubbed at it frantically until I realised it had hardened and wasn't coming off. I needed to use some water, but it was a public bathroom. I couldn't just rub my vagina next to the sink, could I?

Praying to God no one would walk in, I hobbled to the sink with my knickers and jeans halfway down my legs. I quickly started rubbing away at it with water and a runny pink soap I squirted from the plastic dispenser. The wax went gloopy when it was mixed with the hot water, and it spread across my skin. I had made it worse.

Feeling panicky, I rubbed as hard as I could and then tried

to peel it off. The sticky wax caught under my fingernails and I tried to scrape it off with loo roll, but the paper stuck to the skin on my hands and vagina.

I looked at myself in the mirror, bent down with my legs spread open and my hand on my vagina, stuck there with wax and loo roll. This was not how I'd imagined the start of my first ever grown-up date.

The door swung open and a middle-aged woman wearing a brown fur coat stood in the doorway, staring at me in disgust.

My mouth dropped wide open and our eyes met in the mirror. There was a squeal and I looked down and saw the child next to her.

'Mummy,' he asked, 'why is that girl rubbing her front bottom?'

The woman put her manicured hand over the little boy's eyes and spun him around. She looked at me with something close to revulsion and shook her head slowly.

'You're disgusting,' she hissed under her breath as she propelled her son out of the bathroom.

I stared at myself in the mirror, wondering how this was my life. I could hear her hushing the boy outside: 'Orlando, sweetie, are you feeling OK?'

I snorted. Orlando was five years old and didn't have a vagina covered in dried wax. He was bloody fine. I, on the other hand, wanted to crawl back into the loo cubicle and never leave.

I stood inside the restaurant, looking nervously for Jack. I had tried to sort out the mess as best as I could, eventually resorting to my Vaseline lip balm and scarf to scratch the wax off. My skin was now raw and had a couple of actual blood spots on it. I ignored the itchy feeling of the lace rubbing against the sore skin and scanned the room.

The restaurant was a tiny little Japanese place with a conveyor belt. I loved sushi but my experience was limited to YO! Sushi with its nice commercial chains and coloured plates. This place looked kind of grimy but it had Japanesey plates on the belt and there were loads of Asian people, which could only be a good sign. It still looked as if it had pretty low hygiene ratings, though.

I saw Jack sitting on a stool by the belt and I walked over to him. My heart started to beat wildly and the nerves crept up on me. In a way, the wax crisis had been a blessing because it had distracted me from my nerves, but now they were swooping back to me in full force.

I smiled shakily and called out 'Hi,' as I approached him.

'Hey, Ellie,' he said, standing up to give me a hug. 'Did you find it OK?'

'Yeah, it was easy, thanks,' I said as I took my leather jacket off and sat on the stool next to his. I awkwardly laid my jacket across my lap as there was nowhere else to put it. It slid off my legs and fell onto the floor.

'I'll just, um, leave it there,' I said and kicked it gently against the side of the counter.

'Right. So, how was your week?' he asked.

'Not bad, thanks. Hung out with a friend—you remember Emma, right, my friend from that party? She was back from holiday last night so we ended up having a six-hour coffee. How about you?'

'I've never understood how girls can chat for so long,' he said, shaking his head. 'I've had a quiet week. Just at work, then as much writing as I could during the evenings.'

'That's so cool you've been writing so much. Is it more of the political columns and stuff?'

'I've actually started a series of short stories—which aren't political, for a change.'

I perked up. 'Ooh, I love creative writing. What are they like? Can I read some?'

'Sure, I'll show you one now,' he said and pulled a Moleskine notepad out of his pocket. I looked at him in surprise.

'You have them with you?' I asked curiously.

'I was writing earlier,' he explained. 'You're welcome to have a read, but shall we order first?'

I took the laminated menu he offered me. We quickly realized sharing dishes wouldn't work as we wanted totally different things. Relieved that we wouldn't end up fighting over the last maki, I happily selected my own choices.

'So, can I read it now?'

He grinned. 'OK, but you can't be cruel. Deal?'

'Deal!'

I picked up his notebook and absent-mindedly nibbled on a fried prawn roll from the conveyor belt as I read. It was a six-page story about a young boy playing by a spring and enjoying nature. It was Wordsworth meets Enid Blyton, and it was the exact opposite of what I had expected him to write.

'Wow, Jack,' I said. 'I had absolutely no idea you could write about things like this. I'm so surprised. It's not at all political—unless the whole thing is a metaphor and I've completely missed the point of it?'

'Don't worry, there's nothing political in there at all. It's all just memories. So did you like it? What do you think of the writing?'

I hesitated. I had enjoyed reading it but parts of it were a bit clichéd. The line *drops of dew hanging off his lashes* hovered in my mind. I decided to be honest. 'I really liked it, Jack. It's well-written and it's…it's calming. It makes me think of…childhood. There's a couple of lines I would change but on the whole I like it.'

His face broke out into a beam and he looked so hopeful and sweet that I felt a rush of affection for him. 'Thanks, yeah, that's exactly what I was going for,' he said enthusiastically. 'It's supposed to be kind of lyrical. I don't know—I just thought I'd do something different and take a break from the political satires. This is a bit out of my comfort zone.'

'I think it's really good you're trying new stuff, and that you have all these ideas. It took me almost three years of university to get my act together and apply to write for the magazine.'

'Oh shit, I forgot to ask—did you get the columnist position?'

I sighed. 'I still haven't heard back. They said they'd let us know by the end of the week so I guess I haven't got it.'

He squeezed my arm and I smiled at him from over my sashimi. 'You never know, they might still give it to you,' he said. 'And even if they don't I'm sure you'll find something else.'

'Yeah, maybe I will,' I said. 'I applied for a bunch of internships so hopefully one of them will reply at some point.'

'Hey, get you,' he said, looking genuinely impressed.

I was enjoying his admiration. I took it a step further. 'And I kind of started an anonymous blog with my friend.'

'Tell me more.'

Shit. I couldn't really tell him any more without giving away that I was a virgin who spent a lot of time freaking out about vaginas. 'Um, it's kind of just about womensy things. Strictly girl stuff.'

'You're not really selling it to me here, Ellie.'

I laughed. 'Yeah, there's a reason I prefer writing to speaking. I'm not so good with the latter.'

'Ah, I don't know, I think you're doing pretty well,' he said, looking straight into my eyes.

His eyes were so green I was momentarily distracted from the fact that he was flirting with me. I closed my mouth and pulled myself back to reality.

'Um, thanks,' I said. Damn, that wasn't the come-hither response I'd been aiming for.

He grinned. 'But, if you're done with talking, I know something else we can do instead…' My eyes widened and I stared at him. Oh my God, sex. He was about to invite me back to his and I hadn't even finished my sashimi. 'Drinking. Do you fancy a couple of pints?'

CHAPTER FOURTEEN

TWO HOURS AND way too many pints later, I felt bloated and uncharacteristically giggly. I wasn't used to drinking beer but hadn't wanted to come across like a girly princess who could only drink rosé or vodka and Coke. Now I was twenty-five quid down from buying a round along with my half of dinner, and he was about to do his next round.

'Wait, Jack,' I said, and put my hand on his shoulder as he stood up with his wallet in his hand. 'I really can't have another one.'

'OK,' he said, 'I'll just get the one, then.'

He walked to the bar and I sunk happily into the leather sofa. It was going well. He was really funny, and he seemed to fancy me. OK, so he loved splitting bills equally, and he hadn't swept me off my feet the way I'd always imagined guys would on dates, but life wasn't an eighties movie. Besides, we were having great banter and the more beers I had, the more I fancied him. His eyes were undeniably attractive and he had more stubble than usual.

I was definitely going to give him access to my untouched hymen tonight.

He came back with his beer and sank onto the sofa next to me. I turned to face him, looking up at him from my slouched-down position. I hoped my face didn't look moon-like from the unflattering angle. He looked at me, taking in my very unsubtle *please kiss me* body language, and obligingly leant in. I moved my face towards his, and we started snogging. Feeling tipsy, I wrapped my hands around his face, kissing him gently, whilst imagining Audrey Hepburn kissing George Peppard in *Breakfast at Tiffany's* and wondering if we looked as romantic as they did. I wished we were outside in the rain.

He put his arms around me and grasped me hard. Whoa. I was getting turned on and, judging from a look down at his trousers, he was, too. I couldn't help grinning excitedly, and as a smile spread across my face, he murmured, 'What are you smiling at?'

'Nothing,' I whispered, not trusting myself to say anything else, and tried to stop from smiling. We carried on kissing a bit more gently, and then he pulled away from me. 'Right, I'd better finish this drink so we can get out of here before we get thrown out.'

I smiled back, suddenly very shy. He picked up his pint, and as I finished the last inch of mine, he drank the entire thing. I watched him down the full pint with my eyes glued to his face, feeling an animal attraction that made me want to rip his clothes off and shag him right there.

I grinned in anticipation. Tonight I would finally lose my virginity and act out the dirty things I'd been imagining ever since I'd watched *Basic Instinct* at the age of thirteen.

He took my hand and we walked out of the pub, ignoring the leers from a couple of old men in the corner. Outside on the street, he took my face in his hands and kissed me again. I literally swooned. It was so romantic and now, out in the cold air, I was totally Holly Golightly. Except maybe a bit more turned on than Holly was.

Jack pushed me against a wall and we leant against the bricks, snogging like teenagers. Except I didn't ever snog like this back when I *was* a teenager. I had *really* missed out.

'OK, so do you want to go back to mine or yours?' he asked, eventually breaking away from me.

Oh my God, this was it. I had dreamt of this moment so many times that for a second I was so overwhelmed I didn't know what to say. Then my brain kicked into gear, and I told him to come back to my room in Camden, which I had already prepared earlier that day, pre-wax. There was even a singular condom in my top drawer that I'd had since Freshers' Week when the student reps gave them out for free.

We jumped on the 29 bus and I noticed he swiped his Oyster card on the pads even though we got on at the back of the bendy bus. He was so honourable. I swiped mine, too, and we sat near the back, kissing gently. We almost missed my stop, but managed to jump off just in time.

Drunkenly, I guided him up the stairs to my room and gave him the one-second guided tour. Then I stood in the middle of my room, with my eyes flickering uncertainly between Jack and the double bed. He walked over to me, and started kissing me again.

We collapsed on the bed and kissed more passionately than before. He pulled his white T-shirt off and started unbuckling his jeans. Was he going to take my clothes off, too, or should I do that?

While he fiddled with his jeans I figured the most practical thing was to take my clothes off myself, so I pulled my jumper over my head. Then I started peeling my very skinny jeans over my legs, praying he wouldn't notice the beads of perspiration appearing on my forehead as I tried to make it look as casual as possible.

When I turned around, he was lying across my bed. I stared at his body. It was very pale, and he was thin, but with broad shoulders. He looked a bit like the nineties cartoon Johnny Bravo, and was structurally very top-heavy. His pale skin was covered in moles and he had sparse, curly chest hair.

I suddenly felt self-conscious in my black bra and pants and decided to turn the lights off, after switching a lamp on. I got back onto the bed. He ran his hands all over my body as we kissed. I was so drunk I had no idea what my tongue was doing, but decided that the fact that I wasn't thinking about its every move was probably a good thing. Maybe this was the 'natural' part of kissing that had never come to me before.

He moved his hands up to my boobs and squeezed them hard. I bit my lip so I wouldn't yelp out in pain and hoped he would stop being so forceful with them. They weren't used to so much human contact. He started fiddling with the clasp at the back of my bra, but after a few tries, I stepped in to save him any humiliation, undoing it myself. He whipped it off me and started kneading my breasts.

I ran my hands across his body, trying to distract myself as I explored the slightly hairy region of his lower back, where it met the top of his boxers. I realised I should probably touch him down there. I cupped my hand over the bulge poking out from under his boxers. I rubbed it gently but suddenly felt a jolt of fear run through my body as I remembered James Martell. Last time I had tried to rub a penis, I had been so clueless that I had tried to put it in my mouth and practically bitten it off.

I couldn't handle risking it again. I would have to miss

out on the oral or hand job part, so hopefully we could skip straight to sex.

But after about fifteen minutes of hard-core making out, he hadn't taken off his boxers or tried to remove my knickers. The Playboy wax was going to waste, and I had no idea how to progress from snogging to sex. Wasn't this meant to be *his* job?

I was lying on my back and he was on top of me. I could feel his penis pressing into my tummy and thighs when he moved around. He started moving his body up and down, rubbing his dick against my vagina—but *with our underwear still on.*

What was this? What were we doing?! A phrase popped into my head. Dry humping. We were dry humping.

This carried on for a while, until his body trembled and he gasped and collapsed on top of me.

He had come. Into his boxers. Lying on top of me. Why hadn't he done this *inside* me?!

I sighed in total confusion and he rolled off me. I lay there, trying to convince myself that maybe this was a good thing, that we hadn't actually had sex. We had eased into it slowly and now, next time, we could do the actual deed and it would be better because we'd be familiar with each other.

After a few minutes of listening to him breathe heavily next to me, he finally spoke. 'You're a virgin, aren't you?'

My mouth fell wide open and I started choking on air.

Howthefuckdidheknow?! What about me had given that away? I swallowed, and forced words to come out. 'Um, what makes you think that?' I asked, as neutrally as I could.

'You are, aren't you? It's OK if you are, honestly. You're way younger than me, so it's not that weird.'

Great, now he was giving me a Lolita complex. I pondered his words, and then decided that maybe this was a blessing. I could admit I was a virgin, and wouldn't have to have sex with him without him knowing the truth. Now when we finally had sex, he could do it a bit more gently and hopefully it wouldn't hurt too much.

'Um, yes,' I said eventually. 'How did you know?'

'You kiss like a virgin,' he said.

I stopped moving.

There was a ten-minute silence.

OK, maybe it was less than ten minutes, but that's how long it felt.

I had nothing to say. I was overwhelmed by a million feelings swooping through my mind. The worst was humiliation. It was bad enough that I had to deal with the fact that I couldn't snog properly, let alone the fact that he had figured it out, too. Suddenly I thought back to every guy I'd ever kissed and realised they had probably thought the same. Because I was so shitty at using my tongue, they probably thought I'd barely kissed anyone, either. Fuck, did he think he was my first kiss, too?

Then he broke the silence with a laugh. 'God, I can't believe we just dry humped. I haven't done that since I was a kid.'

A kid? Everything he said made me feel worse. I lay there, feeling crappy and crappier, and closed my eyes, hoping it would make the situation go away.

'It was fun, though,' he added. 'You have an amazing body.'

I looked doubtfully down at my slightly lumpy body but started to feel a bit better. 'Seriously,' he said, 'I love girls with really natural bodies. They're so much sexier than really toned girls.'

I spent the rest of the night lying there as still as I could manage while my mind replayed the entire evening on a loop. I lay awake, even when the sky turned bright and rays of light crept through the edges of the blinds and shone onto the man lying in my bed. I wished I could rush over to my diary and pour out my feelings.

I had no idea if our date had been a success or not. On the plus side, he now knew I was a virgin and didn't seem to care about it. He clearly fancied me, because he had come into his pants, and he liked my body. On the negative side, I kissed like a virgin, didn't have a toned body, made him feel as though I didn't want sex—just dry humping—and now couldn't sleep.

I turned over so my back faced him. I was confused and this whole dating thing was so much more complicated than it looked in movies.

He was a guy, a twenty-six-year-old red-blooded male, and he hadn't even tried to pull my pants off. It was clearly because he'd figured out I was a virgin and didn't want to shag me. It was James Martell all over again. The rejection washed over me and I was too tired to push it away.

The rumour about boys finding virgins sexy was a LIE. It was just some medieval bullshit that old people said to try to make their daughters keep their legs crossed and not get pregnant. The truth was that virginity was just an obstacle. Men didn't think, *Oh, yes! Here's a virgin. Let's shag her!* They thought, *Oh, not a virgin. She's going to want candles and shit. Maybe I'll just find a non-virgin instead. It'll be so much easier.* I didn't even want candles.

He woke up an hour later when the alarm on his phone went off. He turned it off and then lay back in bed, yawning. He turned over and leant towards me. 'Hey, did you sleep OK?' he asked.

'Oh, yeah,' I said brightly. 'Bit of a hangover, though....'

'Fuck, me, too,' he said as he rubbed his head. Then he looked at me and leant in and kissed me on the mouth. He smelt of morning breath but I couldn't complain because I probably did, too. We kissed and I felt my anxiety falling away. He still liked me. Maybe all this crap was just in my head and boys didn't mind virgins. After all, it was just a question of a hymen being broken or not. If he didn't care about my morning breath, surely he didn't care about a tiny bit of physiology hidden way down in my body?

'So, last night was really fun,' he said. 'I'd better go, because it's going to take me a while getting home from yours. Shall we do something next weekend, though?'

I smiled up at him. 'Yeah, that sounds good.'

He got up and pulled his clothes on from the discarded pile on the floor. I lay in bed, too self-conscious in the sharp daylight to be able to get out and find my clothes. He dressed himself quickly and then came up to me. He leant down and kissed me briefly on the lips.

'Bye,' he said with a smile and walked out my door.

I sank back into my bed and smiled cautiously. This was kind of fun. For the first time ever, I'd had a guy back to mine and we had, I don't know—'fooled around', as Americans say.

Now we had plans for next weekend, and he had kissed me goodbye while I lay in bed. It was almost like having a proper boyfriend. The next step now would be going back to his place. Then I might even get to do a walk of shame.

CHAPTER FIFTEEN

'ELENA!' SCREECHED MY MUM as I crept into the house, hoping no one would see me. 'Where have you been? You left yesterday morning and you've been gone twenty-four hours, without any contact. I've been sick with worry.'

'Mum, I told you I was going out and it would be late, so I would stay in Camden,' I replied wearily, dumping my oversized leather tote on the floor.

'You said *maybe.* I expected a message to let me know, but you couldn't even text me? I just don't know what to do with you. You treat our home like a hotel, and you just walk in and out when you please, like some kind of a lodger. You make me feel like your servant.'

'Jailer, more like,' I muttered under my breath.

'Huh? And now you're whispering insults? What is wrong with you?' she wailed. 'How can I have raised a girl like you?'

I assumed her questions were rhetorical, so I kicked off my trainers and started climbing up the stairs to my room.

'ELENA. Get back down here!' she shouted from the bottom of the stairs.

'Mum, I don't know what the problem is. For the past week you've been moaning at me to get my act together and leave the house, but once I finally do, you're furious that I'm socialising too much. Can you just choose what you want me to do and make your mind up, please?' I responded rationally from halfway up the staircase.

'Why can't you do anything in moderation? Your aunts never have these problems with your cousins. I just don't know what to do with you any more.'

'You don't have to do anything *with* me,' I said in exasperation. 'Besides, of course I'm not like my cousins. They live in Greece! We were raised totally differently. You're the one who decided to move here.'

'Because your father and I wanted a better life for you. But then you go and act like this, and throw away all the opportunities we've given you.'

I turned and rudely carried on up the stairs. I slammed the door of my room and collapsed onto the bed. I irrationally hated her. It didn't help that both of us had essentially been living alone for the past three years and were not used to sharing the same space. I knew I shouldn't have walked away like that, but there was something about being back home that turned me into a moody teenager every time I walked through the door.

We had got on better when I was younger. When she and Dad weren't fighting, she'd try to make my life as normal as everyone else's and take me on play dates with the other mums and kids. I'd assumed our relationship would get even better the second she and Dad divorced, but it hadn't happened. The stepdad and older stepbrother I'd always dreamt of never materialised.

Instead, my mum just became stressed, overprotective and anxious. It was still better than life with my dad, though. He'd been a shit dad and an even worse husband. His angry moods were frequent and violent. He seemed better now and had a new girlfriend, who he lived with, but I didn't really want to have anything to do with him.

I put on my staple *Fuck You, World* playlist and let the angry pop-rock take me back to my teen years. Thank God they were behind me. Now I was well on my way to being a normal person and a real adult—well, aside from when I was in my mother's company. I got my phone out and reread the text that Jack had sent me this morning after leaving my flat.

Last night was great. Let's do it again sometime. Jack x

He had even put a kiss at the end, even though he hadn't on any of his earlier messages. I smiled as I read it and clutched my phone to my chest. I knew the message off by heart, as I had reread it the entire journey home. I still hadn't replied though, because it didn't really seem like a text-back text and there were no questions. Also, I didn't want to look needy. For all he knew, I could be on another date right now and was way too busy to answer.

My chest vibrated. I looked down and saw I had an email. It was from the student magazine. Oh, my God. *Breathe slowly, Ellie. It's your first attempt and there will be other opportunities,* I told myself calmly.

Dear Ellie,
Thanks so much for your entry. We laughed out loud while we were reading it, and it was interesting and clever as well as funny. We'd love for you to be our new columnist if you're still keen.

We can arrange a proper meeting for when term begins

but in the meantime we'll use your 'anarchy' entry for our next edition. Look out for it!
Really looking forward to hearing from you.
Sarah, *Pi* Editor
p.s. What do you think of 'Ellie on…[Anarchy, etc.]' as the general column name? Please can you send me a picture you'd like us to use as well.

OH, MY GOD! They actually *liked* my entry and wanted me to write for them. I lay back on my bed and laughed out loud. I wasn't a shit writer. I was actually *good* at the one thing I enjoyed. It was a total relief and I couldn't wait to tell Emma. I still had no idea if I was good enough to do it as a full-time career after uni but this was definitely a positive start. Now I just had to find a decent picture of myself….

Later that evening I lay in bed and my mind wandered to my lower regions. The red dots had totally disappeared, and even though the Hitler moustache was still kind of awkward, it looked very porn star. I had stood naked in front of my mirror that morning, examining it. Post-shower the sticky leftover wax had finally gone and now my vag looked as if it had just walked out of a double-page spread of a *Playboy* magazine. It was a shame Jack hadn't seen it, but at least now I would be fully prepared for this weekend and I'd have a Hitler *sans* dried wax or chicken pox.

I cringed at the thought of Jack going down on me and finding bits of wax down there, or even some stray hairs that Yasmin missed. No wonder boys wanted girls to have hair removed down there—the thought of licking someone's lady bits was bad enough without having to rub your tongue against a hairy patch. Thirty-four quid and an hour of pain and humiliation did seem a lot to ask, though. Oh, who was I kidding. I was desperate for Jack to go down there and if being waxed straight into twentieth-century Germany was what it took to get licked out, then so be it.

Shit, maybe Yasmin *had* left some stray hairs down there.

Alarmed, I sat up straight in my bed. I had to check. I was also curious to get another look at my bald vagina. Yaz had seen it from every angle and if Jack was also going to, then it was only right that I should get in on the action and have a look.

I suddenly remembered reading a Judy Blume book when I was twelve, where the main girl looked at her bits with a small pocket mirror. I pulled my trousers and knickers down and inspected myself. It still looked OK, but when I leaned over to try to pull the lips apart and look at it properly, I realised how unflexible I was. I had no idea if I had a pocket mirror but I could probably look at it in the big mirror. I ran over to my full-length mirror and tried to pull my legs apart. I stood wobbling and realised that wasn't going to work, either.

In the end, I faced my back to the mirror, then stood with my legs slightly apart and bent downwards, with my head falling in between my legs. Then I pulled my bum cheeks apart and got a good look at my bum crack. It was darker than I had expected and the hole looked ominous. The skin was a weird shade of pink and it wasn't very pretty.

By now I was completely intrigued by what the front holes would look like, too. But how was I going to see them properly?

Oh, my God. I had it. Judy Blume characters were from the seventies or something so all they had were pocket mirrors. I, on the other hand, was in the post-millennium era and fully equipped with smartphones and cameras. I also had a MacBook. Feeling like Armstrong about to land on the moon, I opened my laptop and switched on the Photo Booth application.

I was quivering with anticipation. The little green light next to the camera at the top of my screen flashed on. Perfect. I put my laptop firmly on the end of my bed, and then sat in front of it. Gingerly, I opened my legs out and saw my vagina appear on the screen. I angled the screen downwards so I could see the full thing and stared in fascination. This was way better than a Biology lesson.

I spent ages absorbed by the neat folds of my skin. No wonder men hit climaxes so easily. It probably wasn't just the pleasure that did it—I reckoned they were all just overwhelmed by the labia minora.

'Elena, are you going to be at home tomorrow mor— OH, MY GOD! WHAT ARE YOU DOING?'

I stared in horror at my mum, who had just walked straight into my room without knocking. My hand was holding open my vagina and there was a zoomed-in image of it on my laptop screen.

'Please get out of my room,' I said in a strangled voice as I threw a blanket over my naked vagina and slammed down my laptop screen. 'Please.'

My mum's face was frozen in shock. 'Are you sending pictures of yourself to men, Elena? That is *disgusting*.'

'Oh my God, no! Mum how can you even ask that? It's for a uni project…about…um, genitalia in literature.'

She crinkled her brow but looked calmer. 'It's…homework?'

'Yes.' I nodded enthusiastically. 'It's homework.'

The magic word soothed her and she walked out of my

room shaking her head and muttering about schools being too modern for their own good. I collapsed onto my pillow and vowed to buy a lock for my bedroom door.

The Vagina Monologue

Dear Reader,
We have a confession for you: Both of us have had moments of not accepting our nether sisters because, quite frankly, vaginas are fucking weird. However, after years of struggling on the road to vaginal acceptance, we have finally managed to embrace our own smelly and lopsided vaginas.

Here are the vaginal hurdles we have jumped over:

1. The smell. Vaginas do not smell like roses and lavender—even when we used to spritz them with perfume before a night out. They may look like flowers but they do not smell like flowers. They smell like the unique combination of sex, sweat and salmon. And that's when we don't have our periods.

2. Discharge. The first time we found this in our pants we freaked out. EM thought she had wet herself. It is not the most attractive part of female biology, but hey, at least if it gets really smelly or yellow you know you have an infection. Thanks, nature.

3. Wetness. Not to be confused with discharge, the lady juice is the body's natural lubricant. EM used to be embarrassed that her vagina would get too wet the second a boy looked into her eyes. Until she realized no boy is going to complain about your vag being too moist, even if it is dripping onto the carpet.

The same goes for dryness. Every vagina is different. And, hello, what do you think lube was invented for?

4. Shapes. Each inner lotus is a unique composition waiting to be explored. EM used to be self-conscious about her uneven and large flaps—until she realized it was the way Mother Nature intended them to be. And who ever said 'neat' was more attractive than lopsided anyway? Much like EK's acceptance of her oversized nose, EM realized large can be attractive. Small is not perfect. We just need to look at the vagina's male counterpart to prove that point.

CHAPTER SIXTEEN

I HAD STARTED touching myself at the age of seven. Obviously I didn't know what masturbation was and had no idea about the end goal of orgasm, but I knew that rubbing my vagina through my pyjamas felt nice. It stopped feeling nice the second my mum caught me with my hands down my pants and called me 'dirty'.

The word had stayed with me for the next seven years and every time I started to reach down at night, her look of disgust came back to haunt me and I stopped—until I was fourteen and had to build a model volcano with Leah in a Geography lesson.

No one really liked Leah because she was loud and pushy and didn't roll up her skirt or shave her legs. But I was secretly in awe of her for not caring that her skirt reached her knees and her legs looked like furry sticks. When she casually asked me, during that Geography lesson, if I'd ever masturbated, I dropped the plasticine and stared at her mutely. She carried on, unperturbed, and started telling me all about her first experience and what she had learnt from an old book in the library.

I absorbed Leah's advice as though it was old news. I pretended I already knew that women could have orgasms, and when she asked if I was going to try it for myself, I looked at her as though she was disgusting for even suggesting it. I never spoke to Leah or anyone else about masturbation ever again, but I did run straight home to try it out. It ended up being the best Geography homework I'd ever had.

That night I went home, prepared for a little experimentation of my own. I was freshly bathed and I had pink candles lit in my room. I was ready. This was something I had to do privately, just for me. I couldn't even talk to Lara about this because then she'd know I first touched myself at seven. She'd think I was a sexual deviant or a freak like that kid from *The Exorcist*. No, this was my private journey of self-discovery.

I put on my *Now 67* CD so that any sounds I might or might not make would be muffled. I took all my clothes off, and slid my moisturised body under the covers. I lay on my back and put my fingers on my clitoris just as Leah had advised. I rubbed it gently. It felt nice and I closed my eyes. I started by following Leah's advice, but after a while it felt so good that I stopped concentrating and just let it happen.

My fingers moved faster and faster until the familiar feeling of guilt abruptly settled on me. I wanted to stop but Leah had told me lots of people had mental barriers that prevented them from reaching orgasm. She told me that my only option was to break through the wall and keep on going towards the other side. I obliged.

I pushed my mum's disapproving voice aside and forced my mind to imagine a tanned Justin Timberlake on top of me. I bit my lip in excitement and all feelings of guilt faded away. I concentrated entirely on the currents of pleasure zooming through my body. I rubbed faster and faster, my breath quickening. I moved my fingers as fast as they could while my entire body tensed up and I clenched my toes.

Part of me wanted to stop but I forced myself to keep going. Suddenly my entire body spasmed and a wave of pleasure rushed through me. It was like nothing I had ever felt before. Every cell in my body was buzzing and I felt a sense of serene joy. This was bliss. Euphoria. Ohmigod, I'd just had my first orgasm.

My fingers felt damp, still wedged in between my wet lips. I took them out and as I opened my legs, I felt a thick liquid slide out and drop gently onto my mattress.

I sat up straight, all thoughts of serenity gone as quickly as they had come, and bent over to look at it. It looked a bit like discharge but it was see-through and had made a small stain on my bed.

Was it just the watery stuff that appeared every time I rubbed myself there or had I actually just come? I inspected it a bit closer and decided it was definitely the come Leah said women make. I was one of the 70 per cent of women who could come.

I felt my cheeks burn with pride. I had just gone from stage one to ten on my personal journey of self-discovery and I was no longer a child. I was a teenager.

After that, I masturbated once a day for years. I was the female equivalent of those teenage boys who drew penises all over their lunch boxes. It was only as I got older and realised that all my friends were getting their boyfriends to do it for them that I gradually stopped masturbating so often. Every time I did it, it just reminded me of how alone I was.

But maybe now it was time to get back into it. I was so good at it—it seemed like a waste of a talent. Besides, I had a lot of spare time now. I was still writing the vlog, but I didn't need to do any more columns until uni began again. Lara still wasn't speaking to me, and even though Jack had suggested weekend plans, he had postponed them because of 'a family thing'. I desperately needed something to distract me. Masturbating was ideal, but I needed to take it one step further and the only place to do that was in a Hoxton side street.

Which is why I was standing in Sh!—Europe's first women-only sex shop, according to the internet—staring speechlessly at a display of sex toys taking up eight racks that reached the ceiling.

I had no idea where to begin but I couldn't wait to start. I browsed the shelves, trying to look as though I was entitled to be there and spent most of my Saturdays checking out sex toys. I stared in horror at the cock rings and other things you needed a partner for, and looked in fascination at the vibrators. They looked terrifying. There were blue glittery ones covered in little lumps and pink gel ones that rotated and had tiny 'rabbit' ears that stroked the clitoris while you penetrated yourself. Some were even waterproof.

A shop assistant walked over to me and I took deep breaths, preparing myself for her inevitable questions. 'Hiya, are you looking for anything in particular?'

'I'm just browsing for now, thanks,' I said with a tiny forced smile, praying she would go away.

'OK. Are you looking for something to use with a partner or for masturbation?'

'Um, just masturbation, really,' I said nonchalantly, focusing all my energy on trying not to blush.

'The best ones are the rabbits, which I'm sure you've heard about,' she explained, as she gestured towards the plastic monstrosities. 'These are the best because they give you dual pleasure. This part goes in so it can hit your G-spot while the ears stimulate the clitoris. These are the best sellers. I really recommend them—they're amazing. What do you think?'

'OK,' I said evenly, trying to think of a subtle way to explain that I did not want to lose my virginity to a pink sparkly piece of plastic called a rabbit. 'Do you have anything that just stimulates the clitoris? What about these?' I pointed towards a display of tiny vibrators that looked as though they would fit on a key ring.

'Oh, yes. So those are bullets. You can use them on the clitoris, but if you're going to get those, I would just get a rabbit because they do that and penetrate at the same time. So it's maximum pleasure. The bullets aren't bad, though.'

The bullets definitely looked less threatening. I picked up a packet and looked at it curiously. It was metallic silver and it was small and slim and did look like a bullet. 'How does it work?' I asked.

'Well, you just press that little button at the top, and it vibrates. They're all waterproof and come in different colours. I guess it's a good one to start off with if you don't want to go straight for a penetrative vibrator,' she said, shrugging her shoulders. 'They come with batteries, too.'

It was £14.99 and the rabbit started off at £35.99—and this one came with free batteries. My mind was made up. I debated between buying a hot-pink one or a leopard-print one, but decided the latter gave off creepy bestiality vibes. I selected the hot-pink bullet and took it to the counter.

The shop assistant looked at me with disappointment, but I was sure I had made the right choice. I couldn't handle breaking my hymen myself with that huge lump of plastic—I doubted it would even fit inside me. Anyway, if I fancied fingering myself, I could stick my fingers up there myself or…maybe I could even slip this bullet up there, too? It vibrated, so it would probably feel good, and it was about a tenth of the size of the rabbit. In fact, it looked a bit like a tampon, so it would definitely fit. Perfect.

I was dying to try it out, but I had stupidly agreed to go out for dinner with my mum and Nikki Pitsillides and her parents. I groaned at the thought, and considered cancelling, but when I got out my phone to call my mum I already had a text from her telling me there was no way I was getting out of this dinner and I should come home immediately to get ready and make sure I looked nice.

It was 2:00 p.m. and dinner wasn't till seven. Did I really need five hours to make myself look good? Clearly my mum thought so.

'No, you can't wear that,' my mum said as she sat on the edge of my bed with her arms crossed. 'You look like a boy.'

'Mum!' I cried out, exasperated and slightly hurt. 'I'm wearing jeans and my favourite top. I wear this outfit all the time.'

'Exactly, and this is why you are still single.' She saw me open my mouth and held up her hand to stop me speaking. 'Elena, I'm not being cruel. I'm just trying to help you. You have such a nice figure. Why don't you show it off more?' A wistful expression came over her face as she continued, 'When I was your age I had the best legs in the whole town. I used to wear skirts every day and they were so short my mum and I argued constantly.' Her eyes narrowed as she looked at me suspiciously. 'But with you, that's not a problem because you don't wear skirts. Why can't you be more feminine?'

'Oh my God, Mum. Everyone wears jeans,' I snapped back. 'It's normal, OK? Girls don't have to wear skirts to be feminine. Besides, the androgynous look is *in*. It's all over the catwalks, so you're completely wrong.'

'Do you think you have the figure of a catwalk model?' she retorted. 'No. Your figure is different, so you have to dress differently.'

I sighed in frustration. 'Mum, can you just get out of my room and let me get dressed alone, please? I'm twenty-one years old and I don't live at home, so I reckon I'm capable of choosing an outfit for a dinner in Guildford on my own, thank you.'

'I want you to look nice, Elena. You're my daughter and I want to show you off,' she said.

'First, I'm not a pedigree dog. If you wanted something to show off you should have bought a pet and not given birth. Second, why is tonight such a big deal? Nikki isn't going to care what I wear and I doubt her parents will, either.'

'Yes, but we're going out to the new Italian place. So why not make an effort, Elena?' she asked, as she came over to me and started stroking my hair. 'You're so pretty, but you hide it all with these boyish clothes. And you never wear make-up.'

She was being uncharacteristically weird. 'I *do* wear make-up,' I said.

'But you don't wear lipstick or lip gloss like all the other girls. You wear this eyeliner, like some punk-rock star and you never brush your hair and make it all soft and pretty,' she said, still stroking the curly mass that I called hair.

'Yeah, because look at it, Mum! If I brush it, it makes me look like I'm going to an eighties prom. Also, no one above the age of thirteen wears lip gloss.'

'OK,' she said, throwing up her arms in resignation. 'But, can you please just try this on?' She held out a floral dress I had bought years ago on a whim and barely worn.

I gave up. 'If I can still fit into it, I will wear it. But I'm not putting on lip gloss,' I warned.

'OK, OK,' she said, smiling and slipping out of my room hurriedly. 'I'll leave you to get ready.'

I pulled the dress over my shoulders and struggled to get my arms through the sleeves. Eventually I managed to get into it and breathed in as I zipped it up.

It actually didn't look too bad. The muted purples, blues and blacks of the flower print were quite subtle. I could barely move my arms because the armholes were inhumanely small, but as I was only going to be moving my fork from my plate to my mouth, I would probably survive. Wearing the dress was a small price to pay to have my mum stop with the barely veiled insults. Mothers were crazy.

The second I walked into the restaurant, my mum's weird behaviour made sense. Seated at a large round table were Mr and Mrs Pitsillides, Nikki and the druggie boyfriend—which would definitely make dinner interesting—and a scrawny guy who I recognised as Nikki's older brother Paul. This was a set-up, and I had been squeezed into a floral dress because my mum wanted me to date Paul Pitsillides.

'Darling!' Debbie Pitsillides said, as she hugged my mum and then me. 'So nice to see you. Gosh, you've grown so much.' She looked straight down my dress at my cleavage.

I flushed and smiled at everyone, giving Nikki a weak smile and nodding vaguely in Paul's direction. My mum ushered me into the seat in between Paul and Nikki, which had strategically been left empty. I plonked myself into it and braced myself for a difficult evening.

'Hey, Ellie,' said Nikki, flicking her glossy brown hair over her shoulder as she looked me up and down. 'You've met Yanni, haven't you?'

Yanni was tanned with a chiselled face, cropped brown hair and a sparkly earring. He nodded at me and I smiled. 'Hey, Yanni, how's it going? Are you working at the moment?' I asked, knowing full well he was a full-time drug dealer for the privileged and bored kids in the area.

'You know—bit of this, bit of that. Mr Pitsillides is going to try to get me a job working for him, which would be cool,' he said, shooting Nikki's dad a deferential smile.

I rolled my eyes, hoping no one had noticed how bored I already was. 'Nice,' I said, nodding. 'And, Nikki, how's stuff going for you?'

'Not bad,' she said. 'I'm still in my last year of uni at Nottingham, so I'm just enjoying it, really. Loads of going out. Yanni comes up loads, too, though, don't you, babe?' She squeezed his arm and pouted at him.

I didn't know how much of this I was going to be able to handle. I turned over to my left, where Paul was nervously shifting around on his seat. 'Hey,' he mumbled.

I felt a bit sorry for him. He looked as uncomfortable as I felt. I guessed he had been pressured into coming here as much as I had, although it was a bit unflattering that he clearly hated the idea of dating me. If I was an average seven out of ten, he was definitely a five. He could at least pretend he found me a bit attractive, but he was staring intently at his menu, barely looking at me.

'Hey,' I said, flashing him my best smile. 'I've not seen you in ages. How are things?'

'Not bad,' he said. 'You?'

God, if he was going to keep going with these monosyllabic answers, this was going to be a very long night. I racked my brains, trying to think of something I knew he liked that I could talk to him about. I vaguely remembered my mum saying he was studying medicine.

'Good, thanks. You're doing medicine, aren't you? How's that going? Have you almost finished with the seven years of studying or whatever it is?' I asked in my friendliest voice.

'It's five years. I'm going to finish this year.'

'No way, me, too!' I cried. 'I'm graduating this summer. No idea what I want to do, though. I guess you don't have that problem,' I added a bit wistfully. 'Must be nice to have your career path set out so clearly.' His face dropped and he looked even more miserable than before. I changed tack. 'Although, it's probably hard, too, right? Like, having to do medicine.'

He looked up and nodded. 'Yeah. It's not bad, but I really like drawing. I don't have much time to do it now.'

'Drawing?' I asked, struggling to visualise geeky Paul drawing nude models or bowls of fruit. 'I didn't know you drew.'

'Yeah, illustrations. For comics and stuff. I would love to be a cartoonist.'

OK, that made a bit more sense, but still…medicine to cartoons? I guessed his parents weren't pleased with this. 'That's so cool,' I said encouragingly. 'I'm so impressed. Can I see your stuff?' I batted my lashes. I was basically throwing myself at him.

I caught sight of my mum across the table and she threw me an approving glance. That made me feel worse, and I gratefully accepted the glass of wine a waiter poured for me. I probably shouldn't flirt with Paul, seeing as there was no way I would ever fancy him, but I was bored. Besides, Jack hadn't texted to rearrange our date, and even though I was convinced he would, I still felt a bit panicky. I mean, what if he never texted back? I would be back to square one, and he was so cute that I had no idea how I'd ever find someone like him again.

Even thinking about Jack made me feel sick with nerves, so I quickly distracted myself by smiling at Paul again. If my mum wanted me to flirt with Paul Pitsillides, then I damn well would.

CHAPTER SEVENTEEN

I'D GOT THROUGH the entire dinner by practically ignoring almost everyone else at the table and giving Paul my full attention. Seeing as he only ever spoke in monosyllables—even after three beers and endless coaxing from me—it had been pretty exhausting.

It was only 9:00 p.m. when we finished dinner, so Debbie and my mum exchanged an obvious glance and suggested that 'the young ones' go out to the new cocktail bar while they went back to Debbie's place to carry on catching up.

Yanni and Nikki were already all over each other and didn't seem to care if we went or not so long as they could carry on touching. I looked at Paul to see if he was up for it and he shrugged non-committally.

I smiled sweetly at the parents. 'Sure,' I said, as a joyous smile spread across my mum's face.

We walked across the road to the new bar with its faux-crystal chandeliers, soft purple lighting and overpriced mojitos. The second we got there Yanni and Nikki disappeared, so Paul and I walked over to the bar. Without the company of his sister and parents, he eased up and offered to buy me a drink.

Finally my efforts were working, and he had noticed that I was a not-unattractive girl throwing herself at him. Happily I agreed, and while I sat waiting for him to come back with my ginger mojito, I imagined kissing him. OK, he was kind of unattractive and weirdly pale—especially compared with Yanni's impressive tan—but he was male, I was bored and I wanted a backup guy in case Jack never got back to me. Hopefully he *would* eventually message to rearrange our plans, but in the meantime I could get down and dirty with Paul Pitsillides.

I wasn't about to lose my V-card to Paul and his black lace-up trainers, but I would never say no to a chance to improve my kissing technique. I wouldn't even be averse to practising my hand job techniques with him, because even if I messed it up a bit, I'd probably be the only girl who'd ever done it to him so he'd still be grateful. Unlike James-sodding-Martell.

When Paul came back with our drinks, I smiled at him and made sure he could get an eyeful of my cleavage. He looked at me as if he couldn't believe his luck and I glowed with pleasure, feeling flattered in a way I hadn't felt with Jack, or James Martell, or any guy I'd ever snogged. Maybe I should always date guys who were less attractive than me.

'Here you go,' he said, gently handing me my cocktail. 'I think my sister and Yanni have gone off somewhere, so you're going to be stuck with me for a bit. Sorry.' He looked genuinely apologetic.

'That's OK,' I replied, sipping the mojito. 'We can catch up properly. I don't think I've seen you since we were about ten and we were all playing naked in your paddling pool.'

He blushed. 'Yeah. That was fun. How has everything been for you since then?'

'Since I was ten? Wow, erm…well, it's been a long eleven years. Uni is good, though…. Feels weird that I'm in my last year. Like, how did that happen? When I graduate in—oh my God, four months—I'm going to be an actual *adult*. With a job. Except I haven't got one yet.'

He laughed. 'Yeah, you might want to find one. You're right, though—time does go really quickly. I just turned twenty-four.'

I would have been excited that he was three years older than me, but my mind went straight back to Jack, who was a full five years older.

'At least you have your job lined up, though,' I said. 'I wish the field I want to go into was as clear-cut as medicine.'

'What is it you want to do? You study English, right?'

'Yeah, and like every typical English grad I want to be a writer one day.'

'I can see that,' he said.

I looked at him in surprise. 'Really? How?'

'I don't know. You're funny, and…creative. And you talk a lot….'

I laughed, genuinely touched. 'Thanks Paul, that's really nice to hear,' I said. Paul Pitsillides was proving to be very different from how I remembered him.

'Hey, I'm three years older than you and I still haven't figured out what I really want to do,' he said. 'You're doing a lot better than I am.'

'I don't know. You seem pretty impressive.' I grinned. 'In fact, not to be cringe, but you seem so different these days. It's fun hanging out with you like this. Although, dinner was a bit more awkward, huh?'

He smiled. 'Yeah, I guess I find it hard to open up with my family watching. I also had no idea what you'd be like now. I think I was wary of finding another version of my sister.'

'Pur-lease,' I cried. 'Do I look like I want to be snogging a guy with an earring all night?'

We both looked over to the couple in question, who were snogging passionately on a sofa, and burst out laughing.

'That's my sister for you.' He laughed. 'As classy as ever.'

'I think you definitely got the better genes.' I smiled. Paul abruptly stopped laughing and froze. 'Um, are you OK?' I asked warily, wondering why my attempts at chat-up lines always ended in such extreme reactions.

He opened his mouth and then closed it rapidly. I looked at him questioningly and then, out of nowhere, he leant his head towards me. Oh my God, was he about to…

His lips touched mine.

He didn't put his tongue anywhere near my mouth, and instead he kissed me gently and hesitantly. It was sweet and it didn't taste of stale beer or coffee. I put my hands on his face, feeling surprised but confident, and he started rubbing his hands across my back.

Until he stopped and broke away.

'Oh God, Ellie, I'm so sorry,' he said, turning lobster-red and looking down at the floor. 'I didn't mean to do that.'

'Hey, Paul, it's OK,' I said, touching his arm with my hand, feeling a bit alarmed. 'You don't need to apologise. It was…it was nice. I liked it.'

His face fell even more than before and he looked as though he was about to cry. 'Paul, what's wrong?' I asked. 'You're scaring me. Am I that bad a kisser?' I joked weakly.

An actual tear appeared in his left eye and I freaked out.

'Paul, seriously, what's wrong?' I asked, my tone getting panicky.

'I'm sorry, Ellie,' he mumbled and then paused. He took a deep breath. 'I think I might be gay.'

'WHAT?!' I screeched. 'You're gay? And you just kissed me? Why? Oh, my God. Have I turned you?'

'No, of course not,' he cried out. 'I just… Oh fuck, this is so complicated. I don't know how to explain it to you.'

'I don't care how you do it, but please start now!' I said, crossing my arms tightly.

'You're right.' He sighed, staring at his limp hands. 'I think…I kissed you because I wanted confirmation that I was gay. I mean, I've always known I was, but I've never really known for definite because—fuck, this is going to sound so pathetic—I've never kissed a girl before. I've never kissed *anyone* before. Not even a guy. So I never had any proof that I was gay.'

He paused, but I was incapable of responding, so after a while he carried on. 'And you were here, and you're the first girl I've ever felt really comfortable with and… I don't know, I just didn't feel scared for once so I guess I just took the opportunity.'

'Oh, God,' I groaned loudly, as I dropped my head into my hands. 'I've turned you. I knew it. I always knew I'd turn someone gay. My mum told me today I dress like a man. Do I look like a boy, is that why you kissed me?'

'Ellie, chill out,' he said, putting a reassuring hand on my arm. 'You look very much like a girl. You're beautiful, and you didn't make me realise I was gay—I always knew. I just, I don't know, needed something to force me to accept it. You've done me the biggest favour in the world.'

I peered at him through the gaps in my fingers. 'Are you sure?' I asked.

'Positive,' he replied.

I peered at him through the gaps in my fingers. 'Really?'

'Yes,' he said, putting a reassuring hand on my arm. 'I feel really shit about this now. I totally understand if you want to pour my drink on me. I'm sorry, Ellie. It's just—you don't understand how it feels to not know for sure if you fancy men. I mean, I'm twenty-four years old and I wasn't 100 per cent sure if I was actually gay. That's fucking weird. You're meant to figure this out as a teenager, but I never really had the chance. I never got to kiss anyone, let alone sleep with them. I'm a twenty-four-year-old virgin and I feel like a total freak. You wouldn't get it.'

I sighed and twisted the straw around my drink, clinking the ice cubes. 'Paul, I do get it. I'm a lot more like you than you think,' I admitted.

'You're gay, too?' he asked, his eyes brightening up with hope.

'No!' I cried out as my straw fell out of my hand. 'Well, at least I don't think so. I've never kissed a girl before. Maybe I should add that to my "things to do before I'm thirty" list.' His face crumpled in confusion and I resisted the urge to pull out my phone and add it onto my list right there.

'Oh,' he said, looking despondent again. 'So, what did you mean when you said you're like me?'

'I mean that I'm a virgin, too. And you didn't really use me. I kind of used you, too,' I disclosed, biting my bottom lip apprehensively.

'What?' he asked, looking genuinely curious. 'For what?'

'Oh, I don't know.' I sighed drily. 'A self-esteem boost? Who knows?'

'Well, I'm incredibly flattered you thought kissing me would make you feel better.' He smiled. 'But does this mean we're even now? Do you forgive me for the…kiss?'

I rolled my eyes. 'OK, fine. I forgive you,' I said, in a faux-wounded voice. 'Except I seriously think I'm going to need therapy for a few years to get over this.'

He laughed. 'Look who you're talking to. It's taken me twenty-four years to realise I'm gay. But you know what? Now that I'm finally out there…fuck, it feels good.'

'This is huge, Paul,' I agreed. 'I can't believe I'm the first person you've come out to. I don't even know what to say.'

'You don't need to say anything. You've helped me enough.' He paused and then grinned widely. 'Wow, it feels weird to say that out loud. I am gay,' he repeated.

I felt a small ball of guilt rise inside me as I smiled weakly at him. It was probably time to come clean to him. I sighed and sat up straight.

'OK, I'm sorry, too,' I said. 'I can be a self-obsessed jerk sometimes, and I used you on my path to losing my virginity and now I feel bad you're apologising so much when what I did was just as bad.'

His eyes widened. 'You were going to give me your virginity?'

I swatted his arm with my hand. 'No, that would be way too weird. I just…wanted to kiss you so then I'd feel better about the guy I really like not texting me back. He's the one I really want to lose it to,' I admitted.

'Who?' he asked eagerly.

I creased my eyebrows and shook my head, wondering how the hell I'd missed the fact that Paul was gay.

'Just a guy I met at a party. But let's not talk about him. Are we…OK about this whole kiss thing? I didn't mean to try to use you,' I said. 'I guess we were as dumb as each other.'

'Shall we just pretend it never happened?' he suggested. 'It wasn't my proudest moment, either.'

I sighed in relief. 'Deal. But…' I paused. 'Now we've cleared that up, we need to discuss this gay stuff, Paul. Are you…going to tell your parents?'

He looked down at his scruffy shoes. 'Ellie, I'm the eldest son. They have all these hopes and dreams for me and I'm just going to break their hearts. I can never tell them. They won't get it.'

'Paul, I know it's a fucking nightmare, but honestly, they might be more understanding than you think. Parents can be surprisingly supportive, you know,' I said whilst racking my brains for a single example to prove this. Cher's dad in *Clueless*?

Paul nodded in agreement. 'Yeah, I guess you're right. I can't really deal with it all now, though. I think I just need some time.'

'Yeah, Jesus Christ, you're a virgin who just came out at the age of twenty-four. Damn right, you need some time,' I cried out.

'Thanks for reminding me,' he replied drily.

'Sorry, a bit insensitive of me,' I apologised.

'You think?' he said, rolling his eyes.

'I will be very respectful of your gayness from now on,' I replied. 'Anyway, on to more pressing matters. Now that you're gay, does that mean we can go shopping together?'

'Oh my God, I can, like, totally be your GBF,' cried Paul.

I choked on my cocktail. 'Oh my God, really?' I shrieked. 'Because I've always wanted a gay best friend.'

He stared at me. 'Ellie, I was kidding. You do realise that not all gay guys are camp?'

'I know that.' I smiled weakly. 'I was, uh, kidding, too. Obviously. So, um, more cocktails? I'll just, uh…yep, go get more cocktails.'

CHAPTER EIGHTEEN

'…So WE JUST sat there chatting normally, as though he'd been out his entire life. Then I went home and had to listen to my mum going on about how glad she was to see Paul and I getting on so well.' I finally finished retelling last night's escapades to Emma, who had been forced to sit through a one-hour phone call. 'Now I'm a total mess and have no idea what to do.'

'Wow,' she said. 'That's…that's pretty big. God, this is way out of my expertise range, Ellie. Brazilians I can handle, but turning a guy gay? Can't say I've done that yet.'

'I didn't turn him!' I wailed, then finished lamely, 'He promised me I didn't.'

'I know—sorry, babe. That came out wrong. Obviously you didn't turn him *per se*, you just, um, helped him. You know what, fuck it. You're a modern cosmopolitan woman who snogged a twenty-four-year-old virgin and helped him figure out he was gay. You're every man's dream.'

'Ha, I don't think so,' I snorted. 'I'm a fucking mess.'

'A fucking *feminist* mess.'

'Really?' I asked doubtfully. 'Is it feminist to try to use a guy to make you feel better about yourself, then realise he was using you to figure out if he was gay or not?'

'Probably,' she said. 'Everything is feminist. You tried to use him, so that's totally feminist.'

'He used me, too,' I reminded her.

'Exactly! Feminism is just men and women being equal. So you, a woman, used him, and he, a man, used you, too. This is feminism and I should be writing my dissertation on this instead of Charles Dickens,' she said triumphantly.

'Please don't mention dissertations,' I groaned. 'Thank God we did our biggest exams last year and only really have to do our dissertation this year, because I have barely opened a book.'

'Me neither. Why don't we meet up in the library and force ourselves to work? Then we can have consolatory coffee breaks,' she suggested.

'Done. I'm going back to Camden soon anyway,' I said. 'I'm getting nothing done at home, and I cannot face my mum asking me about Paul. If I say it's so I can be near the library she'll be ecstatic.'

'Yeah, come back. I'm getting bored of just hanging out with my housemates.... Oooh, wait, does this sudden desire to have your own place again mean you want to be able to entertain guests without any parents around?' she teased.

I sighed dramatically. 'It would, but Jack still hasn't replied to me. I feel so shit about it. I think that's partly why I kissed Paul—I felt like Jack was rejecting me post–dry humping.'

'Hmm, when did you last speak to him?' she asked.

'He texted me straight after the DH to say he had a good time, then we made weekend plans but he cancelled. Also, he asked me to email him my column entry for the UCL magazine because he said he wanted to read it. So I did, but then he never replied to that, either.'

'Babe, he will. He's probably just thinking what to say.

It's not a casual text situation—he needs to read the column and then think of something amazing to say to convince you to give him your V-card.'

'Meh, I guess.... Anyway, Em, my phone's beeping at me so I'd better go. If you need me I'll be drowning myself in self-pity somewhere.'

'OK, don't overdo it. Let me know when Jack messages. Ciao!'

I hung up and collapsed onto my bed. Why didn't Jack want to see me? Had I done something wrong? Telling Emma the facts was depressing—it made me realise how long it had been since I had heard from him. I felt so rejected and alone. Then I remembered my phone had beeped—maybe it was from Jack? I felt a wave of hope wash over me and grabbed the phone. It was a new email.

Subject: You are not alone.

Oh my fucking God. I bolted upright and stared at the ceiling. Was it...Jack? Or Lara? I looked down eagerly to see the sender and felt the smile plummet from my face as I saw the email address it had come from: subscriptions@islamic-marriages.com. Typical. The only people who wanted to save me from eternal solitude were religious matchmakers.

I was about to exit my emails in resignation when I noticed a second unopened email. It was from jack.brown@gmail.com. I let out a bark of surprise and my fingers raced to open it.

Ellie—sorry it took me so long to reply. Was too intimidated by your superior writing skills to message you in case you'd already realised you're so much more talented than me.

But, if you aren't too busy writing witty columns, then

please can we go out this Saturday evening? Really want to see you—sorry for cancelling last weekend. Obviously would have had way more fun with you than at Aunt Gwen's 60th.

On a more boring note, I've attached my latest short story if you want to read it. And, if you do want some feedback on your piece, I've attached a copy of it with my shitty comments that you should definitely ignore... Hope you're enjoying your newfound columnist fame xx

I squealed out loud. He had actually bothered to read my column and attach constructive criticism—he wouldn't have done that if he didn't like me. And he had sent me his writing, too, so he clearly cared about my opinions. I grinned and collapsed onto my bed happily. He wasn't just a dry-hump-'em-and-leave-'em kind of guy. This was actually happening—I was dating a guy who liked my writing and wanted to see me this weekend. Oh shit, that meant I only had three days before I lost my V-plates.

Ellie's to-do list:

1. Tweeze out the stray hairs that have grown back on vagina since the big wax.
2. Watch porn to figure out how to give the perfect BJ—and also a hand job. But is that too soft for pornos to focus on?
3. Figure out if pornos do hand job clips.
4. Apply for more internships. (The first twenty might still reply, Ellie. Stay hopeful.)
5. Do dissertation instead of just taking relevant books out of the library.

6. Mentally prepare for losing V-card on Saturday.
7. Have some quality 'me time' with my brand-new bullet…

Bullet and I spent an hour together and I came three times in a row. I was officially a serial climaxer. It had taken me a few minutes to figure out how it worked, but the whole thing basically just vibrated when you pressed the button, and you rubbed it over the clitoris. I realised that the best thing for me was to start off by rubbing it gently, with the thick side of it, then go faster and just use the tip. I brushed the tip over the clit really quickly and then the familiar feeling of releasing the built-up tension unleashed over me and I literally *quivered* with joy.

It was amazing. There was only one tiny, very mini, little incident when I got a bit bored and tried to mix things up a bit.

I decided to slip the bullet straight into my vagina for some penetration action. It felt nice, and definitely different, until I pushed it in as far as it would go and it slipped in behind the contracting/valve bit where tampons go. Only, unlike a tampon, the bullet didn't have a string hanging off it to pull it back to safety. Which meant it was vibrating deep inside me, and I COULDN'T GET IT OUT! I panicked until I had a brainwave to squat on the floor, and it slipped out of me. I had never felt relief like that before.

The whole experience was so overwhelming that I put the bullet away in a drawer and spent the next few days focusing on slave narratives. I still hadn't moved away from my Surrey home and was spending each day reading articles on online journals and poring over my American Literature anthology. I figured if I got a start on my dissertation, the ball of guilt in my gut would slowly ebb away, and I could spend the weekend with Jack. I was planning on moving back to my little room in central London on Friday and losing my virginity at some point during the weekend. I'd marked my date with Jack on my calendar by drawing a mini *V* across the Saturday and Sunday boxes.

The only distractions to my dissertation were the constant visits into my bedroom from my mother. She was asking me daily about Paul—if I'd heard any more from him, when I was next seeing him, etc. I could hardly tell her he'd kissed her only daughter just to double-check that he wanted to bone men.

Actually, he had been messaging me, but not in the context my mum thought. He sent me pictures of his latest animations, and I sent him my and Emma's latest vlogs. He was surprisingly easy to talk to and we had made plans to hang out. My most recent snog was on his way to becoming my first gay best friend.

Touched for the Very First Time

I'm sure it was all good for Madonna being touched like a virgin for the first time, but what about when you're a virgin touching yourself for the first time? Because most girls out there were touching their vaginas way before they ever let a boy down there—or even knew that what they were doing had a name.

Which it does. Masturbation. Mmmm. The word alone makes us close our eyes in a warm blur of memory while our clits start throbbing in anticipation. It is the most precious gift Mama Nature gave us and something every woman should explore.

Not that Greek Orthodox mums see it like that. And EK should know because she grew up being told 'touching yourself down there is bad'. Result? She inevitably got a complex and felt waves of guilt every time her hand naturally rubbed itself against her prepubescent vagina from the age of 7 onwards. OK, probably from the age of 5 if she's being totally honest.

Masturbatory guilt is just another issue our darling parents can pass down to us, ensuring maximum angst and minimum self-belief. Telling a vulnerable young person that they can't do what feels natural is pure dictatorship and we reckon it probably goes against the European Convention of Human Rights. Exploring your own body is always healthy—no matter how much anyone tells you it's 'dirty', 'wrong', or even a 'sin'.

We're sure that Jesus/whoever didn't actually say masturbation was bad, so anyone who interprets it like that is plain wrong. It's healthy and if boys discuss wanking the whole time, girls should too. EK has finally let go of her mum's bullshit and has even invested in a sex toy (the beginner's vibrator, AKA a bullet). Her only advice? Don't stick it into your vagina. Not up the hole. Just...don't.

CHAPTER NINETEEN

ON FRIDAY I UNPACKED the last of my bags and collapsed happily onto my bed. I always forgot how much I loved living alone until I spent a few days with my mum. I normally got the bus to Lara's house the second I got back to Guildford, but obviously that hadn't been an option this Easter.

I missed Lara. It had been weeks since our fight, and we'd never been out of touch for so long. The more time passed, the weirder it got, but I couldn't bring myself to break the silence. Whatever. Today was the day before my big date with Jack and I had a lot to prepare for. Especially as my period had just arrived, so the *V* on my calendar was going to have to move back a week.

Positive note? My knickers wouldn't be coming off so I wouldn't have to tweeze the waxed VJ.

Negative note? If any sexual action was going to happen, it was going to have to be the dreaded second and third base—which meant I had to learn the BJ and HJ techniques. Today.

I sat on my bed with a notebook and pen. I was going to take this very seriously and I would succeed in overcoming my BJ fears. I started looking for porn sites. I had no idea where to start—the last thing I wanted to do was find low-quality trash that would give my computer a virus. My mother would kill me if I got a virus on my laptop, let alone a porn-induced one.

I vaguely remembered one of the boys in my halls talking about RedTube, which was like YouTube but dirty. If it was mainstream and well known, hopefully it wouldn't rot my laptop's hard drive.

There were dozens of categories and I had no idea where to start. I picked up a chocolate hobnob from a packet next to me and chewed as I scrolled down. Eventually I decided on 'college girls'. It was better than the 'underage' stuff, and didn't seem as hardcore as 'threesomes'. Besides, I was a college girl so I could probably relate to them.

The first video showed a girl in a Britney Spears–esque school uniform. She was wearing knee-high socks with a grey skirt that was so short she definitely would have got detention in my school. The striking ensemble was paired with a white shirt tied just under her bra. She looked like every middle-aged pervert's dream. The video started with her flirting with her maths teacher, who had asked her to stay behind to look at her grades. She twirled her hair around her fingers against a backdrop of music that sounded like the *Austin Powers* theme tune on crack.

So far this was verging on the 'underage girls' category, and I was far from impressed. Then, out of nowhere, she was on her knees and undoing the teacher's trousers. I looked up eagerly—on my first video I had hit the jackpot and she was about to give the maths teacher exactly what I wanted to give Jack.

I grabbed my pen and held it above the pad, poised to translate any of Britney's tricks onto paper for my future reference. She pulled his trousers down and suddenly his penis was staring straight out at me from the screen. I had seen few penises in real life, but this one was incredibly large. The fact that it was fully shaved just emphasised how big it was. Britney didn't seem fazed; she just giggled in delight—that was *not* going on my tips sheet because she looked ridiculous—and immediately put the whole thing in her mouth. Teacher groaned in delight and she started licking the tip of it.

I wrote down: *1) lick it like an ice lolly*, and then looked up, waiting for more pearls of wisdom.

She started putting the whole thing in her mouth and moving her head up and down. I groaned in frustration. This was the main bit of a BJ—the moving up and down thing—but I couldn't see what she was doing *inside* her mouth. I was doomed to eternal failure. Any idiot could move their head up and down with a penis inside their mouth, but it was only an experienced head-giver who knew what to do with their mouth. Did I curl my lips over my teeth to stop any collateral damage, and what the hell was the tongue doing inside?

These were the crucial questions I wanted the answers to, but damned Britney was just sucking his cock with no explanation whatsoever. When the camera did a close-up of her, I tried to see what she was doing with her lips, but it was useless. Then she went faster and faster and the teacher put his hands on her head to force her to go deeper, which looked very unfeminist and I totally couldn't imagine Jack doing it.

Eventually his groans got louder and he came into her mouth. Dribbles of white goo trickled out of the corners of her mouth but she licked them up as though it was melted Milky Bar and looked up at him sexily as she swallowed.

Then—and this bit made me gag a bit—she licked the tip of his cock to clean up any last drops. I closed the video in disgust and tried another one, hoping it would be more illuminating.

The next one showed a blonde girl at a garage, with two old builders. She had huge tits, and it was boringly predictable. There was barely any plot, and within seconds, they were both shagging her *at the same time.* The cameraman—it had to be a man because no woman would ever focus on this—zoomed in on the penises going in and out of both her nether orifices.

I averted my eyes away from the screen, a sour taste in my mouth. I shoved the hobnobs away, watching out of the corner of my eye. This was definitely hardcore and their groans and moans were just as graphic.

Thank God I lived alone, because these noises would be enough to scare any flatmate. I fiddled with the laptop to turn the volume down, but it was complicated because I didn't have any volume keys any more. I had put my hair straighteners on the keyboard whilst taming my hair and it had melted the plastic keys. Instead of sleek black plastic volume keys, I now had to make do with the white gel button underneath the keypad. I was trying to shove my fat fingers into the space to turn the volume down when there was a banging on the door.

Ohmigod. A neighbour had heard it and wanted to tell me to turn it off. I slammed the lid of my laptop closed but the sounds carried on for the longest five seconds of my life. When it stopped, I crept over to the door and opened it slightly. I peered through the small crack and saw a familiar-looking mop of greasy brown hair.

'Paul?' I asked in confusion. 'What are you doing here?'

'Um…we were meant to meet at two but you're not answering your phone so I figured I'd come over instead,' he explained.

'Oh shit, I'm so sorry,' I cried as my hand flew to my mouth. 'I totally forgot. I was so engrossed in my, um, dissertation.' I flushed and then paused. 'Hang on—how do you know where I live?'

'Your mum told me.' He grinned.

Of course she bloody did. 'Typical,' I said, as I gestured for him to come in out of the hallway. 'Now she's going to think we've fallen for each other and every Greek in Surrey is going to know about it.'

'Perfect cover for me,' he said as he sat on my bed. He was wearing a dirty black hoody and ill-fitting jeans with his awful trainers. If he was going to be my GBF we were really going to have to work on his dress sense.

'So,' he said nonchalantly, 'alone, are you?'

'Um, yes?' I replied, gesturing at my very empty room.

'Oh, right.' He nodded. 'It's just, I thought maybe you were with someone?'

I blushed furiously and tried to convince myself that the wooden door he'd been standing outside was thick enough to block out the porn sounds from earlier. 'Nope, I'm alone. I was just, um, watching a film,' I explained.

He nodded as he looked around the room. 'What was it, *Hot and Steamy in a Sauna*?'

I stared at him in horror. 'What are you talking about?' I asked in a strained voice. 'I was just watching a film for my dissertation. A literary adaptation.'

His face was deadpan but his eyes flickered as he nodded mutely. 'Of course. *The Cunt of Monte Cristo*?'

My mouth dropped wide open and when I caught his eye

we burst out laughing. 'OK, fine, I was watching a porno,' I admitted. 'It's not a big deal so please don't make it one.'

He grinned. 'Sure. I mean, what twenty-one-year-old girl doesn't watch porn alone on a Friday afternoon?'

I rolled my eyes at him. 'Yes, OK, it's not exactly the norm. But it was for a good reason.'

'Research?' he asked, and a look of understanding flashed between us. I nodded and he replied, 'I've been there, too, Ellie. But honestly, porn films are a waste of time. No guy wants a girl like that.'

I opened my mouth to try to say something along the lines of, 'How would you know?' but he beat me to it.

'I know what you're thinking,' he said. 'But I'm not a total freak. I do have guy friends who talk about this sort of stuff and I don't think any of them want a porn star. I mean, sure, they get off on it and they'd love it for one night, but I think they'd be overwhelmed to have a girlfriend like that, and not overwhelmed in a good way. You know?'

'Yeah.' I sighed. 'I reckon you've got a point. And I don't really want to be the kind of girl who gazes at a guy in pure joy while she has his dick in her mouth and he grabs her head. I mean, I'd be way too preoccupied with concentrating on the mouth part to be able to smile at him, too.'

Paul laughed. 'Yeah, I kind of know how you feel,' he admitted. 'I'm terrified to get out there and have to start figuring out stuff like that. At least you've known your whole life that you fancied men, but I've only just realised, and all of this is new to me.'

I looked at Paul with respect. Who knew he'd be so comfortable talking about sex—or the lack thereof—and be so honest with it? Jeez, he was almost as skilled as me when it came to self-deprecating and that wasn't something I came across every day. A vision of us lying on a sofa watching *E!* and bitching about celebs formed in my mind. Only, in the daydream, Paul had better clothes and my hymen was no longer intact.

'Anyway,' said Paul, pulling me out of my engrossing daydream, 'who is this lucky guy you're watching porn for?'

'Blaghh,' I groaned. 'I don't know where to start. He's a graphic designer and he's twenty-six and he likes me and I need—no, I *want*—to do stuff with him, but, um, I don't really know *how* to do stuff….' I trailed off. I couldn't explain why I was so nervous about third base without telling him the whole story. I squeezed my eyes shut and decided Paul had a right to know. I was, after all, the first person he had come out to and kissed. Both at the same time.

I took a deep breath and told him the James Martell saga in all its teethy glory. He didn't even laugh or wince when I got to the biting bit. Or the 'Sorry, I can't take your virginity' part. His expression barely changed and when I got to the end, he just shrugged his shoulders and said, 'Shit. Well, good thing that was years ago and now you're going to try again with a decent guy.'

'That's all you can say?' I asked, my eyes wide. 'It was the most traumatic moment of my life.'

'Try being bullied for being gay when you don't even know if you are,' he retorted. Then his voice got softer and he carried on. 'Seriously, Ellie, it was a disaster with this James guy because you didn't really like him. He was just a nice guy who fancied you, but you weren't comfortable with him so things didn't work out. I think if you take things slower, and make sure you're comfortable with this guy first, things will be better.'

I nodded, realising Paul was more intelligent than his

haircut suggested. I was sure I would feel comfortable with Jack, and if not, I could definitely make myself feel comfortable. Maybe there was a WikiHow on it.

We spent the rest of the morning hanging out on top of my bed. It was nice to spend time with a guy without freaking out about whether he fancied me. And Paul was a nice guy. At one point I even found myself wishing he were straight. The thought died when he told me that he had gone to a gay bar during the week, on his own, and he had met a guy. I was too impressed to say anything other than shriek in response.

He told me they had kissed and then swapped numbers. Now Vladi, the guy in question, wanted to meet up with Paul, but he was too embarrassed about his lack of sexual experience to agree. I nodded compassionately when he explained how embarrassed he was for Vladi to find out about his virginity.

'I'm also nervous about, uh, well, going down on him, too,' he admitted. 'Have you picked up any tips from the porn videos you can share?'

'I'm sorry. So far my list pretty much just consists of licking it like an ice lolly.' He looked crestfallen and I realised I had to help. 'But maybe we can learn together?' I offered. 'I have a bit of a skill when it comes to looking up this stuff, so if it isn't too weird, we could, like, watch a video together?'

'Um, what kind of video?' he asked cautiously. 'I don't really want to watch a porno with you, Ellie, no offence.'

'None taken, thanks very much,' I said primly. 'Besides, I wasn't suggesting we watch porn…'

We opened a bag of popcorn and wordlessly ate it as we stared at my laptop, transfixed. A blonde American woman called Gabby was educating us on how to give the perfect blow job. She was seated on a stool in a white room.

'Welcome,' she said. 'Today I am going to share something with you. I'm going to share the glorious secret of how to give your partner that perfect moment of pleasure. A blow job.' Her mouth lingered in an O-shape as she emphasised the vowels. 'I don't want you to think of it as just a blow job, though.' There was a dramatic pause before she carried on. 'I want you to think of it as a *blow gift*.'

Paul and I exchanged a glance and burst out laughing. We paused Gabby as we cracked up. Bits of popcorn sprayed out of my mouth as I repeated, 'It's not a blow job, it's a blow *gift*,' in my best American accent.

'Oh, man,' said Paul, rubbing his eyes on his jumper. 'This woman's fucking insane. We have to watch more.'

We unpaused her and Gabby took us through each step of giving the perfect blow gift. Apart from the occasional snort of laughter, we listened avidly and took notes. By the time we got to the end of the video, my notebook was filled with a systematic list.

1. Take the penis into your mouth with plenty of saliva, or use a lubricant.
2. Suck up and down the shaft and DO NOT GRAZE WITH TEETH.
3. Vary rhythm, speed and intensity.
4. Gently caress his testicles with your hand, then up the pace a bit.
5. Tease him—go fast and then when he gets revved up *(Gabby's choice of phrase, not mine)*, slow down.

6. Use your tongue—if you can multitask, lick it while you're sucking. Or just lick and play with it when it's erect *(the ice-lolly technique again).*

7. Listen to his reactions so you can see which bits he likes.

8. Linger on his sensitive areas—the penis tip, the testicles and the perineum *(that last one seemed a bit more up Paul's alley than mine).*

9. Use your hands and mouth together—put your mouth at the tip end, and suck up and down, and use your hand at the shaft end to do the same, to save you having to deep-throat. *(It also seemed like the perfect way to combine doing a BJ and a HJ. Maybe I could revisit both fears in one slick move?)*

10. Maintain lots of eye contact during the blow gift.

11. If you gag, tell him it's because he is so massive *(making the best out of a bad situation. Well done, Gabby).*

12. Very, *very gently* suck his testicles one at a time.

13. Then the final goal—the ejaculation. It's up to *you* to choose where you want him to come, said Gabby. Either tell him to withdraw, and come on your body, breasts or even a tissue *(seemed kind of sad)*—or let him come in your mouth and choose whether to spit or swallow.

She ended the video with a quick reminder. 'Remember, girls and guys, a blow gift is something *you* should enjoy, too. Share the pleasure and enjoy the gift that keeps on giving.'

CHAPTER TWENTY

AFTER PAUL LEFT, I started to think about Lara. That was the kind of thing she and I would have done together. Paul was lovely and had the best sense of humour I'd come across in a guy, but he was no Lara. She could make me sob with laughter with descriptions of Jez's penis—he had what was known as an almost-chod, which meant it was weirdly thick and the width was almost bigger than its length. Lara told me it was like sucking a loaded tree stump.

I missed her. She was my oldest friend and we once stuck needles in our palms to be blood sisters. Our bond was too strong to be ruined by a hung-over fight, and I was determined to revive it. I grabbed my phone before I could chicken out.

'Hello?' she answered cautiously.

'Hey,' I said, suddenly realising I had no idea what to say to her. Fuck. The nerves rose in me and I tried to make my voice sound normal. 'How are you?'

'Fine, thanks,' she said. Why was she being so formal? She must still hate me. 'You?' she ventured.

'Yeah, fine, too, thanks,' I lied, fighting the urge to start crying and say how much I missed her. Instead I stated the obvious. 'We haven't spoken in ages.'

'No, we haven't.' Why was she making this so hard for me? I'd taken the first step by making the phone call. Didn't she want to speak to me? 'How have you been?' she asked neutrally.

'I…I've been good,' I said. I wanted to tell her about Jack and Paul and Emma but I didn't know how. 'What about you?' I asked lamely.

'Me, too, thanks,' she said.

'Have you seen Angus again?' I asked, bracing myself to hear that they were officially a couple.

'Uh, no, that didn't really work out. But, you know, things are good,' she replied.

'What about stuff with Jez? And uni? Are you still in Surrey or back in Oxford now?' I asked.

'Yeah, everything's good. I'm back in Oxford, just getting some work done. How is work going for you?'

'Errrm, the dissertation is going well, thanks.'

'OK, that's good,' she said as I racked my brains on what to say next. This was worse than small talk with one of my mum's friends.

After a pause, I gave in and let my feelings rush out of me. 'Lara, this is so weird. I don't want to fight. Let's go back to normal. Please?'

She sighed. 'I want to, as well. I'm sorry I didn't call earlier. I didn't mean to let things get so weird between us.'

'Hey, now you sound like you're trying to get back with me after a break-up,' I joked.

'There is no way I'd ever date a male version of you,' she retorted, and it started to feel a tiny bit more normal. Except we hadn't spoken about all the hurtful things we had said to each other. I didn't want to bring it up. It seemed as though Lara didn't want to, either.

'Sooo, what's been going on with you?' I asked.

'Meh, just…you know…life,' she said. 'It's too boring to bother you about.'

'Um, we're beyond that, Lara. The whole point of our friendship is that we're allowed to bore each other.'

'Yeah, you're right.' She paused and then carried on brightly. 'So, what's new with you? Any progress on your mission?'

'I don't know. I've kind of started seeing someone, if I can call it that. It's really new.'

'Amazing, I'm so happy for you!' she cried out.

Cheered on by her warm response, I carried on. 'Yeah, it's good, I guess. And I've made a new friend, Emma, who is really fun. No replacement for you, obviously, but we've been going out, which has been really nice.'

'That sounds so fun,' she said. 'Ellie, I'm so sorry but I have to go. I need to get ready for a ball tonight—don't ask, it's another weird Oxford thing.'

'Oh, OK. No worries. Well, if you want to talk properly, you know where I am.'

'Yeah, and the same goes for you. I promise we'll catch up soon, OK? Bye!' she called, and as I replied with an equally cheery 'Bye!' we hung up.

I suddenly felt very alone. This was the first time Lara and I had ever had such an intentionally short phone call—especially since one of us had boy gossip. I felt empty. I pushed Lara out of my mind. She would call me again when she was ready; she had pretty much promised she would. In the meantime I had a whole season of *Beverly Hills 90210* to get through.

It was Saturday evening and I was ready. It was time to face my fears and have fun with a very cute guy who might definitely become my boyfriend. I met Jack in Soho and we wandered to a pub off Carnaby Street. He was wearing the worst shirt I had ever seen. It was possibly worse than Paul's black hoody and grunge-meets-geek look, although at least Jack's hair always looked washed. The shirt had short sleeves. I hated short-sleeved shirts on men. But he was the only person I could see half working it, and when he grinned at me in his cute half-Irish way, all I wanted to do was rip it off him.

Instead I asked him how his week had been.

'Oh, you know,' he said, 'it's been pretty busy. I've been writing a lot so that's taking up a lot of time. I work these really long days, then go back to my flat and write.'

'It's so impressive you make the time to write after a day at work. I sometimes struggle writing in my diary after a day of half-hearted revision.'

'Yeah, but that's student life for you. I guess because I finished uni a couple of years ago, I know what I really want in life now so I find the time to do it.'

'Either way, it's still very impressive.' I smiled at him. 'So have you been doing your political stuff or the, um, short stories?'

'Bit of both,' he said. 'I'm getting so into the creative writing, though. I really feel like I've discovered my voice.' I laughed without thinking at his cliché but he just grinned. 'OK…I know I sound like a dick, but seriously, this inner-voice thing makes so much sense.'

'No, I do think it is really cool that you're getting into creative writing. I would love to do that some day, but I think I'm just going to stick with journalism for a while. I don't think I'm ready to write a novel or anything yet.'

'You could always start with short stories,' he suggested.

'Yeah, maybe I could,' I mused. 'With your expert guidance, of course.'

'Oh, well, with my wisdom and your wit we'd definitely have a bestseller on our hands. You wouldn't even need to find a job.'

'Thank God, because none of the places I applied to intern for have got back to me.'

'Why don't you just take a gap yaaah,' he drawled in a faux-posh accent as we walked into the dark pub. For a split second I wished that was his normal accent and he could afford to take me to fancy restaurants.

'What? The working-class socialist is encouraging me to spend a year wandering around Third World countries in multicoloured native clothing?' I asked in mock horror.

He laughed. 'Yeah, well, I would have thought it would be right up your street, going on a gap yah. What with the kind of TV programmes you love.'

'Darling, a gap yah? I think you mean a five-star yoga resort,' I replied and he winced at my horrendous posh accent.

'What can I get you?' The barmaid interrupted us and saved me from further humiliation. We both ordered a pint of cider because, as his short-sleeved shirt demonstrated, it was the first really warm day of spring.

At our table, he sat on the leather sofa next to me and put his arm around my shoulders. 'You look pretty today,' he said simply. I looked up at him in surprise, feeling pleased. I was wearing the same floral dress I'd worn to dinner when I turned Paul gay. For a girl who hated dressing up, it was a noticeable effort.

'Thanks.' I grinned. 'No one has ever said that to me before,' I added, immediately regretting it. Now I just sounded like a total no-hoper who never got compliments.

'Seriously? No one's ever told you that you look pretty?' he asked. 'I mean, I know I can be a bit of a dick, but you must know some serious wankers.'

I blushed. 'Yeah, that could be it….' Or it could just be the cold, hard reality that he was the first guy I had ever properly dated. 'You're not a dick, though,' I said. 'Unless there's something you're not telling me?'

'With me, what you see is what you get. If you don't think of me as a dick then I reckon we're doing pretty well. I know I go on way too much about politics and occasionally talk too much, but those are my only flaws, I promise.' He grinned, and I had a sudden urge to kiss him.

I leant over and gave him a kiss on the lips, feeling ridiculously daring and femme fatale. I almost felt like the kind of girl who could pull off blood-red lipstick. He kissed me back gently, and when we broke away I looked up straight into his green eyes.

'That was nice,' he said, smiling, and I hoped he hadn't been analysing the virgin factor of the kiss I'd just given him.

I went an unattractive shade of beetroot. 'Um, thanks,' I replied, looking at the floor awkwardly.

'Anyway, I'm going to stop making you blush now,' he teased, which made me blush more. 'How was your week?'

'Um…' I racked my brains for something normal to say. I couldn't tell him about yesterday's porn session or the Lara fight, so I was at a bit of a loss. 'I think I turned someone gay,' I blurted out.

He looked at me and then burst out laughing. 'What the fuck are you talking about? Please don't say you mean me…. I knew this shirt was a mistake.'

'No, someone else. A family friend. He…he kissed me and then told me he was gay.'

'I know I should be focusing on the fact that you turned someone gay—and I should probably be scared you're going to do the same to me…' he said as I slapped his arm in mock annoyance. 'But I think I'm just jealous that you kissed someone else.'

Ohmigod, he was *jealous*. This was possibly the first time in my entire twenty-one years that I'd made someone jealous, and it felt *good*. I was like a female Austin Powers with my unstoppable mojo.

'Well, in my defence, it was Paul who kissed me,' I offered innocently, with my most flirtatious eyes.

'Right, well, do I have to be worried about any other Pauls trying to take you away from me?' he asked.

He was so confident and sexy that my clitoris started throbbing. It was like a female erection. I tried to make it stop pulsating and crossed my legs, wondering if other women got hard-ons, too.

'I think you're more Paul's type than I am,' I answered back, desperately trying to ignore the clit throb and hoping he wouldn't figure out what was going on down south for me.

'Am I just Paul's type, or yours, too?' he asked as he leant in towards me and I felt his breath on my neck. My knees turned to jelly and I felt like a Judy Blume character—except she never would have talked about the side effect of the vaginal throb.

He kissed me before I had a chance to answer and I melted into his arms. I was a living, walking cliché and I was on cloud nine and three quarters. The words MARRY ME kept flashing across my head as he kissed me without tongue and then put his hand on my vagina and discreetly rubbed it under my dress. I gulped. He was groping me in public. This would be such good material for a game of Never Have I Ever.

I slipped my hand onto his crotch and rubbed him a tiny bit, too. The alcohol was already doing wonders for me and I was imbued with Dutch courage. I'd read all the rules and now it was time to *live them*. He pushed a bit harder on my vag and I suddenly felt the tampon string rub against my skin. OH FUCK, the tampon. I shifted my position and gently moved his hand away from there.

He broke away from me and grinned sheepishly. 'Sorry,' he said. 'Probably a bit inappropriate for the pub.'

'Maybe just a bit,' I acknowledged. 'Maybe, um, maybe we should get out of here?' I was an actual femme fatale. A go-getter, a woman of the world. A Samantha, not a Charlotte.

'Let's go,' he murmured and his breath tickled my skin again and I knew that my vaginal hard-on was making me very damp down there. Or maybe it was just my period.

There Will Be Blood

Yes, Daniel Day-Lewis, there will be. For about five days every month. Bet that's not quite what you were thinking when you directed your well-named blockbuster.

Which brings us onto period sex. EM is going to take over here because EK hasn't had any kind of sex yet, let alone period sex. She is, however, all for it in theory.

EM:

I have had a lot of negative experiences with men who have rejected sex with me when I was on my period. It was horrible.

It was also fucking stupid of them.

When I am on my period, I am generally hornier. It's how Mother Nature made us. Unlike the bastards who rejected me, she clearly thought we should be shagging away while our uterus sorts out its lining. Also, the blood is basically free lube.

It makes the sex better.

A lot of the men I've been with seem to think that when girls are on their periods, the blood gushes out of us. Well, listen up, men, it doesn't. I am not Moses splitting the Red Sea. My red sea is more of a trickle.

If you have sex with me while I'm on my period, I will not bleed all over you. Especially if it's at the start or end, when periods are generally lighter. You might have a bit of blood on the condom but aside from that, I doubt you'd notice.

If you don't want to go down on me, that's OK. There will be days when I don't want anyone near my bleeding chalice. But, when I suggest period sex I don't want you to wrinkle your nose at me and turn away in disgust. It's fucking natural.

It's also the best sex you've never had.

CHAPTER TWENTY-ONE

WE GOT THE BUS back to his flat in East Dulwich and I followed him up the stairs, my heart beating rapidly. I just about took in the wooden floors, spacious living room and relatively tidy kitchen before we got to his room. I noticed the single bed with pre-emptive disappointment about the quality of sleep I was going to get, but I was too full of adrenaline to care.

He put his arms around me and started kissing me again. We both sank onto his bed and began pulling our clothes off so we were just in our underwear. I hoped he wouldn't notice I was wearing the same black bra and pants as last time—freshly washed—and made a mental note to buy some more boy-appropriate underwear that didn't have colourful patterns all over it like everything else I owned.

His hands wandered all over my body, and this time I was prepared for the boob squeeze. The pain even felt sexy and I briefly wondered if maybe I was a sadomasochist. Once we'd had sex a few times, I would ask him if we could try S and M—except without the whole whipping thing because that looked too painful.

'I want you so bad,' he whispered into my ear. Oh, my

God: dirty talk. There was no way I could do that yet. I was a virgin, forchrissake.

'Same?' I said awkwardly, and then decided that talking while fooling around—or during sex, when the time came—wasn't for me.

He must have got the hint because he carried on snogging me in silence. His hands met behind me at my bra clasp and I felt him struggling. I was going to do it for him like last time, but then I remembered it was a *Cosmo* golden rule to let the man feel masculine. I didn't want to emasculate him by helping him. Instead I let him struggle for a few minutes until it triumphantly fell limp against me and he pulled it off my arms.

He burrowed his face in my sizeable cleavage and started licking and sucking on my nipples. I made little gasps, which I hoped sounded sexy, and took note of his sucking techniques so I could use them later on his own erogenous zones. For a second he stopped completely and I momentarily panicked that he'd suffocated in my cleavage, but he quickly came back with full force and was licking everywhere like a happy puppy.

His hand slipped towards my pants and my hand reflexively jumped on top of his. He paused and looked up at me.

'What's wrong?' he asked, his brow all creased up.

'Oh, um, nothing.' I laughed nervously. 'It's just that you can't go there.'

'I...don't get it,' he said. 'Why not? I thought you wanted to?'

'Oh! It's not that,' I said. 'It's just that...' Why couldn't I say the word 'period'? I said it enough in my daily life but the one time I needed to say it aloud, my brain got all coy and refused to comply.

He looked at me questioningly.

'Um, it's just, that, uh, Venus is visiting?' I finally said. He stared blankly and I mentally yelled at myself to stop being so awkward. Venus is visiting? Where did my brain get this stuff from? 'I mean, I have my, um, lady time,' I said in a jokily posh voice, hating myself for not being about to say the word out loud.

A look of comprehension mixed with relief dawned on his face. 'Right,' he said. 'Well, there're other things we can do to keep ourselves busy….' He grinned and leant back in to kiss me again.

We carried on kissing and by now I was sure I was ready to take the plunge—quite literally. I was feeling tipsy and all the kissing meant I was running low on oxygen so I took advantage of my head rush and pulled his boxers down. He jolted in surprise, and I realized I could have probably done that a bit more slowly and sexily, but I looked straight into his eyes like Gabby said, and gave him such intense eye contact that I felt his penis literally *expand* against my thigh. I slipped my hand around it and gently moved it up and down.

OK, this was fine. I didn't have to worry about the pace because I was going to go down and sort that out with my mouth. I distracted him from my unrhythmic hand movements by excessive snogging, until I felt confident enough to venture down south.

He was sitting on the bed, and I had been half sitting on top of him, and half draped over him, but now I stood up and bent down onto my knees. I gently prised his knees open, and moved my head into the groin area. His pubes were shaved like the teacher's from the Britney porn video.

He leant back on his elbows, clearly making himself comfortable while I tried to ignore the cold wooden floorboards bruising my knees. I stared at his member. It was pink and long and hard. It looked like a normal length and size. I turned my head to the side, inspecting it, and decided there was nothing chod-like about it. Phew. It didn't smell either, thank God.

I took a deep breath and prayed to Gabby, Queen of Blow Jobs, to guide me through this. I slowly released my breath and moved in. I put the tip of it in my mouth. He groaned in pleasure. Encouraged by this unexpected confidence boost, I started swirling my tongue around the tip whilst making sure my teeth were nowhere near it. He almost screeched in pleasure, and I remembered that Gabby had said we had to mix things up a bit to make it last. I pursed my lips around my teeth, stretching them out so much it kind of hurt, and pushed more of him inside my mouth. I went right down to the end, which was called deep throating. I didn't gag—I was clearly a natural. I started moving up and down, as slowly and as rhythmically as I could handle. I tried to suck at the same time. As I sped up, I realised I wasn't immune to gagging.

I started going a bit slower, and didn't go right down to the end. I put my hand round the base of him and used it for support. Every time my mouth got down towards it, it felt comfortable to see my own hand there instead of his pale, pubeless groin. Now he started to really moan in pleasure. I slipped my hand under his cock and felt his balls. Their texture was unlike anything I had ever touched. They were wrinkly and I could feel sparse hairs on them.

I carried on with my up-down movements, occasionally using my tongue, and when his breath quickened, he put his hands on my head, just like in the porno, and made me go faster.

I wanted to feel like an angry feminist and yell at him, or at least not enjoy it, but oh my God, I loved it. He was actually helping me out and telling me what he wanted. I wasn't in it alone and he was making me feel appreciated and wanted. I let him guide me and bobbed my head faster and faster until his entire body tensed up and…he came. Inside my mouth. A gloopy warm liquid.

Immediately, I knew I was not going to be a swallower.

I grasped around for a tissue to spit into, but all I found was my dress. Jack was barely acknowledging me and seemed to be basking in his own pleasure so I bent down and spat into my clothes. I felt sad as I saw the liquid stick onto my flattering floral dress, but breathed a sigh of relief that at least it had been inside out so I wouldn't go home with stains all over me.

'That…was amazing,' he said as he sank onto the bed, and I flushed with pure, unadulterated joy and pride. I was good at blow jobs. Fuck you, James Martell. I was *good* at this. I had a talent, a skill, and oh my God, I had conquered my fear! I was every woman, I was Chaka Khan and I was euphoric.

'Glad you enjoyed it,' I said flirtatiously and lay down next to him. I wasn't sure what came next. I'd never given a successful blow job. I hoped he would spend a few minutes telling me how great it was so I could ignore the weird salty taste in my mouth and not feel sad about my dress. He didn't oblige, but instead, he leant over and kissed me. I thought of the salty taste being transferred to his mouth and giggled mid-kiss.

'What's up?' he murmured.

'Oh, nothing,' I said quickly, and started kissing him more passionately, pressing my boobs into him again. My fail-safe move wasn't having the desired effect because he stopped to yawn.

'Fuck, I'm knackered,' he said, and before I knew it, he had closed his eyes and was falling asleep.

I lay there in silence. I wanted a glass of water, but I couldn't bring myself to put my dirty clothes on or risk seeing any of his flatmates. I closed my eyes and tried to sleep, but instead I relived the whole night. I grinned stupidly to myself, feeling a liberating sense of happiness as I realized I had finally given a proper blow job, and basically tossed someone off at the same time. I wasn't a failure. I was normal.

P.S. to 'There Will Be Blood' by EK

For all the girls out there who don't care for period sex—especially if you're a virgin and don't fancy adding more blood to an already delicate situation—try not to feel weird about telling the guy you're bleeding down there. 'I have my period' is a very normal thing to say. Getting shy and telling him you have your lady time, you're 'on' or—wild card—that 'Venus is visiting', will only confuse him. Yes, I am talking from personal and recent experience here.

CHAPTER TWENTY-TWO

IN THE MORNING, I knew I had to take out my tampon or I was going to get toxic shock syndrome and die in my prime. I also knew that I didn't have another tampon in my bag.

I sat on the loo seat, wondering what I should do. I was wearing one of his jumpers and would normally jump at the chance to feel like a sexy romcom heroine with my legs out, but I was too preoccupied. I had opened every bathroom cabinet, because I knew he had a female flatmate, but the bitch hadn't left a single sanitary pad floating around.

There was a knock on the door and I froze. 'Um, who is it?' I asked.

'It's Cat. I need to go to work. Will you be long in there?' a girl's voice called out impatiently.

Ohmigod, it was her—the female flatmate. I ignored the mild irritation creeping up my veins at the fact that she was saying I was taking a long time. I flushed the loo, adjusted the jumper that barely covered my pants and opened the door. She had short dark hair, a nose piercing, and looked angry.

'Hey…sorry,' I said. 'Um, I'm a…friend of Jack's and was just wondering if you maybe have a tampon or something I could use?'

She looked at me with fake sympathy and tilted her head to the side. 'Aw, sorry, I don't. I'm a moon-cup girl,' she said and pushed past me to get into the bathroom.

I stood there in silence, frozen to the spot. A moon-cup girl? What the fuck was a moon cup? And now she was in the bathroom and hadn't even given me a chance to shove some tissue into my pants. I walked back upstairs slowly, and when I opened the door, Jack was awake.

'What's up?' He yawned.

'What's a moon cup?' I asked.

He blinked slowly and sat up. 'What the fuck?'

'Exactly!' I said as I sat down next to him, too confused to bother hiding period talk from him. 'I asked your flatmate Cat if she had a tampon and she said she's "a moon-cup girl".'

'What the hell is that?' he asked.

He really wasn't the brightest of sparks in the morning. 'That's what I want to know,' I replied. He reached for his phone.

'What are you doing?' I asked.

'Something that is hopefully not going to make me wish I hadn't,' he said as he tapped on his phone. 'I'm looking it up.'

'Oh, yay,' I said as I cuddled up closer to him to look at his phone over his shoulder. This was *sooo* boyfriend/girlfriend of us. I grinned again as I waited for his phone to load. Then we both let out noises of total disgust as the Wikipedia entry came up. A moon cup was a reusable plastic bowl-type thing that girls shoved into their VJs to collect blood, and then washed out. It was good for the environment.

'Oh my God, that's disgusting,' I shrieked.

'Fuck,' he said slowly, shaking his head to the side. 'That is messed up.' Then he looked up at me and pulled me close to him. 'Thank God you don't use that shit,' he said as he kissed me and wrapped his arms around me. I smiled happily and sank into his arms.

I sat on the bus, tissue wedged into my knickers, shifting my legs uncomfortably. I was sitting on the 179 back to Tottenham Court Road, and it was stuck in traffic. I was still a million miles from Camden, and the girl I used to be. OK, I was still a virgin but I was finally the kind of girl who could give a BJ without blinking an eye. I had just shared a blow gift with a guy who was definitely about to become my boyfriend.

The thought of Jack asking me out was enough to distract me from the tissue situation or the dried-up come itching my back. I listened to my iPod and chewed on the gum I'd just bought. I wanted to text Lara to tell her the good news but that wasn't an option yet, so I decided I should text Paul instead. He had, after all, been my BJ learning partner.

I sent him a text. I just gave a man the greatest gift of his life and am wearing his dried-up joy on the inside of my dress.

He replied back, immediately saying, Congratulations!! I have a date tonight and may be doing the same. You'll have to share your tips with me soon.

I grinned and sent the same text to Emma. I got a reply just as I was swapping buses.

Woo hoo! Can I come over to hear the dirty details? Can't handle revision.

Yes. I'm en route to Camden now and will definitely not be revising or dissertationing today. Bring snacks.

I closed my eyes and leant against the bus window. Jack had been so sweet this morning. He had made me coffee using his fake-retro latte machine, and had barely stopped kissing me. I'd freshened up with his toothbrush and shoved loo roll into my pants when Cat had gone out to work, and we had spent an hour sitting in his kitchen, chatting. I loved that he didn't think I was weird for bringing up the moon cup. We were clearly a good fit and we already had plans for next week. By then Venus would be gone and we could consummate our relationship. I smiled sleepily in anticipation and spent the rest of the bus journey pretending I was still curled up in his arms.

Emma elbowed me as she pulled the duvet over our legs. 'Budge up,' she said and I obligingly rolled across my bed to make room for her. I yawned, glad we were having such a lazy afternoon. We were already halfway through the packs of chocolate mini bites and rocky roads that Emma had brought.

'These are so good,' I mumbled, my mouth full. 'Thanks for—' I was about to carry on but a spray of chocolate crumbs flew out of my mouth and Emma hit me in disgust.

'Ellie, you're so gross!' she said. 'But yeah, they are amazing. I'm in major need of chocolate—I'm sooo tired.'

'Does that mean your date with Mr Waiter went well?' I asked, raising my eyebrows. She blushed and actually went quiet. I was shocked. 'Oh my God, Emma, do you actually like him?'

'Erm, maybe,' she said. 'OK, we had loads of fun—and oh my God, is he talented in *le sac*—but he is also just a really nice guy.'

'This is amazing, Em! I'm so happy for you!' I shrieked,

accidentally releasing the next fleet of chocolate crumbs from my mouth. 'Oh shit, sorry,' I added, brushing them off her jumper.

She rolled her eyes at me and grabbed another two mini bites out of the plastic tub. 'He's just a truly decent guy,' she explained. 'OK, he took a while to text me, but that's because he was ending something with some other girl. And he didn't want to cheat on the other girl, or mess me around.'

I nodded wisely, as if this happened to me on a regular basis. She carried on. 'I think it's because he is a bit older—he's thirty. He's called Sergio, by the way, and he is doing an MA in Creative Writing while he works in the bar. He is originally from Spain, even though he's lived here for, like, six years. I've seen him a few times now. Also, he is just so fit and he's six-foot-something. You know I *love* tall men.'

'Me, too,' I said wistfully, imagining how great Jack would look if he had a couple more inches on his average five-foot-ten height. 'So what did you do on the date?'

'We went to a bar in Bloomsbury, got drunk together, and he even bought a few of my drinks, which he really didn't have to do. But,' she continued with her familiar naughty smile, 'the fun didn't really start until we got back to his Brixton flat.'

I lay down on the bed, pushing the box of snacks away. 'OK, I'm ready for the real story to start,' I said, snuggling into the duvet and yawning. 'Bedtime story, please.'

'"Bedtime" is definitely the right word,' she said, 'considering we spent most of our time in, on or around the bed. . . .'

I laughed. 'Why doesn't that surprise me? Start at the beginning, please. I want a step-by-step account.'

'Jeez. Demanding, much?' She paused to shove more chocolate in her mouth. 'So we walked into his flat, snogging loads. Then we walked into the bedroom—which was *so* nice, by the way. He has this huge bed with comfy pillows and a weird glass wall thing in between his room and the bathroom. He lives with a South American guy, who was so nice.' She must have heard me yawn again, because she then said, 'Ellie, you brought this on yourself. I thought you wanted every detail. I've just been listening to you go on about Jack's penis for the past half hour.'

'I didn't discuss the interior design of his flat, though.'

She rolled her eyes at me. 'So *anyway*, we were just getting with each other, sitting on the bed for a while, and then he pulled my dress over my head and the real fun began. It was just incredible. His body isn't as perfect as the last Spanish guy's but his penis is *huge* and my God, does he know how to use it.'

I opened my eyes wide and absorbed her every word, as transfixed as if someone was telling me the winning lottery numbers.

'It's all a bit of a euphoric blur but I remember him pushing me up against the glass wall and doing me from every position imaginable. He lasted for sooo long, it was incredible, except…there is one tiny problem,' she added. 'I am *so* sore right now….'

'What, from the sex?' I asked stupidly.

'Yeah. Like, he was so big that it genuinely hurt my vagina and that never happens to me. It was like losing my virginity again—it was *agony* at times. I'm just not used to being with someone so well endowed. I had to actually tell him to go more gently at times, and I'm not a gentle kinda gal.'

I wished I'd already lost my virginity to Jack so I would be able to empathise or at least have some idea of how to respond to comments like these. 'Can't you just practise, though?' I asked. 'And then you'll get used to it?'

She sighed. 'Yeah, I guess. It was just a bit embarrassing, having to tell him we needed to go more slowly. Especially because he's so amazing in bed. I am definitely up for more practice sessions, though….'

'And I'm sure he is, too. I can't think of any guy who would be offended that you thought he was too big. Isn't that the ultimate compliment? And now he gets to have sex with you for as long as it takes for your vag to get used to having him inside. It sounds ideal to me.'

She laughed. 'Well, that is one hell of an optimistic spin on the situation but you're right.' She blushed. 'In fact, I'm actually seeing him again tonight so I guess we can practise then.'

I felt a twinge of jealousy, but then remembered I had Jack, and this was what being a single girl was all about: the dating, and the stories to share with your girlfriends. It wouldn't stop just because Emma was hanging out with Sergio now.

'Em, yay! That's amazing. But seriously. Are you guys, like, going steady now?' I teased.

'Shut up,' she replied. 'Of course not. He's great, but it's way too soon for all that crap. Besides, I'm having way too much fun being single—why would I want to stop now?'

CHAPTER TWENTY-THREE

WHEN EMMA HAD left to meet Sergio, I was still lying in the same position on the bed. I'd swapped the chocolates for beans on toast, and now had an empty plate on the bed next to me while I watched TV shows on my laptop. I was watching a particularly boring episode of *Gossip Girl* when Emma's story popped back into my head. I started getting a bit panicky about the pain I would have to go through to join the post-V club. Now that it looked as though it was going to be a serious possibility with Jack, I was going to have to try to come to terms with the approaching pain.

I put my thoughts into a mental list.

1. He knew I was a virgin already. This was good because it meant he would take care and not shove it inside me with full force.
2. Almost everyone lost their virginity. It couldn't hurt that much, surely?
3. The blood bit. What if I bled all over the sheets? It would be *so* embarrassing. I wouldn't be able to live it down.
4. Horse riding! It broke hymens. If I horse-rode, I would break my hymen, then sex wouldn't hurt and I wouldn't bleed everywhere. I could skip straight to the fun bits.

5. How on earth was I going to start horse riding in central London?

6. Maybe I didn't have to horse ride to break my hymen. Maybe I could do it myself? I could just penetrate myself…

7. I should have bought a dildo instead of a tiny little bullet. Or the rampant rabbit. I was clearly going to have to lose my virginity to some piece of plastic, and it was now or never.

With grim determination, I went into my bathroom and started running a bath. I needed to do this in a warm, lying-down location, and seeing as I had my period, it would probably be best to do it in water and not on my white sheets. It also had to be now or I would keep going over it in my head. I would use whatever I could find instead of an actual dildo, and I'd continue all week, or as long as it took until Jack and I had sex. Then, by the time it came to the real deal, my hole would be the perfect size.

While the bath ran, I scanned my bedroom for something suitable for self-penetration. I considered and eliminated the handle of my hairbrush (too thick) and a selection of mascaras (way too thin). The courgette in my fridge briefly flashed into my head, but the thought of putting a vegetable inside me freaked me out.

I went into the bathroom and looked at all my toiletries. The shampoos and bottles were all too big. I dug deep into the cabinet, and to my utter joy, I found an old set of bath stuff my aunt had given me for my eighteenth birthday. I had forgotten all about the Champneys set, but the four pink-and-white bottles containing body lotion and shower gel were going to come in handy. Each bottle was about five inches long, and the diameter was strangely similar to that of Jack's penis. I had hit the jackpot.

Triumphantly, I selected the bubble bath one then stripped off and eased myself into the warm bath. I added a bit of the bubble bath stuff to the water first, ignoring the fact that it was three years old. I laughed nervously to myself. The bottle looked a bit intimidating, considering it was about three times the size of a supersized tampon. I took a deep breath and put it into the water. I tried to ease it into my hole, but it wouldn't go in. I pushed harder and yelped in pain.

Bollocks. Now what? I needed to turn myself on, so I would get wet and the valve bits would relax and open up. I lowered my fingers and started fiddling with my clit. I closed my eyes and let myself think of giving Jack head and how good and exciting it had felt. I moved my fingers faster. Then I had a brainwave. I would slip a few of my fingers into my vagina and try and open it a bit, fingering myself before using the bottle.

I put one finger in and it slid up easily. The skin was a totally different texture than the rest of my body, and it felt almost rough up there even though it was also warm and damp. Ew, that was probably my period blood, I thought. I ignored the grossness of the image and carried on. I withdrew the finger, and then put two in together. It was a bit tighter this time. I tried to move them around, trying to stretch the hole a bit. Then I took them out and added a third one. I shifted a bit and wiped my brow with my other hand. This was hard work.

The three fingers clumped together couldn't go in as far as the two, but I pushed them around a bit, writhing like a demented mermaid in the bath, then screeched when I accidentally pushed them in too hard. The pain was excruciating and I wondered—was this it? Had I finally torn my hymen?

Anxious to know, I grabbed the Champneys bottle. I breathed slowly, trying to relax myself and get back in the zone. After a while, my heartbeat calmed down, and with the help of my fingers working away on my clit, I started to feel my vagina open slightly. To my surprise, the bottle slipped in. Not all the way, but a little bit. I tried to wiggle it around, to expand the hole and make sure it would be able to cope with a penis inside. It started to feel slightly sore, so I decided I'd done enough for today. I would just do this once a day until Jack and I met up again, curling out my inner lotus, to prepare myself for the ultimate deflowering.

I slipped out of the bath, wrapped myself in a huge fluffy towel and waddled out into my room. My bits still felt a bit sore, so I walked with care. I put on my large Barack Obama T-shirt. Then I walked over to my chest of drawers where I kept all my knickers, and bent down to open the bottom drawer.

To my shock and horror, when I bent down, a gush of water FELL OUT OF MY VAGINA ONTO THE FLOOR. I stared at the damp patch that was quickly spreading out on the green fluffy rug beneath me. It wasn't blood. It was 100 per cent water.

I screamed.

I didn't know how long I was crouched there, frozen in fear above the wet puddle. It felt as if my waters had just broken, as if I was a modern day Virgin Mary. Pregnant without penetration.

If my baby Jesus was fathered by a Champneys bottle, would he get free spa days?

I leant against the wall, my mind clearing up a bit. I didn't understand why this gush of water had just come out of my vagina. Then it hit me.

It was bathwater. I had opened up my VJ and the bathwater had crept in through the open hymen. It was just like sperm swimming up my woman's canal. Then when I'd taken the bottle out, the hymen had closed back up, sealing the water inside. It was only when I'd crouched down that the stream of water had seized its chance and gushed out. I'd finally realised how female drug mules smuggled drugs onto planes.

Great Sexpectations

When Charles Dickens wrote about the weight of expectations society imposed on gentlemen, he had no idea what it would be like for girls a century later when there weren't any gentlemen left. Now a girl trying to get laid has to put on an entire show for a man just because it's what he sees in pornos.

Proof? Here's a list of the things men have expected from our friends and us over the past few years.

[Note: We have slightly changed their words]

1. No pubes. None. In fact, no hair anywhere below your neck. 'But what about the fine hairs that grow around my nipples?' you ask. Get rid of them. We don't know how, but do it.

2. Lots of sounds. Moaning is ideal and softly crying out his name is a guaranteed plus.

3. Wild sex. Depending on the sub/dom roles you're going for, you should either be riding him and whirling a lasso around, or begging him to do you from behind.

4. Dirty talk. Tell him how huge he is and you've never seen one like it, blah, blah.

5. No condoms, ever. Get on the pill, already. STDs? You're just gonna have to risk them.

6. Give plenty of blow jobs and look like you're enjoying it.

7. Don't expect any emotional, loving words. You're *fucking*—not making love.

CHAPTER TWENTY-FOUR

JACK TEXTED ME that evening. He said how much he had enjoyed the night before and wanted to see me next Sunday. That was precisely six days from now, and enough time for my period to go away. I wondered if he'd calculated this, too.

I waited till the morning to reply because I was trying to play hard-to-get. All the books said it was the thing to do, *Sex and the City* loved going on about it, and at this point I was so terrified of buggering things up with Jack when I was so close to losing my virginity that I was willing to play by every rule. Eventually I sent a casual reply, saying I'd be happy to see him on Sunday. It wasn't exactly a Keatsian Ode but it had taken me twenty minutes to compose, with three punctuation edits.

Clearly my playing hard-to-get had worked because he texted back immediately, saying he couldn't wait, and asked me—get this—not one but *two* questions. He had basically told me he desperately wanted me to text him back. Twice.

I basked in my joy before remembering I should do a bit of work or I would end up a failed university dropout. That would potentially be worse than being a twenty-four-year-old male virgin who only just discovered his sexuality. Poor Paul. I would have to remember to send him a text.

* * *

Paul didn't just text me back. He called me. He had been on a date with Vladi, who was a Czech economics student in London, and things had gone well. Unfortunately he wasn't willing to give me a blow-by-blow account of his night—even though blowing had occurred—but he was happy to listen to my in-depth descriptions of Jack's groin area. Eventually he cut me off.

'Ellie, I know I don't need to be saying these sorts of things to you because I'm not your dad, or your mum or your best friend, but, have you, um, thought about contraception?' he stammered.

I shrieked down the phone at him. 'Paul! Of course I have. I've had twenty-one years to prepare for this—I'm not going to forget about pregnancies and STIs.'

He sounded relieved. 'OK, thank God. Because when you were talking about, uh, your blow gift, you didn't mention anything about putting a condom on…and I just thought, you know, you should.'

I paused. No one put condoms on before giving a guy a blow job, right? I mean, all you could get was mouth herpes from that, and Jack's penis didn't have any herpes on it. So I was fine, right? 'Well, no. I didn't,' I said uncertainly. 'But do you know that most people don't?'

'Yeah, I know. But it does mean that a lot of people do end up with STIs and I really don't want you to be one of them.'

'Well, I appreciate the concern, but I'm definitely OK for now,' I assured him, 'and I promise I'll use proper protection when he actually pops my cherry.'

'OK, so long as you do….'

'Oh my God, and you, too!' I added quickly. 'If you get

HIV I will literally die. I'll be like those people who get sympathy illnesses and I'll get phantom symptoms for you.'

It was his turn to laugh. 'All right, I'll be careful, too. Sorry, I just feel like I should say these things to you because we're both in similar positions.'

'No, don't apologise! I love that we have such huge things—well, virginity—in common and that we can both be really open about stuff.'

'Yeah, me, too,' he said. 'I never really expected this friendship to happen, but I'm glad it did. Even if it started off on a pretty weird note….'

'Um, that never happened. Remember?' I replied. 'Anyway, did I tell you my mum's convinced we're dating now?'

'Yeah, about that…' he said sheepishly.

'Paul, what did you do?'

'I told my mum I saw you that Friday and she got all excited…. I denied everything, I swear, but she didn't believe me so this is probably my fault.'

I sighed. 'Oh well, at least my mum's being nicer to me now. It's going to be awkward for your parents when they realise you're gay, though.'

'If that ever happens,' he replied with a sigh. 'Anyway, good to catch up, Ellie. I'm going out now but keep in touch. Hope it goes well with Jack.'

'Thanks, Paul. Same for you and Vladi!'

I hung up and got back to work. I was meant to meet Emma in the library that afternoon so we could work solidly all evening and get dinner together, but the dissertation wasn't going so well. Besides, I now had more urgent things to think about. Obviously I'd thought about protection. I didn't want to be breaking my waters for real any time soon, and there was no way I wanted lumps of gonorrhea all over my precious VJ. I'd always figured I'd go on the pill, but that would require a trip back to Dr E Bowers. I shivered at the thought.

The pill could wait awhile. It was definitely more boyfriend-style contraception, and even though Jack and I were on target and slowly creeping up the relationship ladder, it seemed a bit premature. Condoms would be sufficient. Besides, I was kind of excited to use a condom. We'd spent years learning how to put them onto plastic penises in secondary school, but I'd never had a chance to put my skills into practice. It seemed like a rite of passage I had to go through, and soon I could be one of the sassy girls-about-town who keeps a spare condom in her wallet. The vow I'd taken after visiting Gower Street Practice was going to be completed. I would use a condom on an actual penis and it would actually go inside me and I would never ever *ever* be a virgin again.

Then I realised I only had the one condom I got free in Freshers' Week. Shit. Why hadn't I picked some up from the floor of the surgery weeks ago when I was surrounded by them? It was too risky to have only one in case it broke—and once I started, I planned on having as much sex with Jack as possible. I couldn't leave it up to him to have them, either. What if we had sex at mine and he didn't bring them with him? It was safer to just brave a trip to a pharmacy to get some. Thank God I wasn't in Guildford, where someone would be sure to see me and report back to my mum. Here I could just slip into the chemist, another anonymous student practising safe sex, and no one would ever know.

A few hours later, I was ready to go. I had put a lot of thought into my outfit. It needed to be subtle, but not so subtle that it looked as though I bought condoms every day.

I wanted it to shout out Girl Next Door meets Ambitious Young Woman. In the end, I decided to go for black tights, a black skirt and a cream polo neck jumper. I looked as if I was going to a job interview.

I wandered down Camden High Street to the pharmacy, where I quickly found my required aisle. It wasn't hard to miss. There were rows and rows of family-planning items looking at me. Alarmed, I realised how many types of sexual accompaniments were available in the local pharmacy. Surely all these lubes should only be available in dark shops in Soho?

I browsed the condom selection, trying to ooze casual calmness as I read the labels. Fetherlite… Jesus, what did that mean? Ribbed for extra pleasure? I stared in confusion at the array before me and decided to start eliminating. Coloured condoms were not for me. The flavoured ones seemed a bit too intense. Ribbed would just add width to the penis and that would create extra discomfort, not pleasure. In the end, I decided to go for the thinnest ones. It meant I would hopefully not notice it.

I was about to reach for the package when I realised they came in different sizes. Oh, God. How the hell was I going to be able to buy the right size? First, I had no sodding clue what size Jack would be, and second, even if I did, wouldn't whatever I chose just offend him? He probably wasn't a large because James Martell had been bigger than him, but to get a small seemed rude. I took a deep breath and decided that the only possible solution was to buy a medium pack. Why couldn't they just make them 'one size fits all' like with woolly hats?

I picked up the pack and glanced at the price. Nine-fifty?! For one tiny little pack? These had to be the most expensive condoms available. It was going to cost me almost a tenner to lose my virginity. I could do an M&S dine-in for two with that *and* it came with a bottle of wine. Maybe the shop did own brand condoms? With renewed excitement I scanned the shelves, but to my dismay the only ones I could find were a pound cheaper.

Resigned to the expensive reality of sex, I took my condoms over to the counter. If they did a Meal Deal, you'd think they would at least consider doing a Sex Deal. I wouldn't mind paying ten quid if I got a varied selection of condoms, with maybe a free bottle of lube. I made a mental note to find out exactly what lube did and if I needed some.

I put the singular packet of condoms on the till and the cashier looked me up and down. He was in his fifties, Indian, and he shook his head at me as I defiantly crossed my arms, waiting for him to challenge me.

'Nine-fifty, please, madam,' he said in a strong Indian accent. Ooh, I was *madam*. Clearly my outfit was having the intended effect.

I handed over my card, feeling successful and entitled to be there. I punched in my PIN, felt sad because they were the first four numbers of Lara's date of birth and waited for the transaction to come to an end.

The cashier sighed and looked at me with an expression of…disgust? Jeez, why was he so mean? Buying condoms was what responsible young adults were meant to do.

'Yes?' I snapped at him, putting my arms on my hips. 'Do you have a problem?'

'Your card has been declined.'

Oh. Crap. It was rent day and my loan wasn't coming in till next week, so I had no money in my account. I felt the blush launching across my face at the speed of shame. 'Oh, right, sorry,' I mumbled.

A queue had formed behind us and people were starting to look round curiously. I knew I should leave the condoms there and come back for them, but I needed them for Sunday, and I didn't know if I could handle another day like this. I opened my purse and started looking for loose change.

'So, you would still like the condoms?' he asked in his faltering but pronounced accent.

'Um, one sec, sorry,' I said as quietly as possible, pulling a fiver and pound coins out of my purse. I made up nine pounds thirty from the change in my wallet but I was short twenty pence. Oh, God.

'You need twenty pence more so you can buy the condoms, madam,' he said. 'There might be a smaller pack there that is a bit cheaper.'

'No, there isn't,' I said through gritted teeth. I opened my handbag and began rummaging around for more change. I was now breaking into a mild sweat. 'OK, got it!' I said triumphantly as I pulled out a pound coin. Oh, bollocks…

'That is a euro,' he affirmed.

Please, God, please give me a break here, I prayed, as people behind me started tapping their shoes. An old man behind me stepped forward. 'Here, take this,' he said to the cashier, handing him a twenty-pence piece.

I whirled around to look at my saviour and was repulsed to see the pensioner *wink* at me. I whispered, 'Thanks,' and grabbed the plastic bag from the cashier's hand. I took it and ran. All the way down Camden High Street. The second these condoms ran out, I'd be going straight onto the pill.

CHAPTER TWENTY-FIVE

I LOOKED AT MYSELF in the mirror and held onto the edges of the porcelain sink.

'Ellie,' I said out loud. 'Today you are going to become a woman.'

It was Sunday, 20 May, 2013. I was ready to lose my virginity and enter into the next stage of my adult life. Britney Spears was singing 'I'm not a girl, not yet a woman' and never had her words rung so true to me. I was an African tribal boy, about to kill my first lion. I was the Jewish girl I'd always wanted to be, about to have my Bat Mitzvah complete with a cringe retro theme. My 1993 Vintage Virginity had mellowed beautifully with age and I was about to let Jack pop my cork.

I was plucked to within an inch of my life. The Brazilian had miraculously managed to last—with the help of my Tweezerman and a few hours of vigorous plucking. My outfit was a masterpiece. I had finally decided to embrace myself and stop trying to be someone I wasn't. I was wearing my trusty black skinny jeans with a pair of new heeled boots. They were simple black suede, born out of the Mrs Kolstakis emergency cash fund, and made me feel sexy. My top was simple, too. Black again, because it had worked for Sandy in *Grease*, and it slid easily off my head so we wouldn't get stuck undressing each other. My hair was freshly washed, bouncing along behind me as I walked, and my lips were freshly anointed with pink Vaseline. I didn't even need a self–pep talk in the mirror to be able to half-heartedly admit I looked good. I knew I did.

I smiled to myself, realising how far I'd come in the past few weeks. I, Ellie Kolstakis, no longer hated looking in the mirror. I was finally leaving behind my teenage angst and blossoming into womanhood.

I bounded down the high street, high on life. There was nothing that could make this evening better, other than an emergency girl chat with Lara. But she was still being weird and hadn't texted so I was going to:

1. Get on with my life
2. Be grateful for the few friends who still spoke to me, and…
3. Have the most important night of my adult life with Jack.

He was sitting in the pub, waiting for me. He was wearing simple dark grey jeans, a white T-shirt and a navy hoody. I breathed a huge sigh of relief that was heavily interlaced with lust. When I walked in, his face lit up and he stood to give me a hug.

'Ellie, hey,' he said, kissing me. It was a brief peck but to me it was the height of sophistication. I was finally one of those girls who was 'seeing someone' and was greeted with kisses. On the lips. In public.

I sat down, glowing. I picked up the glass of wine he had already bought for me. It was a far cry from his counting out the change on our first date. *He must really be falling for me.* I sipped it gratefully and listened as he launched into an account of his week.

'I've been looking forward to this so much,' he announced as he sank into the worn couch. 'I'm so fucking sick of my job. They're all such pretentious wankers sometimes and they go on and on about being "cutting edge" and *avant garde*, but at the end of the day, they conform just as much as the next company.'

'As much as you?' I offered, grinning at him so he knew I was kidding.

'Ha ha, Ellie,' he said, nudging me playfully. 'If you think I'm pretentious, you should have a look at these guys. . . .'

'Oh, no, I couldn't bear it,' I said, wincing in feigned pain. 'It's bad enough spending time with *one* of you.'

'Yeah, yeah, you know you love hanging out with me. No one else is as infuriating or charming as I am.'

I burst out laughing. 'Mate, could you be any more arrogant or deluded?' Ugh, why did I have to call him 'mate'? Talk about putting him in the friend zone.

He laughed. 'We're all deluded, Ellie. Haven't you read any Camus?'

'Um, sure?' I said hopefully, batting my lashes at him.

'Ellie, are you fluttering your eyelids at me?' he asked curiously.

'Oh my God, no,' I shrieked, humiliated that he'd caught me out. Boys weren't meant to comment on the lash-flutter. They were barely meant to acknowledge it. Maybe I was doing it wrong.

'OK.' He grinned. 'Clearly I was wrong. Although, I could have sworn there was some major fluttering.'

I bit my bottom lip while the flush spread over my cheeks.

He smiled at me, and leant in to give me another kiss. I kissed him back, surprised, and tried to calm my nerves. I was ridiculously excited, but also terrified. I just wanted our little pub session to be over so I could stop flirting so appallingly and get home so he could bang me.

He seemed to read my mind. 'So, how do you feel about gulping our drinks down and heading back to yours?' I jolted. I didn't think it would sound so seedy out loud. He saw my expression and quickly added, 'That definitely came out wrong. Honestly, I have a surprise for you I want to show you. Oh, man, that came out wrong, too. I promise I'm not a total creep and there is a very wholesome reason why I want to go back to yours.' He grinned. 'And also some not very wholesome reasons….'

I smiled. 'Who knew you were so romantic?' I asked, wondering what he could have on him that he wanted to show me.

He gave me another kiss on the lips. 'I'm so romantic I'm going to pay for a black cab for us to get all the way there.'

I looked at him in mock astonishment. 'Oh my God, you're going to pay for us to go all the way up the road? You're surprising me more and more with everything you say.'

We finished our drinks, flirting outrageously, before we finally left. We tried to get a cab, but all the drivers refused when I explained I lived a thirty-second drive up the road. We ended up walking back to mine, laughing all the way. I nervously let him in and we went upstairs. I couldn't remember the last time my heart had pounded so much and wished we had stayed longer in the pub. I was still way too sober to lose my virginity.

When we arrived, we sat down on my bed and I asked him, 'So what's this surprise you have for me?'

'You don't waste much time, do you?' he said, opening his canvas bag and pulling out a bottle of wine. 'I've brought some Beaujolais for us, and…'

I leaned in curiously as he pulled out a pile of papers. I wrinkled my face in confusion as he handed them to me. 'Um, you brought me some crumpled sheets?' I asked. They were covered with writing in a typewriter font.

'My writing,' he said, looking very pleased with himself. 'I finally finished my short stories and really want your opinion on them. You're the one person I really trust, and I can't wait to hear your opinion on them.'

I was touched. 'Jack, that's so sweet. I'll read them right now.'

'I think it can wait till tomorrow.' He grinned. 'Now, let's get some glasses and start with the wine.'

Smiling, I grabbed a couple of clean mugs and poured us both generous portions. I hoped it wasn't obvious I still had knots in my stomach. This was going to be the night when I lost my virginity. I took a deep breath and remembered the time I passed my driving test. I had been a bag of nerves but I had done it the third time around, and I could do it this time, too. If I could steer a wheel, I could let someone penetrate me. Jack put his empty mug down and started kissing me again. This was it; we were heading up to fifth gear and going all the way.

I snogged him slowly, trying to enjoy every second of the most important evening of my life. He was lying on top of me on the bed, kissing me and moving his hands around my body. We sat up together, our bodies moving in sync. He pulled the top over my head and I congratulated myself on choosing such appropriate shag-wear. I pulled his T-shirt over his head, mirroring him. Then he undid my bra and I realised my mirroring actions couldn't go any further.

We each unbuckled our own trousers and pulled them off. I was only in my black lace pants now. Jack pulled off his boxers, and his erect penis poked out at me, proud of its naked pinkness.

He leant back and I felt his eyes take in my totally naked body. It was the first time he was seeing me completely starkers. Worried, I looked down at my semi-Hitler to see how it was doing under his intense scrutiny. I'd tried to maintain it, whilst letting it grow a bit so it would be a bit thicker and more strip-like, but the lines weren't as straight as when Yasmin had done them. I looked up at him to see if he'd noticed. He was staring at my semi-Hitler as though he was solving an algebra problem.

'What's up?' I asked in a strained voice whilst desperately not wanting to know.

'Oh, nothing,' he said. 'It's just I didn't expect you to have pubic hair like that.'

Was he fucking kidding me?

Why did this ALWAYS happen to me?! And WHAT WAS WRONG WITH MY SEMI-HITLER?

'Um, what?' My voice came out strangled and distorted.

'I don't know, it's just I've always thought of you as natural. I didn't think you'd be into all…that.' He gestured at my vagina.

I stared at him in total disbelief. 'It's called a *Brazilian*,' I retorted. 'Well, a Playboy Brazilian. But that's not the point. Everyone has one. '

'I didn't have you down as the kind of girl who did what everyone else did.'

Was he motherfucking kidding me?! How had I ended up with the one guy in London who preferred girls *au naturel*? I sighed in frustration and semi-humiliation, wondering if a guy would ever see my naked body and not feel the need to comment on my pubic situation.

Jack didn't notice that my cheeks were no longer flushed with lust but with shame. He slipped his hand into the middle of the Hitler as though nothing had happened. I gasped and forgot my eternal pubic dilemma. He leant over and carried on kissing me as his fingers slid around my vagina.

It wasn't as good as it was when I did it alone, but it was enough to make me so damp I wondered if I would drip onto the bedspread. I ran my fingers across his back, exploring the little moles and avoiding the patch of hair at the bottom of his back that spread onto his bum. While his fingers were getting familiar with my female orb, I moved my hand onto his penis and started gently rubbing it. He groaned in pleasure and I glowed with pride. I was getting quite good at this.

We were sitting up and kissing, my back against the headboard. He started to slide down the bed. I froze in total fear. He was going to go down on me. He spread my legs apart and held my lips open. Then he put his head in there, right inside my vagina, with his nose smelling everything, and started licking.

I was too stressed to enjoy it. He was more up-close with my bits than I ever would be. This was the most intimate a person had ever been with me, and I hated it. He licked around and on my clitoris, but the slow movements of his tongue were nothing like the fast vibrations of the bullet I was used to.

This was not going to make me come. I prayed to God he

wasn't planning on staying down there till I came. I was still lying in silence. Should I respond? Should I make sounds?

'Mmmm,' I muttered. What the hell was that? I sounded as though I'd just had a spoonful of crème brûlée.

I couldn't handle this. I pulled him up by his shoulders, and he stopped in confusion. 'What's wrong?' he asked. 'Are you not enjoying it?'

'Oh, no, of course I am!' I lied. 'It's amazing. I just thought you…might not want to stay down there for too long.…'

'No, I love licking girls out.' His tone was deadpan as he stared into my eyes. Bollocks.

'I want to make you come,' he continued. 'Then I want to be inside you and come in you.'

I gulped. This was intense. He had a whole agenda worked out.

'Cool,' I said eventually. I tried to smile. He grinned and went back down.

'Ahh, that's amazing,' I said. God, this was so embarrassing. I felt like a third-rate actress. I felt like a blonde porn star. I felt like a virgin who was going to have to fake an orgasm.

'Mmm,' I groaned. 'Ohhh, that's so good.'

He seemed excited by my encouragement because he licked faster, like an eager puppy with a bone. I wrinkled my face in disgust. I tried to remember the scene in *When Harry Met Sally* where Meg Ryan faked an orgasm. I could totally do this.

'Ohhh, yes, yes! That's it, keep going,' I said whilst wondering how the hell I had managed to get into this situation. 'Ohh, ohhhh, yes!' my voice crescendoed. Then I stopped and tried to simulate the vibration-tension thing my body did when I made myself orgasm. I breathed heavily and gently pushed him away with my toes, so he was forced to move away.

'That was so good.' I sighed dramatically. He smiled at me, looking as chuffed as I probably had when I'd successfully given him head.

He leant over and started kissing me. Oh my God, ewww! I could taste my vaginal juices. I wanted to gag. I pulled away and leant over his shoulder, hugging him while I tried to spit subtly and scrape my teeth with my tongue. He leant towards me and kept kissing.

I took a deep breath and lay down. He lay on top of me, his body squashing mine. Then he stopped. 'I guess I'd better find a condom,' he panted.

'Oh, I have one over—' I started to say, but he had already got his wallet and was pulling one out. Great. I'd gone through all that humiliation in the chemist for nothing.

He opened it and started unrolling it over his penis. And there went my chance of putting sex ed into practice. Oh well, at least this was finally it. IT WAS HAPPENING.

He finished putting it on, and then brought his dick near my vagina. He grinned at me, gently poking it in.

'OWWW!' I screeched. It felt as if he had hit a brick wall inside me and was thwacking against it.

'Sorry,' he said, looking genuinely concerned. 'Try and open up a bit.'

I tried to breathe deeply, and he pushed himself in again, but my closed vag valves refused to let him in. This was not going well.

He shrugged and gave up. He pulled me towards him, and started kissing me again. Oh my God, no. How could this be happening? Why was my body not letting me fulfil my dream? This was so unfair. I was *so close*.

I had to try again. 'No, let's keep trying,' I urged.

'Ellie, it's not working....' he said.

'Please,' I begged, then realised how unsexy that was. 'I want you so bad,' I whispered, channelling the teacher/ Britney porno I'd witnessed. Who knew their minimal dialogue would be so useful?

'OK,' he said with a grin. 'Try and sit on top of me.'

'Um, OK,' I said, and started manoeuvring my body uncertainly. I eventually sat on my knees, one on either side of his body. Then, gently, with his help, I lowered myself onto his still-erect penis. I was descending on him. Slowly, I felt the tip of him rub against my lips. With a deep breath and a prayer to every god out there, I descended. Bit by bit, millimetre by millimetre, he was inside me. I gasped in agony as I felt him go right inside, further than the Champneys bottle had gone. He groaned in delight and my face lit up.

I WASN'T A VIRGIN ANY MORE!

Then I remembered we had to keep going.

Shit, what was I meant to do? Like, go up and down? Ride him like a cowgirl on a wild buffalo? I tried to go up and down but I had no rhythm to speak of. With every attempt the pain got more uncomfortable and I realized how much my thighs lacked muscle.

He took charge. Careful not to let him slip out of me, we rotated so I was on my back and we were in the missionary position. He put a hand on either side of me, as if doing a press-up, and started pumping himself in and out. It felt mildly sore but not agonising. It was more mechanical than pleasurable, but my face broke into a smile that spread across my face and wouldn't stop growing. Jack caught my eye and grinned.

I started to wonder how long it would last. I'd spent so long preparing myself for the moment of penetration that I hadn't got round to imagining this part. In my head, a penis entering a vagina was accompanied by an explosion of confetti and balloons. That hadn't happened in reality. Now he was pushing himself in and out of me, his face winced up in a cross between pain and twisted euphoria.

He groaned loudly and I knew I should start making my little moans again. Whenever I had a real orgasm I barely made any sounds, but I felt silence wasn't an appropriate form of climax. I stifled a yawn and tried to release low, sensual sounds. He gave a particularly enthusiastic thrust and one of my sexy sighs turned into a loud grunt. I cleared my throat and pretended it hadn't happened.

'Are you OK?' he breathed heavily, his voice husky and masculine.

'Mm-hmm,' I replied, my lips pushed together as I breathed through my nose to try to lessen the discomfort. I tried to recall what the yoga teacher at the five-quid student class I'd once attended had told us. *Breathe through the pain. Long deep breaths, in and out of your nose.*

'Are you sure?' he asked again. 'You're breathing kind of funny.'

Damn you, yoga instructor. I gave him a little smile and switched back to breathing through my mouth. Both his breathing and his thrusts became quicker and I bit my bottom lip in anticipation. He was gearing up to release his man-load.

His penis pushed into me harder and deeper than before and my mouth dropped open in shock, gasping at the sudden pain as he sped up. It went in and out again, faster and faster. He was unaware of my agony and within seconds his body was shaking. He let out a groan and collapsed on top of me. His five-foot-ten, average male body fell on top of my exposed boobs. I felt my windpipe crunch into my organs and I gasped for breath.

He held me tightly as he carried on coming into me and gradually his breathing lessened. We lay there for seconds. Me, unable to breathe, and he, regaining his breath.

'That…was…amazing,' he gasped. 'You're so tight.'

'Um, thanks?' I managed as he untangled his arms from around me and pulled himself off my body. His manhood fell out of me, limp and shrivelling. It got smaller and fatter and the damp, cloudy condom crinkled itself around it like used cling film. I stared in fascination at the small bald creature withdrawing into its layers of natural habit.

He pulled the condom off, pulling his penis at the same time, and my eyes grew rounder as I realised how much force the penis could withstand. It stretched out and then bounced back. It was like play dough.

He collapsed on the bed next to me, dropping the condom onto the floor, where I heard it plop onto my soft green rug. I grinned at the fact that I was a twenty-one-year-old girl with a naked man in her bed, a dirty condom on the floor and a sore vagina. I was finally a normal student. I had achieved the dream.

I couldn't stop smiling. I lay my head on his naked upper body, nuzzling my face into his chest hair and breathing in his sweat. I closed my eyes happily. I was cuddling up to my boyfriend post-sex. I'd just lost my virginity to a perfect guy in the most perfect way. I had to text my friends.

I shifted away from him, and in the dim light, searched

the floor for my mobile. My hand hit something smooth and hard, and I grabbed it. I switched it on and immediately tapped out a message.

I LOST MY V-PLATES HALF A SECOND AGO. I'M A REAL WOMAN. I'M EVERY WOMAN. AH!!!!!!

I started typing in Lara's name, but then remembered we still weren't back to the way we were before the fight. I felt a pang of pain and guilt and sickness and sadness. Where was the fun in losing your virginity if you couldn't share it with your best friend?

'Babe, what are you doing over there?' Jack called out.

His voice yanked me back to reality. This was MY moment. I wasn't going to let Lara's weirdness spoil it. I was typing Emma's and Paul's names into the 'to' box when Jack's leg kicked against mine.

'Ellie?' he asked, his voice incredulous. 'Are you texting?'

'Oh my God, no,' I said, throwing my phone back into my bag, 'I'm just, um, checking the time.'

There was a pause. 'Right, OK. What's the time?'

'Like, eleven twenty-three?' I said.

'Cool,' he said and we looked at each other. 'So, how does it feel to not be a virgin any more?' he asked.

I grinned shyly. 'I don't know. Good, I guess.'

He smiled back at me. 'Glad to hear it. Now come here and give me a snog.'

I obliged and we lay intertwined on my white bed sheets until I suddenly remembered the post-virginity blood. I looked down, panicked, but there was nothing there. I turned my back to Jack, pretending to search for my knickers as I quickly put my finger into my vagina and pulled it out again. I squinted. In the light it looked as if there was nothing on it. Thank God. The Champneys bottle had worked.

Relieved, I pulled my pants on, just in case, and climbed back into bed. Jack spread his arm out so I could lie right next to him, resting my head on his chest. He squeezed my boob and I giggled, slapping him in feigned annoyance. He gave me a kiss and then we fell asleep. We spooned all night, our sweaty bodies sticking to each other. We were the couple I had always wanted to be a part of.

CHAPTER TWENTY-SIX

I WALKED INTO university the next day feeling as if I owned that campus. I put my headphones on but even my *Girl Power* playlist couldn't live up to my mood. The sun was shining and I wasn't a virgin any more. As I walked down Gower Street, it felt as if everyone's eyes were on me. The big scarlet *V* I'd been wearing emblazoned across my chest for twenty-one years was gone, and now I exuded sex appeal. My skin was practically alight and I was high on endorphins. It was better than heroin, probably. I bounced up the stone steps where Girls Aloud once did a chocolate advert and plonked myself down in the very middle, gazing out onto the quad in front of me.

I'd spent the morning with Jack. We'd gone to the supermarket across the road and bought muesli because he couldn't handle having a bowl of Coco Pops for breakfast. We bickered like a proper couple in the cereal aisle and even the angry shop owner tutted fondly at the image of young love browsing his shelves. Jack made the teas while I poured the cereal into bowls and we slurped up our breakfast whilst lying in bed next to each other. He eventually went off to work and I showered and got myself ready, casually sauntering into university for my twelve o'clock lecture, having missed my 9:00 a.m. one.

I sat on the steps watching the world go by, wondering if anyone else out there could possibly be as happy as I was.

I closed my eyes and let the brisk May sun warm my skin. It was still cold so I was wrapped up in my leather jacket with a scarf I'd hand-knitted. I was cocooned and warm in my chrysalis. I was a newborn butterfly.

'Guess who?' trilled a high-pitched voice as a pair of cold, clammy hands covered my eyes.

'Emma, get off!' I shrieked. 'You scared me half to death.'

She laughed. 'Well, you shouldn't sit here like a total creep with your eyes closed. What were you doing, babe? You looked like you were praying….'

I swatted her shoulder. 'Obviously I wasn't praying. I was just, I don't know, feeling grateful, and warm, and happy and in love….'

She stared at me.

'In love with the world,' I clarified.

Her forehead creased and she looked at me dubiously through her huge tortoiseshell Jackie O. shades. 'Um. What's wrong with you?'

I looked at her and beamed. 'Nothing.'

Her mouth dropped open and she shrieked, 'OH MY GOD, you did it, didn't you?! You're not a virgin any more!'

'Please, tell the whole campus.'

'Oh, sorry,' she said, lowering her voice but throwing her arms around me. 'This is just such a huge moment and I'm so happy for you! How was it?'

She sat on the steps with me and I sighed blissfully. 'Emma, it was amazing. Not the actual sex—that was a bit uncomfortable but obviously it will get better with time. But the whole not being a virgin thing. I feel so *free* and normal, like now I can be in a conversation with anyone and not have this flashing *V* over my head that I'm constantly trying to hide.'

She smiled at me, nudging me with her elbow. 'This is so good, El. It's just…nice to see you really happy in yourself.'

Hadn't I always been happy in myself? I was happy as a virgin, and I was happy now. I was just a bit happi*er*. I smiled back at her. 'Thanks, Em. So, how's Sergio?'

Her cheeks flushed and she pushed her sunglasses down her nose so she could peer over the rims. 'So, last night Sergio told me he isn't seeing anyone else…and would like me not to see anyone, as well….'

'Oh. My. God,' I said, putting down the Coke can so heavily the froth spilt over the edge. 'Are you and him exclusive?'

'Um, maybe.' She blushed.

'Are you…in a relationship?' I asked.

She sighed dramatically and took the sunglasses off. 'I can't believe you asked me that, Ellie. You know I don't do *relationships*,' she said, practically spitting out the word. 'I'm just seeing him exclusively. We're hanging out. For a while. If and when I get bored, I'll hang out with some more people. I'm just temporarily hanging out *à deux*.'

I stared in silence. Emma had a boyfriend. 'Oh, Emma, this is amazing! I'm so happy for you!' I finally said. Except why did I have a heavy, sinking feeling inside me?

A line from my childhood flashed into my head. I used to love reading *What Katy Did Next*, when I wasn't reading *Pollyanna* or *Anne of Green Gables*. My favourite Katy line was when she got jealous of her friends: *How heavily roll the wheels of other people's joy.*

That was my life. Emma's joy was rolling very heavily over me. What was wrong with me? I should be happy for my friend just as she was happy for me. Instead I was being typically selfish and wishing Jack would ask *me* if we could be exclusive. I sighed and forced myself to be a grown-up. I hugged Emma.

'Uff, what's this for?' she asked, her voice muffled as she spoke through the holes in my scarf.

'It's a congratulations hug. And a thank-you hug, for listening to all my crap about Jack. I promise I'll stop soon.'

She laughed. 'Um, please don't stop. Where else would I get such brilliant stories about bad waxes and awkward dates?'

I shrugged. 'Meh. I guess you have a point. Did I tell you Jack had never seen a Brazilian before?'

Her eyes widened, 'No way! He didn't like the Hitler?'

'Only I'm allowed to call it that,' I barked. 'But yes…he was freaked out by it.' She started to laugh and I scowled in response. 'Emma,' I moaned. 'Do you not think it was embarrassing enough having to be there and see him freak out at the sight of it, without you making me relive the humiliation?'

'It's good for you,' she advised and then broke down into laughter. 'Oh, man, just imagine if it had been you, and he'd pulled his trousers down and there was a man-Brazilian staring at you.'

'Oh my God, don't,' I cried. 'It's too close to the truth. Jack was completely shaved down there. It was so unexpected—James Martell had a full-on bush.'

'Oh, yeah, a few years ago hardly any guys even trimmed

but now they're really getting into shaving and removing it all,' said Emma. 'I guess it evens things out with women.'

'Really? I find it so odd. I'd rather we all just left it *au naturel* and no one had to bother about any of it.' I sighed. 'Anyway, thank God the Boy-Brazilian hasn't become a trend yet.'

'Here's hoping.' She clamped her hand to her mouth. 'Oh my God, I can't believe I almost forgot to show you. Are you ready for your present?' I looked at her in confusion as she rooted around in her leather tote and pulled out a rolled-up magazine. 'Ta-da!'

It was the new edition of the student magazine. 'Oh my God, my column!' I screeched. 'Have you seen it? What's it like?'

She grinned and brandished the relevant page in my face. 'It's amazing—and you look beautiful and clever and funny and I could not be more proud.'

The column was on the left side of the centrefold. It was headed 'Ellie on ANARCHY' and they had used the picture I had sent in where the sun's rays naturally airbrushed my skin. I quickly scanned the column and realised they had barely edited it. At the bottom it said, 'by Ellie Kolstakis'. 'Oh, my God,' I cried out. 'I can't believe it's finally in here and it actually looks good!'

Emma whooped and hugged me. 'It looks more than good, and I'm very proud of you. I've already seen a bunch of students reading it. Just think—you're going to be famous. A total BNOC.' I raised an eyebrow questioningly and she sighed. 'Big Name On Campus, Ellie. Keep up with the slang.'

I laughed. 'Yeah, I can't see that happening any time soon, Em. Anyway, we're late for Chaucer.'

* * *

For one more day, my mood was euphoric. Then it wore off and I started my comedown. I was sitting in the library on Tuesday morning when it dawned on me that I hadn't heard from Jack since we'd done the deed two days earlier. He hadn't sent a single message, and OK, we didn't exactly text every day, but I'd given him my *virginity.*

His silence was disconcerting. Every time my phone vibrated, I pulled the screen open expectantly. Eventually, mid-Tuesday, I decided to take matters into my own hands and send him a message. I was a twenty-first-century female—why should I sit here waiting for *him* to message? Hell, he was probably twiddling his thumbs at home wondering why I hadn't messaged him yet. I asked him how he was and if he wanted to meet later in the week.

After ten hours of tension and stress, he finally replied, saying it would be good to meet up this weekend, but he'd have to let me know when, and that he was well and how was I? My face lit up the second I got his message. He wasn't blowing me off—he was just busy and he still wanted to see me. I decided not to reply for a while, so I could prolong the feeling of calmness and contentment his message had provoked. I knew the second I replied, the tables would turn, and I'd sit in a state of angst waiting for his response. Seeing as I had a dissertation to finish and hand in at the end of the week, I needed my emotional levels at optimum tranquillity. I put my phone in a drawer, sat down with pen poised in hand and proceeded to edit my dissertation.

Midway through a particularly dry paragraph on imagery, my emotional levels dipped. Drastically. I needed Lara. I couldn't go on any more without her knowing the biggest thing that happened to me in my entire life. Our horrible fight had been freaking me out since it happened, but I was no longer a virgin and she didn't know. My medical records were now lies, I was a Post-V and my best friend had no clue.

I needed to tell Lara. This was ridiculous. One of us had to be the bigger person and reach out to cross the gulf that had appeared in our friendship. This time I would actually apologise to Lara; I would cross the Rubicon just like Alexander the Great. I would be a Greek hero. I started flinging my work into a folder, before I remembered the dissertation was due on Friday. I had to finish editing it, do the whole bibliography, print it out again and get it bound. I let out a very long sigh. I would have to postpone the Rubicon crossing.

CHAPTER TWENTY-SEVEN

THE NEXT FEW DAYS passed dismally. I texted Jack back, moaning about my work, but he replied with a simple Cool, good luck x. There were no TMBs in that. With each day that passed, my comedown got worse and I realised what it would be like to be a crack addict with no crack.

I'd been so ecstatic the whole weekend, but now, with the reality of uni, an AWOL best friend, another friend with a fabulous boyfriend and, most important, a semi-boyfriend of my own who wasn't being as boyfriend-y as I wanted, things were officially shit.

I wasn't a virgin. I was meant to be happy. So why wasn't I?

OK, I knew why.

It was because Lara and I weren't speaking. Because Sergio happened. Because Jack wasn't messaging me. He wasn't exactly ignoring me, or cutting me out as men did on TV, but he was hardly being the dream boyfriend who should be making me mixtapes. Or at least a Spotify playlist.

I spent the next few days in exactly the same way. I woke up at 8:00 a.m., I showered, I walked to the library and I stayed there till 6:00 p.m finishing my dissertation. Then I walked back home, bought a reduced sandwich from the supermarket and ate it in bed while watching a crappy TV series on my laptop until I fell asleep. My pubes were growing back and they were itchy. They seemed to know I'd robbed them of more prime time in the spotlight, and were coming back larger and longer than ever. Even my pubes were on bad terms with me.

I had gone for one lunch with Emma, but our dreams of revising together with excess breaks were shattered by Sergio. Deep down, I was happy for her, but the timing couldn't be more off. Double dates couldn't have been further from my reality. Instead I was a sad, spurned woman of the world living in a state of solitude. I didn't even have my virginity to distract me any more—all I had was a copy of my magazine column taped on my wall.

Sarah, the editor, had asked me to do another column for the following week. The theme was 'Romance'. It felt like an ironic kick in the face. Initially I had wanted to write one based on Jack and me, but as the days went by and I still hadn't heard from him, I changed my mind. Hours before my deadline, I cobbled together 400 words on Jane Austen and the lack of romance in our modern lives. It was more 'anti-technology' than 'romantic' but luckily Sarah liked it.

The column was the only thing going well for me at the moment. I glanced over to the wall to look at magazine Ellie, reminding me of my success, but my eyes caught on the clock. It was 3:00 p.m. and my dissertation was due in an hour. I jolted upright and grabbed my bag.

'TAXI!' I shrieked, waving my bound dissertation in the air. I probably had enough time to take a bus before the deadline, but on my tight budget I never got black cabs so it seemed like an opportunity to grab with both hands. All the black cabs ignored me but a dark red one pulled over.

Great, the one time I wanted to take a black cab, a *red* one pulls over.

I climbed in, telling him where to go, and then on a whim, added, 'And step on it!' I felt as if I was in a movie. In a movie, he would have said 'Yes ma'am' and slammed his foot on the accelerator. In real life, he spent the next eleven minutes giving me a lecture on road safety and following speed limits.

When he pulled into Malet Place, I paid him a tenner and jumped out in relief. I ran up the stairs, pushing open the doors to the staff room, and dumped my finished dissertation onto a large pile. There were a couple of other students there, but I decided to make an early exit in case Hannah or someone worse came by. As I walked out of the door, I bumped into Luke, the painfully hipster guy who threw the Never Have I Ever Party.

'Hey, Ellie,' he said. 'Just handed yours in?'

'Yeah, thank God,' I said, smiling way too much. *God, why couldn't I just be normal around men?* 'So glad to be rid of it.'

'Tell me about it. Now I can actually read Kerouac without having to think about his relation to the modernist movement.'

I laughed politely, relieved that I'd never be the kind of person who would reread Jack Kerouac for fun.

'Anyway,' he carried on, 'are you coming to our big party tomorrow night? To celebrate handing in the dissertation?'

'Party? Um, no, I hadn't heard anything about it,' I replied honestly.

'Oh, it's just a Facebook thing.... I'm sure you'll have the invitation on there. We're having a party at Matt's, Opal's and mine. It would be cool if you could come.'

I shrugged my acquiescence. 'Sounds good. See you there.' I smiled at him as I edged towards the staircase. The essay was in and now I had time to focus on fixing my friendship with Lara. I'd wasted weeks avoiding this. Now it was time to get my best friend back. I walked quickly out into the quad and sat on my favourite steps overlooking the front of the university.

Lara, are you free to chat? Really want to talk! xxx

I sent the text and sat waiting anxiously, tempted to imitate Lara's childhood habit of biting her nails even though I'd never done it myself. A few minutes later, my phone beeped.

Hey, Ellie. Sorry but now isn't a good time. I'm home in Guildford with the fam. Will speak soon though. xxx

My heart sank in disappointment. Why didn't she want to talk? I hated that she was still avoiding me—our fight was so irrelevant. If I could get over it and try to be the bigger person, why couldn't she? Then I reread her message. She'd responded quickly, and she'd sent the same number of kisses back. If she *was* mad at me, she wouldn't have done either of those things.

She was in Guildford and she didn't hate me. I suddenly realized that this was perfect. I could go to hers today, right now, and see her there. It was only an hour or so on the train. I grabbed my bag and headed for the tube.

I walked down the familiar road to Lara's parents' home. The silver sports car was outside the house so I knew they were in. My feet crunched on the beige gravel of their driveway. My heart was beating nervously and my palms were sweaty. I told myself to calm down. I was visiting my best friend; I'd spent half of my life in her house, and her family was basically my second family. I could do this.

Biting my lip anxiously, I buzzed the bell and closed my eyes, saying a very quick prayer. *Please, God, or gods, or karmic spirit, help me. Make her not hate me. Make me brave. Alexander the Great, if you're up there, can you help a bit, please? I know it's not as big a deal as you conquering Asia Minor, but—*

The door opened and Lara's mum stood there, looking flustered. Her normally immaculate hair was tied up in a ponytail and she was wearing a fleece over leggings. I didn't even know she owned a fleece. Her trademark pearl stud earrings were nowhere to be seen.

'Stephanie?' I asked cautiously. 'Is everything OK?'

She looked at me, relieved. 'Oh, thank God, Ellie,' she breathed out. 'I was hoping Lara would come to her senses and call you. Come in. She's in her room.'

I looked at her in confusion as I stepped into their marble hallway. 'She kind of…didn't call me,' I disclosed. 'But can I just go up, anyway?'

'Oh…' said Stephanie, her face falling. Then she shook her head gently and smiled at me. 'Sorry, what am I doing? Come in, come in. You know the way.'

I shot her a smile and went upstairs to Lara's room. I was officially confused. How come Stephanie knew about our fight? I knew Lara and her mum were close, but not *that* close. Lara and I always used to say mums and daughters who got on too well were creepy. I knocked on her door.

'Yeah?' she called.

'It's me,' I said, tentatively pushing the door open. Lara was sitting on the bed, her long blond hair pulled into a messy bun on top of her head. She was surrounded by stuff. Clothes, make-up and books were spilling out of large brown boxes.

She stared at me in complete shock. 'Ellie, what...what are you doing here?'

'We... I wanted to talk to you,' I said numbly. 'But what's going on? What's with all the boxes?'

She looked at me and her face crumpled. She burst into tears. In all our years of friendship, I'd never seen her cry in front of me. I stood dazed, frozen in shock, before instinct kicked in and I ran over to hug her. We sat on the bed, my arms wrapped around her. I held her as she cried onto my striped grey jumper. Eventually her sobs subsided and turned into sniffles.

'I'm so sorry,' she said. 'I...I didn't mean for...'

'Lara, stop,' I interrupted. 'Everything's fine. We're fine, I'm here, you don't need to apologise. Cry as much as you want. And when you're ready, explain what's wrong and I'll be here for you.'

She smiled at me gratefully and I squeezed her tight. 'Ow,' she gasped. 'Stop squeezing so hard.'

I laughed, and she joined in between her sobs. 'Oh God, Ellie,' she breathed out. 'Everything is officially shit.'

'What's wrong, Lar?'

She sighed and started fiddling with her hair, which she always did when she was nervous. 'My dad left my mum over a month ago. I found out about it a few days after we, I...after we went out that night to Mahiki. He's sleeping with some skank. It's so sodding typical. I don't know if I hate him more for that, or for being a total cliché. Anyway, Mum's freaking out. We can't live here any more so we're going to move somewhere but we don't know where, and we don't know if we're going to rent or… I'm so confused and it's so complicated.'

'Oh, my God. I'm so, so sorry, Lara. I can't believe it. I'm so…shocked, and disappointed with your dad. How can he do that to you and your mum?' I asked.

'I know,' she said simply. 'I can't figure it out, either. It's too surreal.'

I hugged her again. 'It's going to be OK, babe. I know it is. You have your mum and she's amazing.'

'I know,' she said. 'But even though she obviously earns a fair bit as a barrister, it's not enough for us to live here. Especially because she was the breadwinner so they have to split money in the divorce and it's so messy. I think she also doesn't want to live here any more because of the memories…'

'I get it,' I said softly. 'Is there a plan?'

'Meh…there are some options. We either rent somewhere in London, or go and stay with Aunt Charlotte and have some kind of girls' pad, but I don't know if I can handle the thought of living with my newly single mum and her single sister in Hertfordshire.'

'Oh, my God,' I cried suddenly. 'Why doesn't your mum go and live with Aunt Charlotte—they're like best friends anyway and she probably needs her sister right now—and you come and live with me?'

'Ellie…I can't,' she said quietly. 'I need a home. I can't just crash with your parents, or with you in Camden, or… I don't know.'

'OK,' I said, disappointed that I couldn't fix everything. 'You're right. It was a silly idea. But you're always welcome, you know. I mean, I know you're at Oxford during term anyway, and we only have a couple of months left, so this summer you could stay with me in Camden. We could have one last summer in London together before my lease runs out. Then by the end of summer, maybe your mum will have somewhere sorted.'

She looked up. 'I…I mean, maybe that could work. I was dreading a summer in Hertfordshire. But, Ellie, I've been a shit friend.'

'Lara,' I said, putting my hand up in the air as a signal for her to shut up. 'You've been going through so much and I haven't been here for you at all. I'm a way shittier friend than you. Your life is falling apart, and I've been so selfish….'

She slapped my arm, smiling at me through her tears. 'Jeez, stop telling me how crap my life is.'

I smiled sheepishly. 'Sorry…. Honestly, though, Lara. Even though we were going through all that weird stuff post-Mahiki, why didn't you tell me about this?'

'I was jealous,' she whispered. 'You always pick yourself up whenever bad or awkward stuff happens to you—which is like *all* the time—and you're really strong. And I felt really weak and lame and I couldn't tell you.'

My eyes welled up. 'You're an idiot,' I said, wiping away tears. 'I'm a bloody mess.'

She shot me a smile. 'I can tell. But seriously, back when your parents divorced, you were so calm about it. You never cried, and you didn't make a big thing about it like I am now.'

'Lara, our situations are totally different,' I cried. 'I grew up in a dysfunctional home with my parents constantly arguing. They were so shit together it was a relief when my dad left. Your family is different. Your parents seemed genuinely happy together and your dad leaving has changed everything. It's normal for you to be sad—it would be fucking weird if you weren't.'

'Really?'

'Of course, you idiot,' I said, squeezing her arm. I had tears in my eyes now. I couldn't believe Lara had been going through all this alone just because I had been too stubborn to apologise. It was a month too late but it was time to finally say sorry. 'Lara, I really am sorry, you know. I never thought you might actually have needed me all this time. I just thought you were angry with me and I avoided you because I was scared. I should have been more brave.'

'I wasn't brave, either,' she conceded. 'I just kind of ran away from life and holed up here with my mum.'

'That *is* brave. She needed you and you were here for her. Is that why you're not at uni?' I asked.

'Well, you know us Oxbridge kids…we get long holidays so I'm still not actually back at uni.' She grinned.

I swatted her. 'Well, some of us handed in our dissertations yesterday because we actually *went* to uni at eighteen and didn't sod off on a gap year.'

She laughed. 'Glad to see you haven't changed.'

I blushed and stared at her in silence.

She stared back. 'What?' she asked. 'Why are you doing, poignant eyes?'

I bit my bottom lip and grinned in silence. Her eyes got wider as comprehension dawned on her face.

'SHUT UP. YOU DIDN'T! YOU'RE NOT… OH MY GOD, YOU'RE NOT A VIRGIN!' she screamed.

I burst out laughing and squealed, 'I KNOW! I DID IT!'

We screamed together and hugged, laughing. 'I literally can't believe this,' she said after we'd stopped yelling. 'With that guy? I don't even know his name. I'm a shit friend.'

'I thought we'd got over the shit-friend thing. We're as bad as each other, so it neutralises out. Anyway, it only happened last week so you're not too late finding out about it—don't worry. He's called Jack. It didn't hurt much and we've been seeing each other…well, um, four times, and we're still texting and… Oh, I don't know.' I sank onto her pillows with my legs up in the air.

She sank back with me. 'This is insane,' she said. 'I'm so happy for you! But oh my God, I haven't known about your newfound state of womanhood for a whole week.' She sighed theatrically. 'I should have seen it the second you walked in. You're totally PCG-ing.'

'Huh?'

She grinned. 'Oh, finally I know an abbrev you don't. Post-coital glowing, obviously.'

I laughed. 'Well, I was actually majorly PCG-ing on Monday, but it's worn off every day since. In fact, it's basically dead now because he isn't messaging as much as I want him to, and I, like, don't know if he wants to be my boyfriend,' I finished quietly.

'Was it…ever suggested that he wants to be your boyfriend?' she asked cautiously.

'No. But we'd been on three dates. I just assumed, because he was always so cute, and he seemed to like my personality—not just my boobs like the typical wankers on TV. And he was so keen before, and now he's totally bailing and I don't wanna be that girl who loses her V-plates to a guy who abandons her. So what do I do?' I looked at her hopefully.

'OK,' she said. 'Let's take this slowly. I don't know the details, but you'll obviously fill me in all night because you're staying over. But it sounds like you need to ask him.

I mean, fuck it, the worst that can happen is he says he's not interested and then you can move on, and at least you didn't lose it to a stranger.'

I nodded gradually. 'Right, OK. I mean, I'd rather die than ask him outright, but I see your point. I need to know. Fuck it, I can do this. Tomorrow.'

She nodded and wrapped her arms around me.

'So tell me everything,' I said. 'Every tiny irrelevant detail I've missed over the past few weeks. I miss you.'

'Ugh, you're so cringe. But fine. I kind of missed you, too.' She smiled, her eyes still red, and lying there on her bed, she told me everything. About her dad, about Angus never texting her back and how Jez was still being a dick. The gap between us narrowed until we'd forgotten there ever had been one. I'd crossed the Rubicon.

CHAPTER TWENTY-EIGHT

OVER CROISSANTS AND COFFEE the next morning, I had the brainwave of inviting Lara to Luke's party. Next thing I knew, we were on our way back to my flat in Camden, carrying a selection of dresses and shoes from Lara's extensive wardrobe.

'Are you sure you want to go tonight?' I asked Lara worriedly.

'Ughhh, how many times are you going to ask me before you believe I want to go out and get trashed?'

'But I know you're going through a lot and I don't want to force you to go to some random party where you won't know anyone,' I continued.

'I think maybe you're the one who wants to get out of going to the party, not me,' she said, touching on the exact problem, as she always did.

'Fine,' I grumbled. 'I feel weird. I hate mixing social groups. What if you don't like Emma? What if she doesn't like you? And Jack is still AWOL and I hate my life.'

'First, please can you give Emma and me a bit more credit? We're both your friends, and I'm sure we can get on for one night, especially with the aid of alcohol. And second, we spoke about Jack. You're going to find out what's wrong, and then put it to rest and move on with your life.'

She was right. She and Emma were amazing and I was lucky to have them both. If Jack was going to ditch me, I would survive. But he probably wasn't—he'd been so keen before, and I couldn't imagine he would lose interest. His last text had had a kiss at the end, so he clearly still liked me. I just felt weird because…well, because I wasn't a virgin any more. Things were different now.

'Is that my phone or yours?' asked Lara as we lay exhausted on my bed and my phone beeped.

I checked my pocket. 'Oh my God, it's from Jack,' I cried as I opened it.

'I told you that you were being overly dramatic,' she said. 'Go on, what does it say?'

'He says, "Hey, how was the diss? Are you going to that party to celebrate tonight? Eric is going with your favourite person and invited me. I'll go if you go." And it has a kiss on the end,' I finished triumphantly.

Lara nudged me. 'You're ridiculous. He always liked you. He wants to go to this party with you.'

I closed my eyes and let out a massive sigh of relief. 'Thank God I'm not one of those girls. He still likes me post-sex. And you get to meet him tonight!'

She rolled her eyes. 'Great, now I'll be a third wheel.'

'Or you can take this chance to get over Angus and Jez and those rubbish men and find someone new,' I said, my eyes sparkling. I added smugly, 'Although, now *you* get to know what it feels like to be third wheel.'

She groaned. 'Oh my God, I couldn't bear it. I'm gonna text Jez and get him to meet me afterwards. At least then I'll have a backup booty call if I feel depressed while you go off with Jack.'

'Or you could pull someone new at the party,' I suggested again.

'No,' she said. 'I really can't deal with someone new right now. I'll just go to Jez's tonight as I'm guessing you'll be bringing Jack back here.'

I did my best innocent face. 'You and Jez could always crash in the bath.'

By the time we were banging on the flat door two hours later, my head was so full of cheap Prosecco that I didn't even care that it was Hannah who opened the door for us.

'Ellie.' She smiled at me faux-sweetly. 'So nice of you to come. Hi, I'm Hannah.' She turned to Lara, air-kissing her as she introduced herself. I gagged inwardly. Why was she pretending she was the host when she didn't even live here?

'Hello,' I replied, gritting my teeth. 'How are you?'

'Oh, you know, shattered post-diss.... O-M-G,' she cried out suddenly, spelling the letters out. 'Are you shagging Jack? Eric told me. In fact, he told me *everything*.'

I stared at her in horror. Please, God, let her not actually know *everything*. Please let Jack have kept his damn mouth shut. I turned my face into something vaguely resembling an 'excuse me' face and grabbed Lara's arm. I bolted into the living room, dragging her after me.

Lara looked up at me. 'Ow, can you let go of my arm, please?'

I released her arm, feeling a bit more sober. 'Did you not hear that? She says Jack told Eric *everything*. What if she knows I was a virgin up until a few days ago?' I whispered urgently.

'Don't be dramatic,' said Lara.

'I'm not being dramatic! This could be a total disaster.'

She shrugged her shoulders at me and walked into the kitchen, barely batting an eyelid at the groups of very cool-looking people draped over corners and armchairs. She looked like the kind of girl who didn't care about not knowing anyone at a party. With a resolute sigh, I tucked my hair behind my ears and followed her into the kitchen.

In the two seconds it took me to follow her, she won over Luke. He was in his cream cable-knit jumper that looked vintage, though I had definitely spotted it in the window of Urban Outfitters. His eyes took in her perfect body, hair, clothes, face, wit… The jealousy list started whirring through my brain but this time it didn't feel nasty. In fact, I was kind of proud that my best friend from home was such a hit. Normally home friends were always dressed wrong and ended up bored in a corner. Not Lara.

I yawned and got out my phone to see if Jack had messaged me, but then Emma walked in. She was wearing a sparkly silver dress with shoulder pads and looked stunning. She was holding Sergio's arm. He looked different out of his waiter's uniform.

'Ellie!' she shrieked, not caring who turned to stare, even though Luke was definitely too preoccupied to hear her shriek. She enveloped me in a big hug and pulled Sergio's sleeve to get his attention. As if she'd lost it. 'Serge, you remember Ellie, right?'

'Hey,' he said warmly, giving me a hug, as well. I hugged him back stiffly.

'So, where's Lara?' asked Emma impatiently. 'I can't wait to finally meet her. Also, I'm so glad you guys have made up and I promise I'll love her.'

I sighed and pointed across the kitchen to Lara and Luke. 'She's already pulled.'

'Lara!' Emma said delightedly, tapping her shoulder and beaming. 'I probably don't need an introduction, seeing as I'm Ellie's only other friend who isn't you, but I'm Emma.'

Lara spun round and grinned. 'Emma, of course,' she cried. As they hugged, I realised my two best friends were both blonde and thinner than me. I was also starting to realise why the Prosecco had been reduced to half price. I ran to the sink, pushing past Luke, and helped myself to a glass of tap water.

I downed it quickly and refilled it. I turned back to the girls. 'So nice to meet you at last,' said Lara, smiling prettily, totally oblivious to Luke making puppy eyes behind her.

'You, too,' said Emma warmly. 'We already have so much in common and I'm so impressed you managed to pull within three minutes of getting here. You know, Luke's been staring at your arse this whole time,' she added matter-of-factly.

Lara let out a burst of shocked laughter and whirled around to see Luke turning a deep shade of mauve. 'Fuck off, Emma,' he muttered and walked out of the kitchen, shaking his head.

I turned to face them all, feeling sick. 'I don't feel very well,' I announced.

'Yeah, you don't look great,' confirmed Lara.

'Well, you'd better make yourself look a bit better,' Emma told me, 'because Mr Lover Boy has just walked in.'

I turned around to see Jack standing in the entrance of the kitchen, chatting to Eric and hugging Hannah. He hadn't seen me yet. I faced the girls, my eyes wild and bright. 'Oh my God, that's him,' I whispered, panicking. 'Do I look disgusting? Lara, do you think he's fit? Oh my God, has he seen me? Help!' I said urgently as I grasped both their forearms.

'Seriously, what is this thing you have about hurting my arm?' whined Lara as she pulled her arm away and stroked it. I stared at her angrily.

'Oh, all right,' she said calmly, flattening her hair with her hand. 'You look fine, he looks fine and you're going to be totally fine. Turn around and go get him.'

Emma nodded her assent and leant against Sergio's tall, silent body as I nervously walked towards the kitchen door. Thank God he had come. My nerves started to fade away and I forgot about the Prosecco bubbles that had been defying gravity by making their way up my oesophagus.

'Jack, hey,' I said, trying to sound sexy and mysterious and cool as I tapped him on the shoulder.

He turned around and his face lit up. I pulled my lips into a pout to stop them turning into a ridiculously wide smile. 'Ellie,' he said, wrapping me in a hug. I closed my eyes and grinned as I thought about the last time we had been so close. Without any clothes between us. And his penis inside—

'How have you been?' he asked, pulling away from me and bringing the hug to an abrupt end.

'Good,' I replied with what I hoped wasn't a needy smile. What sort of things did girls say to make boys ask them out? I racked my brains. 'I finished my dissertation.'

'Right, hence the "end of dissertation" party.' He grinned. 'Hey, you should come meet Eric.'

'OK,' I said happily. He was willingly introducing me to his best friend. Hel-*lo*, progress.

'Eric, this is Ellie,' he said, and Eric turned around to look at me. Except he didn't just look at me. He looked me up and down, taking in every inch of my outfit. He was testing me.

'Hey,' he said coldly. The tone of his voice suggested I'd failed part one. I *knew* I should have worn something vintage. 'Jack told me about you,' he continued. 'So, do you know my girlfriend, Hannah?'

OK, a question. That was definitely a second chance. I gave him my most winning smile. 'Yeah, we do English together. She's in my Chaucer module.'

He looked at me as if I was the most boring person he'd ever met. He smiled politely and turned around. Clearly I'd failed part two, as well. What happened to everyone having three chances?

'So, do you like him?' asked Jack eagerly. I raised my freshly tweezed brows at him. He waited expectantly, and I realised he was being serious.

'He seems like a nice guy,' I said cautiously.

Jack grinned. 'I think you guys would get on really well. I feel like you have a lot in common.' This was news to me but I shrugged my shoulders.

'Come meet my friends now,' I said enthusiastically. He followed me over to Lara and Emma. Luke was flirting with Lara, while Sergio and Emma were intertwined in a passionate kiss. I tapped them both on the shoulder.

'Jack!' shrieked Emma as she gave him her typical over-the-top welcome. She introduced him to Sergio, who, living up to his European blood, hugged Jack, who awkwardly hugged him back. Lara turned around and moved her eyes around frantically, gesturing at me to introduce them.

'Jack, this is Lara, my best friend from home, and Lara, this is Jack, my…' Bollocks. I froze. Lara came to my rescue and hugged Jack without bothering to wait for whatever humiliating term I would inevitably have come up with.

'Good to meet you,' she said. 'So, Ellie says you write a lot. That's so cool. I've always tried to write but I've never managed to finish anything. How do you do it?'

He answered readily, and they began an animated conversation about literature while Emma and Sergio pretended to look interested. I watched Lara proudly. She was perfect at introductions and was making Jack feel comfortable and interested. Unlike my earlier exchange with Eric.

I felt something vibrate against my thigh. Disappointed, I realised it was my phone. Paul was calling me. 'Sorry, guys, I'm just going to take this call,' I announced. No one looked up from their conversations as I walked out of the room.

'Hey, Paul, what's up?' I asked.

'Ellie, I need your help,' he whispered urgently. 'I'm with Vladi and we're about to have sex. But he doesn't know it's my first time. I don't really know why I'm calling you. I'm just kind of freaking out.'

'OK, whoa. Don't panic,' I said firmly, rapidly trying to make my drunk brain sober up. 'Look, you don't have to feel weird about being a virgin. I was one, too, until last week and, honestly, now I've had sex, I've realised it's just not a big deal. I think you should tell him.'

'Because it's better to be honest?'

'Um, because it will hurt less if he knows,' I cried out. 'But yes, also that.'

He sighed. 'I know, and I really want to. But what if he rejects me?'

I leant against the doorpost to think. If I was in Paul's position I would be terrified to tell Vladi for exactly the same reasons, but deep down I knew the brave option was the right option. If Paul wanted it to work with Vladi he had to be upfront from the start.

'If he rejects you he is a wanker and you can give your virginity to someone else,' I announced confidently.

'Is that what you'd do if you were me?'

'Definitely,' I lied. 'Now get out of the bathroom and go and tell him.'

'Walk-in wardrobe, actually. But OK, thanks for this.'

'You gay guys… Anyway, let me know how it goes, Paul. Good luck!'

'Thanks, Ellie,' he said nervously and hung up.

I let out my breath slowly. Thank God Jack had figured out I was a virgin without me having to tell him. I couldn't have handled a denouement like that. My virginal kissing clearly had its benefits.

CHAPTER TWENTY-NINE

WE STAYED CHATTING and drinking at the party until my vision started to blur and the voices around me sounded like distant hums. I realised it was time for me to go home. With Jack.

'Lara,' I said as nonchalantly as I could manage, 'do you need to go to the loo?'

'What?' she said, and I realised I'd interrupted her mid-speech. 'No, I'm fine, thanks.'

I gave her a death look.

'Actually, maybe I do,' she said, and we both turned and walked from the kitchen to the bathroom. The second we got in there, I locked the door.

'OK, emergency meeting,' I announced. 'I am officially drunk and am not going to last much longer. I need to leave. So, are you going to get off with Luke, or go and find Jez? Because I'm going to need my bed.'

She rolled her eyes. 'Jeez, is this how it's going to be all summer?'

I felt a pang of guilt. 'No, I promise. Normally I wouldn't mind going back to his. But tonight I think I may vomit at some point and I'd rather vomit in my loo than his and get yelled at by scary Moon Cup Cat.'

'What's a mooncupcat?' she asked. 'Oh, never mind. I'm going to text Jez so he can come and get me. Or at least pay for my cab to his.' She paused. 'Wow, I'm basically a voluntary call girl.' She shrugged her shoulders and started tapping out a message on her phone.

'OK,' I said. 'I'm going to leave you here so I can get Jack on his own and explain we need to go now.'

She grunted at me in response and I walked back out to find Jack. He was chatting to Emma while Luke and Sergio laughed hysterically over something on Luke's phone. Emma and I exchanged a look so silent and subtle that the CIA would have hired us on the spot if they'd seen it. She gave me a tiny nod in comprehension and slipped away.

I grinned at Jack, realising it was the first time during the whole night that we'd been left alone. 'Hey,' I said.

He smiled. 'How's it going?' he asked.

'Meh, I'm feeling a bit tired now,' I said. 'Shall we go?'

He looked startled. 'Go? Um, what do you mean?'

'You know. Let's go. We can go back to mine. I only live a couple of tube stops away. Oh, wait, the tube's closed. Well, there's definitely a bus,' I said.

A look of something I didn't understand flashed across his face. Did he not want to come home with me? 'Um, OK,' he said. I breathed a sigh of relief.

Emma winked at me as we left and I managed to wave bye to Lara before Jack and I walked out into the cold.

'Wow, it's freezing,' I said as I tucked my arm into his so we could walk close together. He didn't say anything in response as we walked in silence.

We walked a bit more and then I tried again. 'So, did you enjoy your night?' I asked finally.

'Yeah, it was good, thanks,' he said amiably, but then

fell silent again. This was definitely weird. Something was wrong. I slipped my arm out from under his and tucked my hands into my pockets. I started to feel cold but this time it was a deep chill that had nothing to do with the weather.

I wanted to ask if something was wrong, but I felt too nervous. What if he didn't really want to come home with me? I shook the thought from my mind as we reached the bus stop. The silence was killing me. I braced my nerves and asked him, 'Jack, is something wrong?'

'No, everything's fine,' he said quietly, and my drunkenness died. Nothing was fine. It was the opposite of fine.

Oh, my God. He didn't want to go home with me. The thought flashed across my head and I realised it was true. I hadn't given him a choice. We hadn't even kissed tonight. I'd completely assumed he wanted to be with me—without asking him. Oh, my God. Now he was on his way back to mine and *he didn't want to be there.*

I was still trying to understand this when my bus pulled up. 'Isn't this the bus?' he asked.

I stood in silence as the urgency of the situation hit me.

'Let's miss this one,' I said finally. I turned to face him. I took a deep breath. I needed to be a grown-up. I needed to ask him straight out. 'Jack…do you not want to come home with me? Because you really don't have to,' I blurted out.

He let out a short, abrupt laugh even though nothing was funny. He ran his hand through his hair awkwardly. 'No, of course I do.'

'Seriously, Jack,' I said. 'Honestly. I can get the bus alone right here, right now, and you can walk back to the party. It will just be nice of you to have walked me to the bus stop. It's fine, honestly. Please,' I said desperately. I didn't even know what I was desperate for. I just wanted this to end.

He paused. Then a look of relief came over his face. 'Really? Are you sure, Ellie? I'm just…I'm just not feeling up to it tonight.'

I felt sick. The bile was climbing up my throat. I swallowed and put on the bravest face I could. 'Jack, seriously, don't worry,' I trilled. 'I'm tired. I want to go home. Just go back to the party.'

He sighed in relief. Oh God, he'd genuinely felt as if I'd forced him into leaving with me. I wanted to cry. Instead I grinned and gave him a hug and smiled extra brightly at him. Then I turned around and pretended to read the bus-stop sign while tears started to swim in my eyes.

'Hey,' he called out in a voice laced with guilt. 'Ellie, no. Don't…don't be like that.'

I took a deep gulp, wiped the space under my eyes with my fingers and forced my face into another bright smile before I whirled round to face him again. 'Like what?' I asked innocently.

'Like…upset, or pissed off. It's not… I don't… It's complicated. I just… I have a lot going on. Seriously, it's not you—it's me.'

My mouth dropped open in disbelief at his clichéd line.

He carried on. 'Sorry. I just… I'm going through a lot at the moment.'

Maybe his parents were dying? My face softened. 'What's going on, Jack? You can talk to me.'

He fidgeted and ran his hands through his hair again. 'It's so complicated. I just can't talk about it. Honestly, you're really great, Ellie. It's just that I can't go back with you tonight. It's because I didn't expect it. I just came here hoping to see you because you're one of the only people I know in this crowd, and obviously I like spending time with you, but I didn't think you'd want me to go back with you.'

Tears were stinging my eyelids. How could I have got it so wrong?

'The thing is, Ellie,' he said, getting swept up in the emotion of his speech, 'I just don't feel like I can go back with you tonight. I can't have sex with you tonight. I'm just going through too much.'

His parents had to be ill. 'But we don't have to have sex. We can…' *I couldn't say cuddle; I wouldn't.* '…hang out,' I finished lamely.

He sighed. 'I just… I don't feel psychologically prepared for it tonight.'

My mouth dropped down. Now I was too shocked to want to cry. I had nothing to say in response.

'Anyway,' he said, 'let me wait here with you while your bus comes.'

'No!' I cried out hoarsely. 'Seriously,' I continued, trying to make my voice come out calmly. 'I'm fine. The bus will be here in a second and I just… Please. Honestly, just go.'

'Are you sure?' he asked, concern sweeping over his face.

'I'm fine,' I snapped. 'I'm a twenty-one-year-old woman. I think I can handle myself. I'm fine.'

He looked taken aback. 'OK.' He shrugged. 'I'll call you tomorrow. If you're free, maybe we could get dinner.'

'Sure, fine, whatever,' I said, and froze while he hugged me. Then he turned around and walked back to the party. I held my breath until he was out of sight. Then I let out the pent-up tears. I sobbed and sobbed. I picked up my phone and dialled Lara's number. 'Lara,' I wept the second she answered.

'Where are you?' she asked automatically.

'Bus stop. By Old Street station. The one next to… Starbucks,' I gulped out between tears.

'Don't move,' she said and hung up.

I cried harder. *I don't feel psychologically prepared to spend the night with you,* he'd said. Psychologically prepared. The words swam around in my head. I sat down on the bench. The other drunken people who had been sitting on it stood up and quietly walked away, leaving me to sob alone. Even the hobos didn't want to be around me.

CHAPTER THIRTY

My body jolted to life. The digital clock on my bedside table said 7:00 a.m. Lara was fast asleep next to me. Everything flooded back. Jack rejecting me on the streets of Shoreditch. Me sobbing on a street corner, sitting alone at the bus stop. Lara taking me home in a taxi. Crying all the way home. Getting home and being sick. Drinking loads of Ribena. Oh God, Ribena. The thought of the magenta liquid made my stomach turn.

My head was banging. Wincing in pain, I crept out of the bed quietly, trying not to disturb Lara.

I tiptoed into the bathroom. I felt disgusting. I took my clothes off and crawled into the bathtub without bothering to look at myself. Everything hurt. I remembered everything. I wished I didn't, but I did. I felt sick. I turned the shower on but I didn't stand up. I sat still in the bath, clasping my knees to my chest while the water sprayed me. I didn't have enough strength to stand up. I put the plug in so the bath would fill up while the water washed over me.

When it was full, I leant back and closed my eyes. The rejection was so awful. I'd never propositioned a guy before, except when I'd asked James Martell to take my V-plates and he said no. It was like a double whammy. It was even kind of ironic. I'd been rejected by the guy who refused to take my virginity, and now I was being rejected by the guy who actually *took* my virginity.

Then it hit me—I had become that girl. The idiot who threw her virginity away on the first guy who showed some interest, and then fell for him harder and harder while he looked at her in pity and wandered off in whichever direction his libidinous dick took him.

I smiled drily at the thought of him running around, pointing his pallid penis at a bunch of girls. The smile helped. It made me remember that it was OK. I was just another girl who got fucked over by a shit guy, and I would get over it. I would never see him again. I had Lara, I had Emma and I would be OK with the fact that I'd given my virginity to someone who wasn't *psychologically prepared* to sleep with me again. Had I really been that bad? I sank into the bath and tried to ignore the throbbing of my head and the sick feeling in my tummy.

I grabbed my phone to distract myself. Oh God, there were so many messages from Jack. I couldn't deal with those right now. I scrolled past them and found one from Paul.

He said he thought it was amazing I was still a V and then we did it! Minimal pain. Thanks for the advice, P.

I smiled to myself. At least not all men were unpsychologically-prepared bastards.

Lara sat on the lid of the loo and looked at me, a worried expression on her face. 'Ellie, are you sure you don't want me to read it to you?' she asked.

'For the millionth time, Lara, I don't want you to read

Jack's message. He rejected me. He infiltrated my private lotus and then he refused to go back there even when I invited him. And quite frankly, I don't want to *know* what he has to say.' I spoke calmly. All this talk of lotuses was making me feel very Zen.

She sighed in frustration. 'OK,' she said after a pause. 'What if I read it, and then if it's an incredible apology that explains everything, I'll tell you, and if it's just more bollocks, we delete it and vow never to mention his name again?'

'Ugh, no,' I said, wrinkling my nose. 'Have you not read *Harry Potter*? By calling him you-know-who, you give him power. You've got to call him Voldemort.'

'Fine,' she said, rolling her eyes. 'So am I allowed to read Voldemort's text?'

She really wasn't getting my metaphor. 'OK,' I said grudgingly. 'You can read *Jack's* text. But not out loud.'

'Oh, thank God,' she said. 'Because I already read it earlier. It's good and you need to hear it.'

'What?' I cried as I leaned forward and bath bubbles frothed up into the air. 'You read it without my permission?'

'You would have done the same,' she said without looking up from my phone. 'So, he hopes you feel better, he wants to take you out for dinner tonight and he really hopes you'll say yes. He's buying.'

I lay back into the bath, mulling this over.

'So, shall I respond with a yes?' she asked.

I didn't reply, still trying to figure out what my instincts were telling me. I closed my eyes and tried to meditate.

'Ellie?' she asked cautiously. 'You've been in the bath for, like, four hours. I really don't recommend you spend the whole day there. You look pruney.'

I sighed, opening my left eye. 'No,' I said firmly. 'Don't

reply. That's not an apology or an explanation. Besides, how dare he assume I can drop everything and do dinner with him? You and Emma and I already have dinner plans.'

'I don't care if you cancel, and I doubt Emma will, either,' she said.

'That's not the point!' I said indignantly. 'He didn't come over when I asked last night, so why should I be at his beck and call?'

She sighed. 'I guess you're right. It's just… It *is* all kind of weird. I feel like there must be some explanation and you need to see him to figure it out. You know?'

The thought of his dying parents popped back into my brain. Maybe Lara was right.

'Well,' I said, 'I suppose it would be good to get to the bottom of it.'

Lara's face lit up and I saw her slide open my phone, ready to type out a message to Jack.

'Wait!' I called out, holding up my right hand. She stopped moving and there was silence. 'If I see him, it's on *my* terms. I have dinner plans with you guys and I want to keep them. So, tell him he can see me for a coffee if he wants. At…at 3:00 p.m. Somewhere I feel comfortable. At Planet Organic. So I can get hangover juice.'

Lara nodded fervently and tapped away on the phone. 'Done!' she announced triumphantly. Within seconds the phone beeped again.

'Oh my God, he's replied already,' she said, her eyes quickly scanning the screen. 'OK, you're going to meet him at 3:00 p.m. outside PO. He says he's looking forward to it.'

I sat at a small metal table waiting for Jack to pay for my Ginger Zinger smoothie. I felt numb and quietly determined.

My head was still throbbing but I had hidden the bags under my eyes with concealer, layered mascara over last night's leftovers and forced myself out of the bath and into my favourite jeans. I now resembled a human being.

'OK, two Ginger Zingers,' Jack announced as he slumped down onto the seat next to me.

I took the plastic cup from him and sipped it thirstily. It was like medicine. The bits of carrot, orange, honey and ginger soothed my throat and I could already feel the oxy-things working their magic on my battered immune system.

'This is fucking good,' he said, slurping his drink.

I smiled tightly at him. 'Yeah, they're really good.'

'I've never been here before,' he admitted. 'In fact, I had to look up this place to know what you were talking about.'

'That's me,' I said lightly, 'always in the know about the best places for hangover juice.'

'Well, you've now officially won my trust. I'll go wherever you suggest.' He laughed.

There was a brief silence while I remembered how last night he had done everything *except* go where I suggested. He went quiet as well, and I knew he was thinking the same thing. I stared at him expectantly, waiting for him to break the silence. I wasn't in the mood for all this small talk. I needed to hear the truth.

He took the hint. 'Um, Ellie, I guess…I guess we need to talk,' he said.

'Please, talk away,' I said, spreading my hands out.

'Last night…things got weird. I really didn't mean for things to come out the way they did.'

'OK, then explain to me how you meant them to come out.'

'I mean, I just… Look, we're fine, right?' he asked quickly.

'We're fine. We're hanging out. We don't need to go over all this, do we?'

I sat back in my chair and looked at him coolly. 'Jack,' I said. 'We *do* need to go over this—this is exactly why I'm sitting here. To hear what you have to say. I want to hear all of it.'

He still looked uncertain as he fidgeted with the straw of his Ginger Zinger.

'You *owe* it to me,' I added.

He shifted on his chair and took a deep breath. 'Yeah. You're right. I'm…I'm going to explain it all to you, right now.'

I crossed my arms.

'Right, OK. Let me just start at the beginning.'

'A very good place to start,' I said. Bugger. *The Sound of Music* lyrics had a habit of popping into my head when I least expected them to.

'Right. So…I've dated a few girls in my time…' he started.

I raised an eyebrow and crossed my arms more tightly, wishing it were someone else's arms holding me safe.

'Anyway, yeah, I've dated people and I've never really met anyone I truly liked. Obviously they've all been great, but somehow, I haven't…I haven't really connected with anyone. I just, I never believed in true love. Do you…do you believe in it?' he asked. He looked worried.

'Uh, I…I guess. I don't know.'

'OK,' he said, his eyes piercing straight into me. 'Well, I didn't. But then it all changed.'

My heart started to lift.

'With all the other girls, the way I felt about them was just a bit…a bit average. A bit nothing. It was no wonder I didn't believe in true love, because these girls were all the same in a way.'

He paused for a while and I stared at him, transfixed. My heart was so hopeful that I couldn't even think. I was totally absorbed. Every cell and particle inside me was hooked on his words.

He carried on. 'Then one day, in a way that was totally unexpected, I went to a party and I met a girl who was completely different. A girl who took my breath away and made me see the world in different eyes. Someone who changed my life with the first word she said to me.'

I felt my knees go weak. I couldn't even remember the first word I'd said to him. It must have been profound.

His voice was full of passion as he kept talking. 'For the first time in my life, I had a totally deep, intense connection with someone. It wasn't just how beautiful she was. It was the way she made me feel. She challenged me, but she liked the same things as me. She made me laugh, but she also made me cry. From the second I saw her I felt a connection with her. Do you know what I mean?' He stared into my eyes.

'Yes,' I whispered softly.

'I'm glad,' he said gently. 'Because I never expected to find that. And it's really thrown me off. I'm a different person from how I used to be, and it's making things really complicated for me. It's why I've been a bit weird and a bit… I guess it might have come across as though I've been a bit hot and cold with you lately, and sending you mixed signals.'

I nodded understandingly. I got it now. He was just scared. He had never expected to fall for me. He was a boy. Boys hated commitment—everyone knew that. And now he'd found me. He really liked me, and it was scaring him.

'It's just this…this connection was so powerful, Ellie. It changed me, totally,' he added.

I felt little vibrations of ecstasy running through my body. He was inadvertently telling me he loved me. I had *changed* him. I, Ellie Kolstakis, was capable of making someone change his life. How could I ever have doubted him? He was just terrified that *I* would reject *him*. I felt like laughing at the irony of it all. He really liked me. I wanted to punch the air triumphantly. It took all my self-control to not jump up and kiss his worried-looking face.

He carried on. 'So, that's why I'm…explaining all of this. She changed me the second I met her and I just fell for her.'

This third-person tense thing was starting to freak me out. Couldn't he just use the pronoun 'you' instead? The Ginger Zinger didn't feel so good in my delicate tummy, either.

'I met her last year,' he said, 'so it wasn't overlapping with you—don't worry. She ended things with me just before I met you.' He paused. 'She's Brazilian.'

I felt my stomach sink. He was talking about someone else. This entire speech. It was about someone else. Not me. He didn't love me. We didn't have a profound connection. He had it with *her*. Someone else. I felt sick. Tears pricked my eyelids.

He kept going. 'It's just… I really liked her and she told me she was only here for a few months and was going to go back to Brazil. So she didn't want anything serious. Which broke my heart. Then I met you, and we hung out a bit, but you and I were obviously never going to be serious. We're more friends than lovers, right?' He nudged me.

My heart fell into my lace-edged socks. Friends, not lovers. The phrase spun round in my head and went into neon green letters bigger than VIRGIN on Dr E Bowers' computer. I was ready to cry. He looked at me expectantly. I gathered together the tiny modicum of strength I had left inside me. I made a big, unnatural smile appear on my face.

'Sure,' I said.

'Ah, I knew you'd understand,' he said, grinning gratefully. 'The way you are with me…really jokey and silly. It's what makes me love you as a friend. You're hilarious. The way you kid about everything, even your virginity. It's nice you wanted to lose it to me as a friend—it's way better than loads of girls who just give it away on a drunken one-night stand or to a guy who breaks their heart, you know? At least this way, we'll always stay friends. I think you're great.'

I nodded mutely. Friends, not lovers. Heart. Broken. Ow.

'That's why I wanted to talk to you about Luisa. I need a girl's perspective. I just… Do you believe in love? Do you think she's the one for me and I should fight for her, or do I just let her go?' he asked anxiously.

I couldn't do this. I couldn't sit here and advise him on another girl. It hurt more than anything had ever hurt before. I wanted to cry hot, salty tears of humiliation. I wanted to undo everything. I wished I'd never met him. I wanted Lara.

'Oh, I don't know,' I said breezily, gulping away sobs before they appeared on my face. 'I reckon…um…if she *is* the one, it will happen. In its own way. If it's meant to be, it will be.'

'Do you really think so?' he asked, leaning towards me. He was so passionate and cared so much…about someone else. Why was I still sitting there, giving him advice? I needed to get the fuck out.

'Oh, my God,' I said loudly. 'Is that the time? I totally forgot—I double-booked myself! I said I'd meet a friend. I have to go. Shit. Call me, though—we can chat about Luisa and, um, stuff.'

'Oh, OK,' he said, looking confused. 'What's the time?'

Bugger, what *was* the time? 'Way later than I thought it was!' I quipped and grabbed my bag. I gave him a quick wave and ran out, leaving him looking around the café for a clock.

I reached a hidden alleyway around the corner and collapsed to the ground. I felt so stupid. How could I have thought he was talking about me? How could I have believed that Jack wanted to be my boyfriend when really he just thought of me as a friend? He hadn't even liked me through any of this. God, I felt so used. When we were sharing our writing, laughing together, sleeping together...he'd probably been thinking about this *Luisa* the whole time. I dropped my head into my hands and cried.

CHAPTER THIRTY-ONE

I LAY ON my bed, clutching a glass of rosé. The girls were sprawled over my duvet alongside an open pizza box. I'd cried all evening but now I was well on my way to the next stage in the grief cycle. I'd done denial, sorrow, and now, fuelled with wine and pizza, I was on ANGER.

'He's a fucking dick,' I said for the tenth time that hour. 'How DARE he lead me on like that and then casually be all, like, "Oh, I thought we were more friends than lovers, right?" I mean, who the fuck even *uses* the word "lovers"?'

'He's a useless, time-wasting, scummy little shit,' agreed Emma. 'You're better off without him. Leave him to this Brazilian bitch.'

'Exactly, Ellie,' said Lara, nodding fervently. 'He's a total bastard. You need to forget him and move on—you deserve so much better.'

I closed my eyes and took a large slurp of wine. It was wine from a box, and you could tell from the taste.

'Guys,' I ventured with my eyes still semi-shut, 'do you think Jack did like me?'

Emma reached out and squeezed my arm. 'Yes, of course he did. It's just that you wanted completely different things and you misread each other's signals. It happens.'

'I guess,' I said. 'It still feels shitty.'

'Of course it does,' she replied. 'But just think, even if you had been in a full-blown "I love you" relationship with him, I doubt you would have married the guy. It would have ended at some point anyway. It's just…this way it ended sooner than you thought.'

Lara nodded. 'She's right. We all build up fantasies about guys. Yours just crashed down to earth sooner.'

'So, it was…a good thing?' I asked doubtfully.

'Oh, who fucking knows,' said Emma. 'Let's have some more wine.' She squirted more rosé generously from the cardboard box into our glasses.

'Also,' said Lara, 'you shouldn't attach too much importance to Jack, Ellie. You're too special to waste even a second of your life caring about him and what he thinks.'

'I agree,' said Emma. 'And you know what? Everything happens for a reason. If Jack hadn't been such a dick, you wouldn't be here getting valuable life advice from your favourite people.'

I rolled my eyes at her but Lara cautiously ventured on. 'Don't hate me for saying this, El, because I love you, but…I think you need to like yourself more. You need to stop letting guys run your life. Don't waste your time trying to preempt what a guy wants. If you don't like having Brazilians, don't get one. Go *au naturel*. If you want to be a virgin, be one. If you want to sleep with every man who smiles at you, fucking *do* it!'

My friends were better than any number of Ginger Zingers. I was starting to feel rejuvenated. 'Fuck it,' I said. 'I'm growing out my Hitler.'

As they laughed their approval, I realised that I'd wanted to embrace my pubes ever since I was seventeen and shaved my vagina for the first time. The pubic pressure to have a waxed, perfect VJ had been weighing down on me for four exhausting years, but I was finally ready to walk away from it.

'I'm never getting a wax again,' I announced. 'I think I'm going to carry on trimming it though, but purely *because I want to*—and also, it's really gross when it pokes out of my knickers, you know?' I paused while they nodded in agreement. 'But this is it, guys. I'm done caring about my pubes. If it means I can never buy lacy knickers because there'll be a mass of squashed hair beneath them, so be it. Cotton pants, here I come.'

The girls cheered and I started to realise I was having more fun with them than I ever had with Jack. When I was with him, I'd constantly been having a second conversation with myself, narrating and overanalysing every tiny thing. On top of that it had been fucking *exhausting* pretending to understand his political views. It was a relief to be around friends who liked me for me.

'Aw, Ellie, I'm so proud of you,' said Lara. 'I'm not being patronising, I promise. I know you try really hard to fit in, but we love you *because* you're not like everyone else.'

'I love you, too,' I cried. 'I've been an idiot, haven't I?'

She sighed in mock exasperation. 'Stop being so hard on yourself. You haven't been an idiot. You've just been *you*. Whatever you've done—caring loads about your virginity, trying to fit in, losing it to a guy you really liked who turned out to be a dick…it's just life. You did what you thought was right at the time and you're moving on. And when you're ready, you're going to turn it all into a funny story to make us cry with laughter like you always do.'

She was right. Yes, I had possibly attached undue importance to what was essentially just biology, but that was because of all the external influences in my life. Hannah Fielding, Never Have I Ever, *Sex and the City*… It was no wonder I'd cared so much about my virginity. But it was really just a hole in a hymen.

Suddenly I felt light and free in a way I hadn't even immediately after losing my virginity. This was different. At the age of twenty-one, I was finally OK with being a virgin. Pity I wasn't one any more.

'Babe, are you OK? Your eyes have gone misty and weird,' said Emma.

'Guys…I think I'm OK with being a virgin,' I said slowly.

Lara and Emma looked at each other, exchanging glances filled with concern. 'What?' I asked.

'Um. You know you're…not a virgin any more, right?' asked Emma cautiously.

'Whatever,' I said, waving my hand in the air. 'I've just had an epiphany. I think…I have finally accepted my virginity. And the fact that it's gone. Oh my God, this is…this is fucking revolutionary.'

Lara looked confused. 'Are you sure you're OK, Ellie?'

'Yes, I'm OK. I'm *great*,' I cried. 'I've just realised that there was nothing wrong with being a virgin. So nobody had penetrated me. So what? *I* can shove a plastic dick in me. Who cares?! Why does the state of my hymen mean so much? It's not defining me. I'm not defined by my skin colour or my weight, because that's racist and fascist, so it shouldn't be any different with my virginity.'

'I don't think you meant fascist,' said Lara.

'Just because you do Law,' I retorted and she held up her hands as if in surrender.

'So, do you guys agree or not?' I demanded.

'Of course we do,' said Emma, 'What do you think we've been trying to tell you this whole time? And you know what? It goes the other way, too. Why should I be judged if my hymen *is* broken? So am I a slut because my vagina has had more than thirty-five different dicks inside? Um, NO!'

Lara's eyes widened a bit at that but she joined in. 'It's true. Why does it matter if I enjoy having sex with an emotionally unstable guy who doesn't want to be in a relationship with me? I don't want a relationship with him, either. I just enjoy sex, and there is nothing wrong with that. I don't want a boyfriend. I want occasional, non-committal, booty-call sex with Jez. Fuck it, if you can finally accept your virginity, then I'm going to stop pretending I want more from him. I'll admit I love our arrangement. It's perfect.'

'You know what?' I added, a grin on my face. 'I no longer care that I was a twenty-one-year-old virgin. I wasn't a drug addict or a uni dropout or anything disastrous. I was just a virgin. And if Hannah really does know I was a virgin, I think I'm OK with it. So I was a virgin at twenty-one. So fucking what? If that's the best gossip the English gang have, then their lives are *dull*.'

'Totally,' agreed Emma. 'It's not even interesting news. No offence, Ellie. It's the kind of thing everyone will forget about in five minutes. Besides, after graduation, we never have to see any of them again.'

'You're so right,' I said. 'It will be embarrassing if people know and talk about it, but I'll get over it. And, while I'm at it, I'm going to accept that I am attractive even with my obvious flaws. I don't need to look like Angelina Jolie to get laid.'

Emma raised her eyebrows.

'Oh, fine,' I said, rolling my eyes. 'I'm not just "attractive", I'm fucking *hot* and so are you two.'

The girls laughed and raised their glasses. 'To Ellie and her hairy hymen,' shouted Emma, and we clinked our glasses.

I kept my glass raised. 'Here's to my future. As a girl who doesn't give a fuck about the state of her pubes, her hymen, and her humiliation. Here's to my vagina.'

CHAPTER THIRTY-TWO

Pubes and Prejudice

Here is our promised entry on pubes. Instead of both of us sharing our knowledge with you, EM has respectfully bowed out of this one because her pubes are blond and she has no ingrown hairs. Instead, EK is going to tell you about her own sizeable bush and her journey to final acceptance of what lies beneath her pants. Hope it helps.

EK:

The first time I showed a guy my vagina, he burst into laughter. We were both 17 years old and it scarred me for the next four years. It was only when I was 21 that I was able to face my demons and let another man down there again. He laughed too.

I do not have a particularly amusing vagina. However, both of these men found my pubes—or lack thereof—hilarious.

Guy 1 saw my pubes in their full glory. Curled to the max and springing out from every follicle. I had done nothing to cultivate my lower garden and he found this hilarious. BUT no matter how much he laughed, he was still willing to let me go down on him. My point being, I may have been more au naturel than a hippy in a commune, but he still wanted a BJ from me.

Guy 2 saw me with a Brazilian that had turned into a Hitler 'stache [warning: a Playboy wax is advertised as a type of Brazilian wax but it does look different. Normal Brazilians have thick landing strips. A Playboy Brazilian is a tiny postage stamp of hair that looks like Hitler's moustache imprinted onto your vagina]. He told me he hadn't expected me to have a waxed VJ because I 'seemed like a natural kind of girl'. He had shaved his own regions into a neat lawn.

I let their reactions bother me. I have been so preoccupied with men's expectations of what my VJ should look like that I have spent hours (and hundreds of pounds) on shaving, creaming, waxing, tweezing and trimming my pubes. I have even cut my clitoris with a razor blade from trying to shave. My vagina has dark dots all over it from the ingrown hairs that are too deep to get rid of. I am permanently scarred.

Which is why I have decided I am finally done with it all. I am no longer going to try to prune my bush into the top of an exclamation mark or yank out all the hairs that are just doing their job and stopping dirt and sweat from getting into my vagina (yes, that's their biological purpose).

From now on, I'm doing whatever I want to my pubes. I'm keeping them trimmed but I'm not even bothering to do my bikini line. Why? Because I'm embracing my pubes. I don't want to cut myself shaving; use creams that don't work on thick hair; lie half-naked in salons; or agonise over stray hairs with my tweezers. I don't care what the next guy says about my pubes and I refuse to be part of the culture that assumes women have no hair down there. WE. DO.

I PRESSED 'PUBLISH' and waited happily while the screen took me to the vlog home page. We already had 750 followers. The past month had been hell while Emma and I forced ourselves to revise Shakespeare and Chaucer when all we wanted to do was keep telling the cyber world about our vaginas.

Most of the comments on our posts were negative. Apparently our posts were patronising and unnecessary. But for every ten haters, there was always one girl who said something positive. It made it worthwhile.

Jack had texted a few times since that night, apologising, but I hadn't replied. He'd taken the hint and finally left me alone. It still hurt, but only because my pride had been dented. It had taken four weeks but I had now fully accepted what had happened. I'd written *I am over him* on my left hand in permanent pen to help me remember and I'd redone it every week so it never had a chance to fade. I'd changed his name on my phone to DO NOT REPLY—REMEMBER LUISA. The thought of the Brazilian part-time model (I'd Facebook-stalked her) put me off every time. I couldn't compete with that.

Instead I had thrown all my energy into passing my degree and vlogging with Emma. It was funny how easy it was to focus on work when I wasn't having an existential crisis about my virginity.

None of the companies I'd applied to intern with had replied yet, so I had sent them all a follow-up email gently pushing for a response. As a last minute decision, I added a link to the vlog to the email. I had no idea how it would go down—especially with the conservative newspapers I'd emailed—but at least I was being proactive.

Meanwhile Paul was shagging Vladi and making his way through the pack of lightweight condoms I had gifted him. Lara was still at university, going to May Balls and glamorous things I didn't understand, and was on track for a First. She was due to move in with me soon. I had a summer with my girls ahead of me and I was moving on from Jack. His name barely even featured in my diary any more. It was only on every alternate page.

There was only one thing I still hadn't done. Go back to Dr E Bowers.

Which was why, after I posted my latest vlog entry, I shut down my laptop and grabbed my leather jacket and sunglasses. It was time to face my fears. I had let go of my status as a barely touched maiden and accepted my new one as a fallen woman. I had a future as a slut ahead of me and I couldn't wait to let Dr E Bowers know.

I was back in the surgery waiting for my name to flash up on the TV screen. I fidgeted awkwardly and wished the air conditioner wasn't on so high. My bare legs, which had looked relatively tanned outside, looked deathly pale under the fluorescent lights. The few leg hairs I'd missed when shaving were standing on end in the cold.

I crossed my legs and tried to pull the white summer dress down over my knees. The waiting room was relatively empty because most people had headed back home after exams or were too busy getting liver disease to care about check-ups.

The television screen flashed. *MS ELLIE KOLSTAKIS. PLEASE GO TO DR E BOWERS' OFFICE.*

Obediently I got up.

'Come in,' said the familiarly terse voice from inside the office.

I pushed open the door and there she was. Her blond Diana

hair had been chopped even shorter into a David Bowie–style mullet and she was wearing a chocolate-brown suit.

'Ms Kolstakis, how are you?' she asked, looking me up and down. Her eyes hovered on the hemline of my dress and then returned to my face.

'OK, thanks. How are you?' I replied neutrally, sitting down in one of the plastic chairs. I knew the routine now.

'Very well, thank you. So what can I do for you today?' she asked expectantly. She pushed her rimless glasses up her nose and peered at me over the lenses.

'Well, I would like to do a chlamydia test, please,' I said confidently, crossing my arms. 'And all of them, actually.'

'All of what?'

'I want to get tested. For all the STDs,' I explained.

'It says on my system here I gave you a chlamydia test last time, but I don't have any information about your results. When did you send it off?' she asked, scrolling through her computer.

'I didn't actually get round to it,' I admitted. 'It didn't seem relevant because I hadn't had sex then. But that's all changed now, so I need to get tested.' I settled back into my chair, watching her smugly.

She turned to face me. 'Right, so you've recently had unprotected sex? Do you have reason to think your partner had any STDs?'

I shifted in my chair. My bare legs were getting stuck to the plastic. 'It wasn't unprotected. I just thought I should get checked to be on the safe side.'

'And your partner—has he been checked lately?'

'I mean, he isn't actually my *partner*, and I don't know if he's been checked.... I didn't ask him.' Jeez, what century was she from, expecting him to be my boyfriend? I bet she was the kind of person who said 'making love' instead of 'having sex'.

'Could you ask him now?' she asked.

'Um, no,' I answered, biting my lip.

'All right,' she said wearily. 'Let me give you another chlamydia test. You can do this one here. And you'll need to get a blood test for HIV.'

'HIV?! Oh my God, do you think I have HIV?' I cried out.

'It's unlikely, but if you'd like to be tested for everything, it makes sense to do an HIV test,' she said, typing away on her computer.

'OK,' I said uncertainly, 'but I've only had sex once, so I think I probably don't.'

She shook her head gently. I could tell she didn't believe me. 'All right,' she said. 'Do you have any symptoms you're worried about? Does your vagina smell? Are there any lumps, or unusual amounts of discharge?'

'Um...' Didn't everyone's vaginas smell? And I didn't think it had any lumps, or I probably would have noticed. Who knew STD tests were so complicated?

'I suppose I do have a lot of discharge,' I mumbled, looking down at the floor. 'And it sometimes smells but I thought that was...normal.'

'Is the discharge white or yellow? Is it thick?'

I had no clue. I had never analysed it. Clearly I should have. 'Erm, I guess it's...a bit of both? Kind of...average, I guess?'

She sighed. 'OK. Well, you may have thrush. Let me give you some thrush cream just in case.'

I looked up, alarmed. 'Thrush? Really? I thought you get it from wearing lacy knickers. I'm more of a cotton pants kinda girl. I don't think I have thrush.'

'Certain underwear can cause thrush, but it can also appear for a number of reasons. It's a very common infection and your body can generally overcome it by itself, but I'll give you the cream just in case. If you start to get particularly heavy discharge or if there's a very fishy smell, you can use the cream.'

'OK,' I answered, trying to process all this brand-new information.

'In the meantime, take this pot and fill it with a urine sample. While you're in the bathroom, do this chlamydia test and then come back for a blood test with the nurse. I'll pass on your information to her. Is there anything else you'd like to talk to me about while you're here?'

'Well, there is one thing,' I said cautiously. 'This is…kind of embarrassing for me to ask, but, um, now that I'm *not* a virgin, do you mind changing it on your computer? So it doesn't say VIRGIN in massive letters next to my name? Maybe you can change it to…SEXUALLY ACTIVE, or HAD SEX. Actually, HAS SEX would be more accurate because I'll probably do it again….' I trailed off awkwardly.

She stared at me and took off her glasses. 'Excuse me?'

'It's just, well, on your computer last time I was here, it said that I was a virgin. And I'm not now. I've had sex. So I was wondering if you could update my records?' I asked. 'Please?'

She furrowed her brow. 'I will update your records, yes,' she said. 'I tend to do that after I've seen a patient. If you go off and do your samples, I'll finish my paperwork.'

She wasn't going to do it in front of me. Typical. Maybe she was going to write SLAG or SEXUALLY VOLATILE.

'OK,' I said with a small sigh, resigned to my new fate as a fallen woman. People were automatically going to assume I had HIV and write things about me behind my back. I picked up the brown envelope and plastic pot and walked off forlornly to the loo.

Right. I just had to hold the pot under my vagina and catch the urine as it came out of me. Except when it trickled out in a pretty solid flow, it went everywhere but into the pot. Bugger. I paused mid-flow, taking a deep breath. Damn. I moved my damp fingers, adjusting the pot. OK, good, this time the pee was filling it up but… Oh no, it was overflowing. Onto my hand. And my bracelet.

I gagged as I withdrew my hand and finished peeing. I quickly cleaned myself and pulled my pants up with the dry hand and flushed the loo. The pot was now soaking wet on the outside and the paper label was peeling off. My name was smudged and there was blue biro all over my hands.

I screwed the lid on and washed my hands in the sink. With a shrug I decided I might as well wash the pot, too. I didn't want the poor nurses to have to touch my pee and the label had pretty much dissolved.

Now for the chlamydia test. I opened the pack and a test tube fell out onto my lap. It had an oversized cotton bud inside. I felt a twinge of panic. This looked complicated. There was a mini-instructions leaflet in there, too. I opened it up and looked at the diagram. Right, I had to take the cotton bud out and make sure it didn't touch anything but the inside of my VJ. Simple.

I unscrewed the tube and took out the long stick. I pulled my pants down again and crouched by the sink. Slowly, I inserted the long white stick into my vagina. It tingled as it pushed in, and I felt my thigh muscles start to wobble under the weight of my body.

I reached for the instructions, trying not to lose my balance. OK, it said to rub the stick around. I rubbed it around in circular motions. Suddenly my thighs collapsed and I fell onto the floor. I lay on my back, my legs and pants hovering in the air, with a long white stick poking up out of my vagina like a surrendering peace flag.

Wincing in pain, I got back up slowly, trying not to disturb the stick. I stood upright and began pulling it out. It broke in half. Fuck. I was holding half a white stick in my hand. The cotton bud bit was still in there. I flung the broken stick onto the side, and put two fingers into my vagina to feel around. I breathed a sigh of relief. I could feel the end of the stick. Gently, I eased it out and inserted it into the test tube.

I put the lid on and screwed it shut. I took a look at the instructions. It said, 'put stick back into tube, and then break off'. I'd just done it in the wrong order. I breathed a sigh of relief, pulled my pants back up and washed my hands. With soap. Twice.

I handed the nurse my urine sample and chlamydia stick. She took them from me gingerly, clearly noticing that the pee pot's label had disintegrated.

'I'm just going to take a blood sample from you,' she said. 'Can I have your right arm, please?'

'Sure,' I said, taking my cardigan off and sticking my arm out. I turned it upside down so she wouldn't notice how hairy my forearm was.

She took my arm into her hand and turned it over.

'OK, you're just going to feel a tiny prick,' she said as she jabbed her huge syringe into the most sensitive part of my arm—the inner elbow.

'OW,' I screamed as pain soared up my arm. She rolled

her eyes at me, tutting. The bitch. Clearly no one had ever done this to her.

I turned away as the blood filled the syringe and she stuck a lump of cotton over my arm. I rubbed the sore spot tenderly. I'd better not have HIV after this.

'There we go. You're all done now. We'll send you your test results next week. Thanks for coming.' She started to open the door for me.

'Sorry, I just have a quick question,' I said nervously. 'You know those, erm, condoms outside? In the box by the water cooler? Are they, um, free?'

She sighed wearily. 'Take as many as you want.'

I obliged. Sex with Jack hadn't been particularly enjoyable but now my first time was over, I couldn't wait to start shagging my way to multiple orgasms. Safe sex, here I come.

CHAPTER THIRTY-THREE

TODAY WAS MY last day as a student. I was going to find out my degree results and finally know whether I was doomed to be a 2:2 failure, an acceptable 2:1 graduate with no prospects, a girl with a First who would go places even without having an internship lined up or—God forbid—a nobody with a Third. I felt my stomach turn. I had done an acceptable amount of revision to get a 2:1 but I was secretly dreaming of a First. I had revised every day from 8:00 a.m. till 11:00 p.m. with only about four breaks a day. Surely people who got Firsts did that much. There weren't enough hours in a day to do more.

I waited anxiously outside the English department. Emma was meant to meet me here but she was running late. Our department was the only one in UCL that made the students come in to collect their results.

On cue, Emma ran up to me, tottering in wedges under a black maxi dress. She looked as though she should be drinking piña coladas on a yacht. I was wearing leggings and an oversized T-shirt with flip-flops. Dressing up had not been on my agenda this morning.

'Sickness on a scale of one to ten?' she asked, hugging me.

'Twelve. You?' I replied numbly.

'Worse. Let's just go in and do this,' she said, taking my arm and leading me towards the building. I nodded my assent as we approached the noticeboard.

There was already a small crowd in the common room, scattering out into the hallway, mostly chatting happily. I bet they'd got Firsts, the bastards. We ignored them and walked over to the noticeboard. My heart pounded as my eyes raced over the board, looking for my candidate number. I'd written mine on my hand over the fading *I am over him*. My hand was right; I was *so* over him.

C2359. There it was. *Upper second-class honours.* What did that mean? That was…a 2:1. Oh, thank God. I breathed in relief, but then felt disappointment race through my veins. I hadn't magically got a First. I wasn't a genius. I wasn't destined to be an academic scholar. There went my chances of getting into the CIA or doing a PhD on Shakespeare.

I looked at Emma. 'Well?' she demanded, her eyes sparkling.

'A 2:1. Average,' I said. 'You?'

'A First!' she squealed. 'I literally have no idea how this happened. Oh, my God. Maybe I shouldn't go into PR any more—I could be a Shakespeare scholar.'

My face darkened. She was stealing the dream I'd never got a chance to live.

'This is so exciting!' she cried out.

I sighed. 'I hate you, but I'm so ridiculously proud,' I announced, wrapping my arms around her.

She laughed, 'Thanks, babe. If it had been the other way round I probably would have only hated you. And a 2:1 is still amazing, you know that.'

Still amazing? Ugh. I hated the 'still'. But she was right. And she was also wrong. If it had been the other way round, she definitely would have been ecstatically happy for me. Besides, I'd passed; I'd done acceptably well. I hadn't really worked as hard as I could have, but fuck it—my friend was a genius.

'Let's go get celebratory drinks,' I announced. 'Drinks are on me!'

'Waheeyy!' Charlie called out from the other side of the common room. 'Let's go to The Fitzroy Arms, guys. Drinks are on Ellie.'

I rolled my eyes at him. 'Sorry, Charlie, but I was just talking to Emma because she went and got a First,' I said proudly.

He looked at her in admiration. 'Fuck. Well done, Emma.'

She grinned, shrugging. 'What, do you think it's hard?' she asked, and put her arm around me. 'Pub, now.'

We all ended up leaving the common room and walking down to the pub in a trickling throng, laughing and chatting as we took up the entirety of Tottenham Court Road's east pavement. Everyone was being completely normal with me and Hannah wasn't even there. It seemed as though no one knew my virgin secret. I decided to forget the whole thing and let myself relax. We were no longer students, I was no longer a virgin and the sun was shining.

I was on my third gin and tonic when my phone beeped. It was an email and the subject line said *Re: Internship.* I slammed my drink down on the table and immediately opened up the email. It was from *London Magazine*—a very cool, hip online magazine that I'd sent my vlog to a fortnight ago.

Dear Ellie,

Thank you very much for your email applying for our three-month internship. As you know, competition is high but we would love to offer you the position, starting from September.

We absolutely loved your 'vlog' and found it hilarious. It would be fantastic if you could write something similar for us, and we look forward to hearing your ideas. Please get back to us to confirm you're keen to take up the internship.
Best wishes,
Maxine
Editor, *London Magazine*

'Oh, my God,' I cried out. 'Emma, look!'

She peered over my shoulder to read the email and seconds later, screeched with excitement. 'Ohmigod, Ellie! This is amazing. I'm so proud of you. They said they *loved* the vlog—I can't believe it! How cool is that?!'

'I know. This is crazy,' I said, grinning wildly.

'What is?' asked Kara, who'd been at the Never Have I Ever Party, nudging me. Now we were all about to go our separate ways and graduate, everyone was being overly friendly. It was the end of an era and we were so terrified to start properly in the real world that we were trying to cling on to the student one for as long as possible.

'I just got offered an internship for *London Magazine*.'

'You have got to be kidding me,' she cried. 'They only give out one internship every year. Well done, that's amazing!'

'Get you,' said Emma. 'Beating all those other aspiring journalists! I'm so impressed.'

'Not just any aspiring journalists, either,' said Kara. 'I know Hannah applied for it, too. She had her heart set on it, actually. She got a rejection email earlier and stormed off home.'

We all exchanged glances and burst out laughing. I couldn't believe I had finally got my own back on Hannah Fielding. Fuck her and her hippy headbands—I was a better writer than her.

'What's so funny?' asked Charlie as he joined us and put his arm around Kara. He gave her a sloppy kiss. I looked at Kara in alarm, waiting for her to shove him off. She kissed him back. Whoa. I'd definitely missed that.

I caught Emma's eye and her mouth fell open. 'Oh my God, how did we miss that gem of gossip?' she whispered as Charlie and Kara walked away, leaving us alone.

'Tell me about it. I'm going to miss these people,' I said fondly, looking at the sun shining on the group and their vintage dresses and skinny jeans. 'I feel like the end of a film. Or the end of a Christmas special, you know?'

Emma laughed. 'I think you've got some serious rosé-tinted and G-and-T-enhanced glasses going on.'

My phone beeped again. 'One sec.' I grinned as I tapped open my screen. 'Probably just another internship offer. It's *so* hard being successful.'

Emma rolled her eyes at me. 'One internship offer and she thinks she's the next Jeremy Paxman.' I didn't reply and she looked at me in concern. 'Ellie, are you OK? I was kidding.'

Wordlessly I looked up from my phone and passed it to her.

'What is it?' she asked in confusion, her face scrunched up. '"Dear Ms Kolstakis. Thank you for visiting Gower Street Practice. Your test results have come back positive for chlamydia. Please call 0207"... OH, MY GOD,' she cried, staring at me. 'Ellie, are you OK?'

I stared at her numbly. OK? Was I OK? I'd got chlamydia on the one occasion in my entire life when I'd had sex. And we'd used a condom. HOW WAS THIS OK?

'Babe, it's fine,' she said soothingly. 'Everyone has chlamydia. It's so easy to treat, and it's symptomless so no one knows. You've caught it early, so they can get rid of it. Seriously, it's fine. Did you not use a condom, though?'

'YES,' I wailed.

'Maybe you got it from oral sex, then,' she suggested.

'You can get chlamydia from blow jobs?' I cried, and then lowered my voice as people turned to stare. 'Why does no one tell me this stuff?!'

'Oh, babe,' she said. 'I'm sorry. It's so unfair. Hardly anyone uses condoms for oral sex, and you've only done it once and caught it. That's such shit luck.' She gave me a sympathetic hug.

'I can't believe I have chlamydia,' I moaned dramatically. 'I'm like the Virgin Mary, except instead of getting a baby Jesus, I got chlamydia. And I'm not even a virgin any more.'

She patted my arm understandingly. 'I'll go and get you another G and T,' she said.

I sat alone on the bench contemplating my news as I waited for her. I was no longer a virgin. I had completed my goal. I'd come into contact with an actual condom on an actual penis, and I'd taken a chlamydia test. In fact, I hadn't just completed my vow; I'd taken it one step further and actually contracted chlamydia.

I laughed to myself as I slurped the last bits of melted ice cubes through my straw. After twenty-one years of surviving virginity, chlamydia didn't really seem like a big deal.

Me, Myself and my Virginity

EK:

When we started this vlog, we told you we were EM, proud slut, and EK, reluctant virgin. Things have changed. I lost my virginity, dear loyal readers. I reached third and fourth base on the same night and couldn't stop smiling for days. At the ripe age of 21, I finally lost my V-plates to no less than an attractive, older guy.

I thought, after all these years, I had finally found the right guy. I was convinced he was falling for me just like I was falling for him. Only it turned out he thought he was just taking my virginity as a friendly favour. Quote: 'We're more friends than lovers, right?' Um. I didn't think so.

The thing is, The Jack Debacle, as I have coined it (because he doesn't deserve anonymity), has taught me a lot about virginity. I've realized that I have never really thought about what virginity means to me because I've been so preoccupied with what everyone else thinks it means. Examples: the American teen movies where the losers are always virgins. Or the ones where the jocks all try and take the hot girl's virginity. TV shows like *SATC*, where everyone discusses sex the whole time. Magazines that have 'Top 50 Sex Tips' on the covers. You get the drift.

I only accepted my virginity after I lost it. I wish I had done it earlier, but either way, I'm glad I finally have. So whoever you are, whether you lost your virginity 20 years ago or you still have it, just accept it. Embrace any STDs you may or may not have, along with the regrets, the disastrous stories, the heartbreak, the pain and the regret. Because, if it weren't for all this stuff, life would be pretty dull. And I, for one, wouldn't have anything to vlog about.

* * * * *

WIN

Anouska Knight's first book, *Since You've Been Gone*, was a smash hit and crowned the winner of Lorraine's Racy Reads. Anouska returns with *A Part of Me,* which is one not to be missed!

Get your copy today at:
www.millsandboon.co.uk